"DEEPLY MOVING....

Mengestu writes . . . with poignancy and
psychological precision. . . . With great lyricism and ferocity."
—THE NEW YORK TIMES

"POWERFUL."
—THE CHRISTIAN SCIENCE MONITOR

"MAGNIFICENT....

Mengestu seamlessly weaves together a disturbing
story of parallel lives and plots."
—COUNTERPUNCH

"Taut and swift . . . with an abiding mystery driving it forward. . . .
One reads to the end . . . with a kind of desperate intensity. . . .

EXTRAORDINARY."
—THE BOSTON GLOBE

"HEART-RENDING....

Both invokes and channels *Great Expectations*—a novel, like
this one, about letting go of myths we'll never inhabit,
so that we might craft new stories that free us to live."
—MILWAUKEE JOURNAL SENTINEL

"The enigmatic Isaac radiates a sense of quiet purpose that makes him both substantial and immensely appealing. Mengestu's assertion of the claims of the self against the ideologies of tribe, nation, or home is all the more powerful for being expressed through paradox."

—*London Review of Books*

"Subtly powerful. . . . We need globe-straddlers like Mengestu to show us that love, like hate, respects no borders." —Boris Kachka, author of *Hothouse*

"Extraordinary. . . . A fierce and tender examination of identity, love, disillusionment, friendship and sacrifice."

—*National Post* (Toronto)

"Writing with the kind of effortless ease suggestive of much painstaking struggle, Mengestu locates the novel's horror not in war per se, but in those seemingly born to its bidding." —*Toronto Star*

"Mengestu portrays the intersection of cultures experienced by the immigrant with unsettling perception. . . . [He] evokes contrasting landscapes but focuses on his characters . . . who are all caught in a cycle of connection and disruption, engagement and abandonment, hope and disillusion."

—*Publishers Weekly* (starred review, "Pick of the Week")

DINAW MENGESTU

ALL OUR NAMES

Dinaw Mengestu is the award-winning author of two previous novels, *The Beautiful Things That Heaven Bears* (2007) and *How to Read the Air* (2010). He is a graduate of Georgetown University and of Columbia University's MFA program in fiction and the recipient of a 5 Under 35 award from the National Book Foundation and a 20 Under 40 award from *The New Yorker*. His journalism and fiction have appeared in such publications as *Harper's Magazine*, *Granta*, *Rolling Stone*, *The New Yorker*, and *The Wall Street Journal*. He is a recipient of a MacArthur Foundation genius grant and currently lives in New York City.

ALSO BY DINAW MENGESTU

The Beautiful Things That Heaven Bears

How to Read the Air

ALL OUR NAMES

ALL OUR NAMES

DINAW MENGESTU

Vintage Books
A Division of Random House LLC
New York

FIRST VINTAGE BOOKS EDITION, JANUARY 2015

The Library of Congress has cataloged the Knopf edition as follows:
Mengestu, Dinaw.
All our names / by Dinaw Mengestu. — First edition.
p. cm.
1. Students, Foreign—United States—Fiction.
2. African Americans—Fiction.
3. Women social workers—United States—Fiction.
4. Identity (Psychology)—Fiction.
5. Alienation (Social psychology)—Fiction. 6. Psychological fiction. I. Title.
PS3613.E487A66 2014   813'.6—dc23   2013031632

Vintage Trade Paperback ISBN: 978-0-345-80566-9
eBook ISBN: 978-0-385-34999-4

Book design by Betty Lew

www.vintagebooks.com

Printed in the United States of America
10   9   8   7   6   5   4   3   2   1

To Anne-Emmanuelle,
Gabriel, and Louis-Selassie

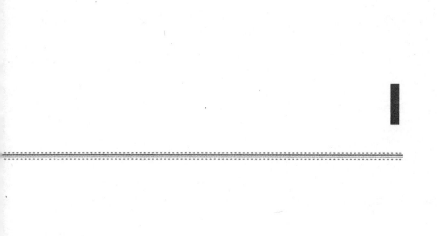

ISAAC

When Isaac and I first met at the university, we both pretended that the campus and the streets of the capital were as familiar to us as the dirt paths of the rural villages we had grown up and lived in until only a few months earlier, even though neither of us had ever been to a city before and had no idea what it meant to live in such close proximity to so many people whose faces, much less names, we would never know. The capital in those days was booming, with people, money, new cars, and newer buildings, most of which had been thrown up quickly after independence, in a rush fueled by ecstatic promises of a socialist, Pan-African dream that, almost ten years later, was still supposedly just around the corner, that, according to the president and the radio, was coming any day now. By the time Isaac and I arrived in the capital, many of the buildings had already begun to show signs of wear, having been neglected or completely forgotten, but there was still hope in the brighter future to come, and we were there like everyone else to claim our share.

On the bus ride to the capital, I gave up all the names my parents had given me. I was almost twenty-five but, by any measure, much younger. I shed those names just as our bus crossed the border into Uganda. We were closing in on Lake Victoria; I knew Kampala was close, but even then I had already committed myself to thinking of it only as "the capital." Kampala was too small for what I imagined. That city belonged to Uganda, but the capital, as long as it was nameless, had no such allegiances. Like me, it belonged to no one, and anyone could claim it.

I spent my first few weeks in the capital trying to imitate the gangs of boys that lingered around the university and the cafés and bars that bordered it. Back then, all the boys our age wanted to be revolutionaries. On campus, and in the poor quarters where Isaac and I lived, there were dozens of Lumumbas, Marleys, Malcolms, Césaires, Kenyattas, Senghors, and Selassies, boys who woke up every morning and donned the black hats and olive-green costumes of their heroes. I couldn't match them, so I let the few strands of hair on my chin grow long. I bought a used pair of green pants that I wore daily, even after the knees had split open. I tried to think of myself as a revolutionary in the making, though I had come to the capital with other ambitions. A decade earlier, there had been an important gathering of African writers and scholars at the university. I read about it in a week-old newspaper that had finally made its way to our village. That conference gave shape to my adolescent ambitions, which until then consisted solely of leaving. I knew afterward where to go and what I wanted to be: a famous writer, surrounded by like-minded men in the heart of what had to be the continent's greatest city.

I arrived in the capital poorly prepared. I had read the same Victorian novels a dozen times, and I assumed that was how proper English was spoken. I said "sir" constantly. No one I met believed I was a revolutionary, and I didn't have the heart to claim I wanted to be a writer. Until I met Isaac, I hadn't made a single friend. With my long skinny legs and narrow face, he said I looked more like a professor than a fighter, and in the beginning that was what he called me: Professor, or the Professor, the first but not the last name he christened me.

"And what about you?" I asked him. I assumed that, like others, he had another, more public name that he wanted to be known by. He was shorter but wider than me, each of his arms tightly laced with muscles and veins that ran like scars the length of his forearms. He had the build but not the face and demeanor of a soldier. He smiled and laughed too often for me to imagine he could ever hurt someone.

"For now, 'Isaac' is it," he said.

"Isaac" was the name his parents had given him and, until it was necessary for us to flee the capital, the only name he wanted. His parents had died, in the last round of fighting that came just before independence. "Isaac" was their legacy to him, and when his revolutionary dreams came to an end, and he had to choose between leaving and staying, that name became his last and most precious gift to me.

From the beginning, it was harder for Isaac than for me to be in the capital. This had never been and, I understood later, would never be my home, regardless of what I imagined. It was different for Isaac, however. Uganda was his country, and Kampala was the heart of it. His family was from the north, one of the tall, darker tribes that a man in Cambridge had decided were more warrior-like than their smaller cousins to the south. Had the British stayed, he would have done well. He had been bright enough in his early years to be talked of as one of the students who when older could be sent abroad, perhaps to a public school in London on a government scholarship. But then the whole colonial experiment ended in what seemed like a single long bloody afternoon, and boys like Isaac were orphaned a second time. And although Isaac had arrived in the capital only a few weeks before me, he knew enough about it from rumors and stories to assume he would easily find his place in it, and then rise to the top of whatever circle he found himself in. The fact that he was poor and completely unknown when we met was his most obvious well of frustration, but I suspected there were other sources of anger and heartbreak that he had yet to acknowledge.

Isaac and I became friends the way two stray dogs find themselves linked by treading the same path every day in search of food and companionship. We had taken up residence in the eastern quarters of the city, in the harder-to-reach, hill-rich region prone to mudslides. He was living with friends of cousins, who had agreed to house him on the floor in their living room. I was renting a cot in the back of a dry-goods store that on the weekends became an impromptu bar for the owner and his friends. On Friday and Saturday nights, I wasn't allowed to return to the store until 2 or 3 a.m., after the bed had been used by the owner and his friends to entertain themselves with some of the young girls in the neighborhood. With no money and nothing else to do, I would circle the neighborhood—a maze of rutted, narrow paths that wound slowly up the side of a hill, at the top of which was one of the city's newly paved roads. From here, one could look down upon our shanty village as it descended into what had been a lush, green valley, rich for grazing cattle but had become, with the mass migration to the capital, a dense cluster of tin roofs and wires, ringed by shallow pits of trash and feces. Twice I saw Isaac up there before we ever spoke to each other. On both occasions he was standing on the side of the road, staring at the passing traffic instead of the city beneath him, as if he were preparing to sacrifice himself to one of the cars at any moment. We acknowledged each other with a quick nod of the head. Neither of us could have done more without alarming the other; had I not seen Isaac at the university shortly afterward, we might have spent years nodding to each other from the edge of the road. A few days after that second meeting, however, I saw him on campus. We were trying our best to belong, standing near but never too close to a group of students. It was the second week of August, and with the start of a new year there were students gathered on every square inch of the central lawn, which was ringed by towering palm trees that gave the campus an air of tropical grandeur far greater than it deserved. When I saw him, I knew he was at the university not because he was supposed to be, but because, like me, he felt that was where he belonged, among the bright, future generation. Like me, he had told everyone he knew and met that he was a student, and at that time both of us were convinced that someday we would be.

It was with this understanding—that we were both liars and frauds, poorly equipped to play the roles we had chosen—that Isaac approached me. We had become part of a crowd gathered around a table in the center of the lawn where one of the boys with the neatly sculpted Afros was reading off a list of demands. Had Isaac and I not been there at the same time, we might have been moved by the young man's call for better teachers, lower fees, and more freedom for the students, but we had noticed each other right away, and so were never a part of that gathering. All we could see from the moment our eyes locked was the vaguely familiar, possibly hostile face staring back. Perhaps only two men meeting unexpectedly in the middle of a desert after having traveled for so long that they've begun to believe the world was uninhabited would know what we felt like. In the province of the slums we meant little to each other. Here we were everything.

Isaac waited for the speech to end. The final words, "This is our university," were followed by a brief applause. Everything back then was supposed to be ours. The city, this country, Africa— they were there for the taking, and, at least in that regard, our approach to the future was no different from that of the English-men who preceded us. Many of the young boys who were stu-dents at the university would later prove the point as they stuffed themselves with their country's wealth.

Once the crowd had thinned, Isaac made his move. He loped. His shoulders descended and rose with each step, almost feral in movement. I felt hunted. I thought, "He's coming for me," and though I knew there was no physical injury at stake, I was right in assuming there was something at risk. He stood next to me for a few seconds before he said, "We should go somewhere and talk."

That sort of conspiratorial language came naturally to him. Over the next few months, I heard him say things such as "We should talk in private," or "Let's talk someplace else." Isaac was gifted at making you feel special.

I nodded my head in agreement. I was victim to his maneu-vers from the beginning, instantly folded into his reality, which, for the first time since I came to the capital, gave me the feeling there was at least one place I belonged.

We walked until we were far away from the campus, in a part of the city I had never been in before. Isaac talked the entire time. He had his own version of history—half fact, half myth—which he was eager to share. He began each of his stories with "Did you know," which was his equivalent of "Once upon a time."

"Did you know," he said, "until a decade ago no Africans were allowed to live near the university. This is where the British were planning on building a new palace for the king. If they had lost World War II, they were going to move all the English people here, and this part of the city was going to be just for them. They were going to make everything look like London so they wouldn't feel so bad about losing. They were going to build a big wall around it and then change all the maps so that it looked like London was in Africa, but every time they started building the wall, someone would blow it up. That's how the war for independence started."

I listened, knowing that Isaac's main intention was to amuse. Whether or not I believed him didn't matter, as long as I was seduced. We stopped at a café on a street lined with single-story tin-roofed stores selling jeans, T-shirts, and brightly patterned ankle-length dresses. There were similar streets all over the city and across the continent. What made this one unique were the four-story concrete buildings that had recently sprung up in pairs every hundred feet. They had been built quickly, and poorly, to house the private businesses that were supposed to come sweeping into the capital. Their vacancy seemed more meaningful than the crowds and the dozens of other stores standing in their shadows, although it was impossible to know if it was because the empty buildings spoke of the imminent future, or its failure to materialize.

I pointed to a pair with blacked-out windows across the street from us. "And who is supposed to live there?" I asked him.

He stretched out his arms. "Those aren't buildings," he said. "Look how ugly they are. Soon everything in the capital will look like that. That's the government's secret plan. We built them to keep the British from ever wanting to come back."

He put one finger to his lip. "This is just between us, of course."

"Of course," I said. I didn't know yet when he expected me to take him seriously.

We took a table outside. Isaac ordered tea for us. When it came, slightly cooler than he wanted, he sent it back and demanded another. He wanted me to be impressed by his ability to command: in this case, a slightly warmer cup of hot water. When the issue with the tea was settled, he crossed his legs, leaned back in his chair, and said, "So—you go to the university, too."

"Yes," I told him.

"Every day?"

"Every day."

It wasn't until that second exchange that we were certain we were talking about the same thing. Isaac's face softened. He dropped the constant, half-forced grin he had been wearing since we met.

"My grandfather wanted me to study medicine," he continued. "But I have other plans of my own."

"Then what will you study?"

"This is Africa," he said. "There's only one thing to study."

He waited for me to respond. After several dramatic seconds he sighed and said, "Politics. That's all we have here."

I hadn't learned to speak with such false though convincing authority. When Isaac asked me what I planned to study, I had to gather my courage before I could respond.

"Literature," I told him.

He slapped the table with his hand.

"That's perfect," he said. "You look like a professor. What kind of literature will you study?"

"All of it," I said, and here, for once, I spoke with a bit of confidence, because I believed in what I said. Many of the writers who attended that conference had already begun to make themselves scarce by the time Isaac and I had that conversation: several were already reported to be in exile in America; others were rumored to be dead or working for a corrupt government. But I still dreamed of joining their ranks nonetheless.

HELEN

When I met Isaac, I was almost what my mother would have called "a woman of a certain age." That in her mind made me vulnerable, though I never felt that way, not even as a child growing up in a house where it would have been much easier to be a boy. My mother was a whisperer. She spoke in soft tones, in case my father was upset or had entered one of his dark moods, a habit which she continued after he had left. We lived in a quiet, semi-rural Midwestern town, and decorum for her was everything. What mattered most was that the cracks that came with a family were neatly covered up, so that no one knew when you were struggling to pay the mortgage, or that your marriage was over long before the divorce papers were signed. I think she expected that I would speak like her—and maybe when I was very small I did, but my instincts tell me that, more likely than not, this was never the case. I could never have been a whisperer. I liked my voice too much. I rarely read a book in silence. I wanted to hear every story out loud, so I often read alone in our backyard, which was large enough that if I yelled the story at the top of my voice, no one in the house closest to us could hear me. I read out there in the winter, when the tree branches sagged with ice and the few chickens we owned had to be brought into the basement so they wouldn't freeze to death. When I was older, and the grass was almost knee-high because no one bothered to tend to it anymore, I went back there with a book in my hand simply to scream.

That Isaac said he didn't mind if I raised my voice was the first thing I liked about him. I had driven nearly three hours, across multiple county lines and one state line, to pick him up as a favor to my boss, David, who had explained to me earlier that morning that, although, yes, tending to foreigners, regardless of where they came from, wasn't a normal part of our jobs, he had made an exception for Isaac as a favor to an old friend, and now it was my turn to do the same.

I was happy to take Isaac on. I had been a social worker for five years and was convinced I had already spent all the good will I had for my country's poor, tired, and dispossessed, whether they were black, white, old, fresh from prison, or just out of a shelter. Even the veterans, some of whom I had gone to high school with, left me at the end of a routine thirty-minute home visit desperate to leave, as if their anguish was contagious. I had lost too much of the heart and all the faith needed to stay afloat in a job where every human encounter felt like an anvil strung around my neck just when I thought I was nearing the shore. We were, on our business cards and letterhead, the Lutheran Relief Services, but there hadn't been any religious affiliation—not since the last Lutheran church for a hundred miles shut down at the start of World War II and all of its parishioners were rechristened as Methodists.

It was common among the four of us in the office to say that not only were we not Lutheran, but we didn't really provide any services, either. We had always run on a shoestring budget, and that string was nipped an inch or two each year as our government grants dried up, leaving us with little more than a dwindling supply of good intentions and promises of better years to come. David said it first and most often: "We should change our name to 'Relief.' That way, when someone asks what you do, you can say, 'I work for Relief.' And if they ask you relief from what, just tell them, 'Does it really matter?'"

Mildly bitter sarcasm was David's preferred brand of humor. He claimed it was a countermeasure to the earnestness that supposedly came with our jobs.

I knew little about Isaac before I met him, except that he was from somewhere in Africa, that his English was most likely poor, and that the old friend of David's had arranged a student visa in order for him to come here because his life may or may not have been in danger. I wasn't supposed to be his social worker so much as his chaperone into Middle America—his personal tour guide of our town's shopping malls, grocery stores, banks, and bureaucracies. And Isaac was going to be, for at least one year, my guaranteed Relief. He was, in my original plans, my option out of at least some of our dire weekly budget meetings and the minimum of two hospital visits a month; last and most important, he secured my right to refuse to take on any new clients who were terminally ill. I had been to twenty-two funerals the year before, and though most were strangers to me when they passed, I felt certain my heart couldn't take much more.

My first thought when I saw Isaac was that he was taller and looked healthier than I expected. From there, I worked my way backward to two assumptions I wasn't aware of possessing: the first that Africans were short, and the second that even the ones who flew all the way to a small college town in the middle of America would probably show signs of illness or malnutrition. My second thought—or third, depending on how you counted it—was that "he wasn't bad-looking." I said those same words to myself as a test to measure their sincerity. I felt my little Midwestern world tremble just a bit under the weight of them.

Isaac and I had known each other for less than an hour when he told me he didn't mind if I sometimes shouted; I had already apologized for being late to meet him, and for failing to have a sign with his name on it when I arrived. Later, in the car, I apologized for driving too fast, and then, once we arrived in town, I apologized for my voice.

"I'm sorry if I talk too loud," I said. It was the only apology I had repeatedly sworn over the past ten years never to make again. The frequency with which I broke that promise never softened the disappointment I felt immediately afterward.

"You don't have to apologize for everything," he told me. "Talk as loud as you want. It's easier to understand you."

I couldn't hug Isaac or thank him for his attempt at humor without making us feel awkward, but I wanted him to know that I wasn't normally so easily moved, that I was a woman of joy and laughter. I tried my best to give him an animated, lively description of our town.

"It's pronounced 'Laurel,' like the flower," but I suspected that wasn't entirely correct, so I pointed to the hulking brick factory, which, other than a grain silo, was the tallest object on the horizon.

"That used to be a bomb factory," I said. There were rumors that it would be converted into the state's largest shopping mall, but I wasn't sure he knew what a mall was, so I left that out.

We drove past gas stations and fast-food restaurants clustered together every quarter-mile with nothing yet built in between them. I tried to think of something else interesting to say. I pointed to a gas station and said, "Fifteen years ago, that used to be a pig farm." A second later, I worried that maybe he didn't know what a pig farm was, or that maybe he thought I was bragging about our town's pig farms to someone who had just come from a country where there were no farms, or pigs. I had to bite my cheek to keep from apologizing. When we reached the old, charming main street that used to be the heart of the town, I asked him if there was anything he'd like to see before I took him to his apartment.

"Thank you for asking," he said. "I would like to see the university if it isn't too much trouble."

I looked at his hands. He had his hands palm-down on his thighs, with his back perfectly straight like a schoolboy trying to prove he was on his best behavior. I thought, Now I know what it means to be frightened stiff.

We made a quick tour of the southern half of the campus. It wasn't the largest or most prestigious university in the state, but I always suspected it was the most beautiful. Like everyone, Isaac was impressed by the trees—hundred-year-old oaks that, especially in August, seemed more essential to the idea of the university than any of the buildings. I felt a surge of nostalgia every time I came there, and offered to take him to the library. "I would appreciate that," he said.

We were standing in the main reading room—a wide, grand hall that a professor of mine had described as a terrible clash of

Midwestern and classical taste—when I decided that, for Isaac's sake, I'd had enough of his formal politeness. He'd been staring silently for several minutes at the wood-paneled walls lined with leather books and supported by marble columns, all of which stood on top of a thick green carpet that could have been found in any one of a hundred living rooms in town. He looked down before he stepped onto the carpet, and I could almost hear him wondering if he should take his shoes off. He was still staring at the walls in awe when I shouted to him, "How do you like America?"—not quite at the top of my voice, but definitely somewhere near it.

There were two weeks until the start of the semester, so the library was nearly empty. The few people there all turned to stare at us, and I could see a librarian on the other side of the hall slowly making her way toward me. As she did so, Isaac walked out of the room and then the library without saying a word. I began to prepare yet another series of apologies—to him, to the librarian, and, if I lost Isaac, to David. I waited until the librarian had almost reached me, before following Isaac out: to run after him, in our town, at that time, would have given the wrong impression.

Isaac hadn't gone far. He was standing a few feet away from the front door, near the very top of the steps, with both hands tucked into his pockets, as if I had caught him in the middle of a late-afternoon stroll across campus.

"I apologize for leaving so abruptly. I didn't understand what you were saying in there. Next time, please speak louder."

I wanted to hug him again. There was a natural, easy charm to his words, and, more than that, forgiveness. No one else I had ever met spoke in such formal sentences. I had been told when given his file not to be offended if he didn't speak much, since his English was most likely basic, but I remember thinking that afternoon that I felt like I was talking with someone out of an old English novel.

At the office the next day, when David asked what Isaac was like, I told him he was kind and had a nice smile and an interesting face, all of which was true and yet only a poor part of what I really wanted to say. David half listened to my description of Isaac. When I finished he asked me, "And what else, other than the obvious?"

"He has a funny way of speaking," I said.

"Funny how?"

"He sounds old."

"That's a new one. Maybe it's just his English."

"No," I said, "his English is perfect. It's how I imagine someone talking in a Dickens novel."

"Never read him," he said.

And neither had I, but it was too late to admit that Dickens was merely my fall guy for all things old and English. From that day on, David and I took to calling Isaac "Dickens." When Isaac and I went to find more furniture for his nearly empty apartment, I told David, "I'm off now to see my old chum Dickens." In meetings, David would ask how Dickens was getting along in our quaint town, which only a decade earlier had stopped segregating its public bathrooms, buses, schools, and restaurants and still didn't look too kindly upon seeing its races mix.

"He's doing very, very well," I said, in what was as close as I could come to an English accent.

A month later, after Isaac and I had spent a half-dozen nights intertwined in his bed till just before midnight, I brought him a copy of *A Tale of Two Cities*. He had a growing stack of books, used and borrowed, around his bed, but none, I had noticed, were by Dickens.

"A present," I said. It was unwrapped. I held the book out to him with both hands. He smiled and thanked me without looking at the cover.

"Have you read it already?" I asked him.

"No," he said. "But I have every intention of doing so right away." I laughed. I couldn't stop myself. He was so eager to please. I had to confess: "We have a nickname for you at the office. We call you Dickens."

Only then did he look at the cover.

"Dickens," he said.

And again I was afraid I had embarrassed him. He flipped the book over and read the description on the back and, as he did so, smiled. It was the same expression he'd had on his face when I found him on the library steps.

"I could do much worse here than that," he said.

What Isaac and I never had was a proper start to our relationship. We missed out on the traditional rituals of courtship and awkward dinners that most couples use to measure the distance they've traveled from restaurant to bedroom. No one watched us draw closer, and no one was there to say that we made for a great or poorly matched couple. The first time Isaac placed his lips on mine was in his apartment after I had shown up unannounced to check on him. He had been in town for two weeks, and we already had a routine established. I picked him up from his apartment every other day at 4 p.m. In the beginning, our afternoons were spent primarily doing errands. I drove Isaac to the grocery store, bank, and post office.

I spent an afternoon waiting with him for the telephone company to arrive, and when it came to furniture, I was the one who picked out the couch, coffee table, and dresser from the Goodwill store two towns away.

Isaac told me he knew how to cook, but not in America.

"The eggs here are different," he said. "They are white, and very big. And I don't understand the meat."

And so I taught him what few domestic acts I had learned from my mother. I taught him how to choose the best steaks for his money from the grocery store. I held a package of discounted beef next to my face for contrast and said, "See those pockets of fat? That'll keep it from drying out," and told him that if he had any doubts he should smother it in butter. Eggs, I told him, were an entirely different matter. "I hate them. You'll have to find a better woman than me for that," I said.

I knew that part of the reason I had been given this job was that David assumed that it would play to my motherly instincts, and that, as the only woman in the office without a family, I had the time. I never had those instincts, however. I watched friends from high school and college grow up, get married, and have children, and the most I had ever thought about that was "That could be nice." My mom had been that kind of mother, and if Isaac had been from Wyoming, I could have dropped him off at her house the day he arrived and never thought of him again until it was time for him to leave.

"She would have made you fat," I told him. "And the only thing you probably would have ever heard out of her was a list of what was in the refrigerator and what time you could expect to eat."

· · ·

That kiss happened September 3, in the doorway between his living room and bedroom, just after we had returned to his apartment from buying silverware and plates. He was on his way to the bedroom and I was leaving the bathroom when we collided in the hallway, which was wide enough for only one person to pass at a time. Forced to stand face to face, what could we do but smile?

"Do you live here as well?" Isaac asked me.

"I do now," I said, and, without thinking, we leaned toward each other, me up and him down, until our lips met. We kissed long enough to be certain it wasn't an accident. When we opened our eyes and separated, what we felt wasn't surprise so much as relief that our first moment of intimacy felt so ordinary—almost habitual, as if it had been part of our routine for years to kiss while passing.

I was late getting back to my office, but had I not been, I would still have wanted to leave on a dramatic note. I grabbed my jacket and thought of walking forcefully out the door, stopping for one final, brief kiss, but once I was close to him, I wanted to press my nose into the crook of Isaac's neck so I could smell him, and that was exactly what he let me do.

"You are like a cat," he said.

"You smell like onions," I told him.

He craned his neck around mine. We held that pose for at least a minute, at which point I pulled away so I wouldn't have to worry about him doing so. When I was back in his apartment two days later, I walked from room to room as soon as I entered. Isaac asked me what I was doing. I took his hand and pinched the flesh between his thumb and index finger before wrapping my arms around him. "I'm making sure you're really here," I said. He lifted my chin up to his lips and kissed me quickly.

"Does that help?" he asked. It did, but it wasn't enough. Compared with others, Isaac was made of almost nothing, not a ghost but a sketch of a man I was trying hard to fill in.

I nudged him backward until we landed on the couch. I felt his legs trembling; I was relieved to know he was nervous.

"I'm still not convinced," I said. My doubt became the cover story we needed to take each other apart. Isaac kissed my neck, and in return, I took off his shirt and placed his hands on the bottom of my blouse so he knew he should do the same. I kissed his chest and he kissed mine. Once we were undressed, he asked, "And what about now?"

I raised my hips and pulled him inside me.

"I'm almost convinced," I said. His right leg never stopped trembling. Knowing he was afraid made me want to hold on to him that much harder, and I thought if I did so, with time I could help color in the missing parts.

With no outside world to ground us, every moment of intimacy that passed between Isaac and me did so in an isolated reality that began and ended on the other side of his apartment door. I had never had a relationship with a man like that, but I understood how easily the tiny world Isaac and I were slowly building could vanish.

"I am dependent on you for everything," he often said during our first two months together. He said it sometimes as a joke, sometimes out of anger. He could say it if I had just told him where his glasses were, or if I had taken his clothes out of the washing machine and hung them to dry because I knew he had a habit of leaving them in the washer overnight, and it would be affectionate and charming and made me think that it wouldn't be so bad to fall in love with a man like this, who noticed the small things you did for him and found a way to say thank you without making you feel like his mother. At other times, he said the same words and all I heard was how much he hated saying them, and how much he might have hated me, at least in those moments, as well.

The list of things he was dependent upon me for grew larger the longer he stayed in our town. In the beginning he needed me only to do my job: to help get him from one point to another, since he had no car or license; to explain basic things, like when and when not to dial 911. Later on, he needed me to sit with him quietly in the dark and hold his hand as he mourned the loss of someone he loved. Once, he called me at work and asked me to leave the phone on the desk, just so he could hear other people talking. He didn't always know how to fill his days. He had his books—dense historical works and biographies along with a smaller collection of romance novels that he kept hidden under his bed. He read obsessively. When I asked him why, he said it was "to make up for all the lost time," because he had never had access to libraries like ours until now; but I suspected it had as much to do with not knowing what to do with all those long empty hours. Isaac had none of the good or the bad that came with living in such close, sustained contact with your past. If there was anything I pitied him for, it was the special loneliness that came with having nothing that was truly yours. Being occasionally called "boy" or "nigger," as he was, didn't compare to having no one who knew him before he had come here, who could remind him, simply by being there, that he was someone else entirely.

ISAAC

Every aspiring militant, radical, and would-be revolutionary in Eastern and Central Africa was drawn to the university back then. They started coming shortly after the president took power and claimed the country was the first African socialist republic— "a beacon of freedom and equality where all men are brothers" was how he phrased it in the radio announcement given after he staged the country's first coup. Millions believed him. He spoke the right language, grand, pompous, and humble merged into the same breath. He was from the military, but he claimed he wasn't an army man, just a poor farmer who had picked up the gun to liberate his people, first from the British and then, after independence, from the corrupt bureaucrats who followed. It was rumored that he had a photographic memory, was a champion chess player, and every weekend returned to his farm to tend to his cattle and crops. Whatever people wanted in a leader and dreamed of for themselves, they found in him. The newspapers ran daily photographs of the president in various guises: the president as father, with a dozen children gathered around him; the president as village leader in a bright red-and-blue costume, using a walking stick, and the president as the intellectual statesman in a three-piece suit that tamed his massive girth and lent an air of sophistication to his bull-sized head.

He gave generously to the university, supposedly from his own pocket. His portrait hung randomly throughout the campus, and for a time it was rumored that the university would be renamed in his honor. For years the patronage kept the students content. They held on to their socialist, Pan-African dream, while ignoring the corruption and violence that touched the rest of the capital, for as long as they could. By the time Isaac and I arrived on campus, the dream had proved rotten and was cast to the side. Among the students there were warring parties split along thin ideological lines. It was Isaac who taught me how to divide the students spread across the lawn in a state of constant protest into two camps: the real revolutionaries and the campus frauds.

"All the battles aren't equal," he said. "If you are going to be a writer, you have to be able to know the difference between the boys who come in chauffeured cars and the ones who fought to be here."

I didn't tell him the difference was irrelevant to me. I belonged to neither camp and had no interest in choosing. Some students wanted war and revolution, while others pretended to out of their own self-interest. Either way there was a place for outsiders like me as long as I watched safely on the sidelines, but if I wanted to do so, Isaac was right, I had to learn to see like him.

As we walked across the campus, Isaac pointed to various student camps and asked what I thought of that person, or that group. "Is that a real revolutionary?"

Our game started poorly. More than half the time, he claimed I was wrong. After a dozen attempts, I asked him what made him so certain he was always right.

"You know how you can tell who they really are?" he said.

He knelt down and took off one of his shoes and wiggled his dirty toes in the air. He held the shoe, which like my own was covered in dust and had been repaired so many times there was hardly anything left of the sole

"Look at the shoes. Anyone who walks to campus has shoes as ruined as ours."

For several days, we lay on the grass and pointed out all the polished shoes that passed us. It took a day before I no longer saw the students as a general, uniform mass. They were a part of the same campus body but it was fractured into dozens of discrete parts that were loosely connected and rarely touched. Once I understood that, I knew what to look for when I studied the students. After two days I told Isaac, "I don't have to see the shoes. I can tell by the way they stand." I pointed to packs of boys on the other side of the campus and said, "Chauffeured car," and according to Isaac, I was always right. Privilege lifted the head, focused the eyes. I knew that before I came to the capital and had assumed there were better rules at the university. After several days of watching, Isaac decided it was time to do more than point.

"We should introduce ourselves to them," he said.

He didn't bother to explain why. He stood up, and as he walked away from the corner of the campus that I had begun to think of as ours, he turned back to say, "This won't take long."

Isaac had taught me how to notice, but not watch. As he drew close to a group of three handsomely dressed boys standing almost within earshot of us, I briefly turned away, both embarrassed and afraid of what would happen next. When I looked up, he was already on his way back to me.

"What did you say to them?" I asked him.

"Nothing," he said.

"Then why are they staring at you?"

"Maybe they didn't understand my question?"

"Which was?"

"I asked them if they had enough room in their fathers' cars for all of us."

That was the start of Isaac's revolution, although neither of us knew it at the time. He posed variations of the same question to randomly selected groups of boys for a week. He called it his "interrogation." He would say to me, "I'm going to interrogate those boys over there." Or, "Who should I interrogate today?" And before I could respond he was off.

After the second or third time, I learned to watch without turning away. I saw that the risk of embarrassment and possibly even pain was necessary to the performance. He was pushed, threatened, laughed, and spat at, and, regardless, he returned to me with only a slightly dampened version of the confident glare he wore when he left. He could do so in part because he knew I was there watching, a witness rather than a mere spectator.

Isaac's "interrogations" ended once it became obvious that enough students knew what to expect when they saw him coming for them.

"I've learned something important," he said after he declared the end to his questioning. "All of the rich boys are named Alex. If they tell you something different, don't believe them. Trust me—their real name is Alex."

That same afternoon, he began to wave at any student who bore obvious signs of wealth, while calling out, "Hello, Alex. Very nice to see you again." Or, "Alex, where have you been? Say hello to your friend Alex for me."

It was an easy game for me to join him in. I followed him around campus yelling hello to the privileged boys; occasionally,

when feeling bold, we approached a pair with our hands outstretched, and greeted them in unison as Alex.

By the time they realized they were being mocked, we had
walked away. If they yelled for us to return, we never acknowledged them. Isaac kept his stride, while I had to concentrate not
to stumble.

The only students on campus we admired were the ones who,
like us, failed to hide the not-so-subtle marks of poverty. When
I wasn't with Isaac, I made a careful study of how they held their
heads, if they looked down before speaking, and if close enough,
what they said, what their voices sounded like when they spoke.

Isaac had other campus heroes as well. Of all the would-be
revolutionaries, there was one group he never mocked. They
were from Rhodesia—independence was still years away. No one
on campus had a more powerful cause, which took the form of
a single white banner unfurled each morning that read: AFRICA IS
NOT FREE UNTIL WE ALL ARE. Isaac had introduced himself to them,
when I was not around to see it.

"They're from Rhodesia," he told me, "but don't use that
word around them. If you say 'Rhodesia' they'll tell you no such
place exists. One boy told me that if I wanted to find Rhodesia I'd
have to live inside of a white man's head. I like them, but they
don't trust anyone."

That was as close as he could come to admitting that they had
not taken him seriously. He continued to watch them, but I never
saw him so much as wave to them or look in their direction.

The real star of the campus for Isaac, and many others, however, was virtually invisible. He was supposed to be tall, young,
handsome, and well read and wore only olive-green pants and
shirts. Isaac claimed to have seen him from afar as he was leaving

the campus. He said he was certain he was either Congolese or Rwandan. "He's tall and serious like a Rwandan," he said, "but it's the Congolese who know how to fight. Maybe he's both."

"Maybe he doesn't exist," I said. "Maybe he lives only in the black man's head."

There was an article in the campus newspaper with the outline of a head and a series of quotes from students who claimed he was a myth. The next week, messages written in black marker began to appear on the buildings and supposedly in the classrooms as well. The most famous of them, which every student knew by heart, read simply:

Marx was a great man, and now he's dead.

Lenin was a great man, and now he's dead.

I have to admit, I'm not feeling so well myself.

Isaac loved that. "That man is something special," he said over and over. He said it was proof that there were still real revolutionaries around, "not only rich boys waiting to be government ministers."

The day after that message appeared, we scoured the campus in search of others. We found six more that day, five the next. On the third, every one had been painted over and replaced with a handwritten poster that said: "It Is a Crime Against the Country to Deface Our University Walls."

"Soon," Isaac said, "everything will be a Crime Against the Country."

"I'm sorry," I told him, "but it's already a crime to say that."

He held out his arms to be arrested.

"We should start practicing for this," he said.

The following Monday, Isaac arrived on campus with a dozen fliers he had made, using stolen paper and markers. When I asked him where the paper came from, he clasped my shoulder and said, "Sometimes revolutionaries have to take what they need. Some take food, and guns. I take paper."

We christened that afternoon the start of our paper revolution.

"Our first act of war," Isaac said, "is to hang these up where everyone can see them."

The fliers contained a new list of Crimes Against the Country.

"Why should they be the only ones who get to say stupid things?" he said.

That first flier listed four.

It is a Crime Against the Country to fail to report any
   Crimes committed Against the Country.
It is a Crime Against the Country not to know what is a
   Crime Against the Country.
It is a Crime Against the Country to ask what is a
   Crime Against the Country.
It is a Crime Against the Country to think or say there
   are too many Crimes Against the Country.

Isaac watched as I read and admired his work.

"I'm no poet like you," he said. "Just a poor comedian."

"We need one more," I said.

Isaac handed me his marker.

I wrote the fifth and final crime on each of the fliers before showing it to him:

It is a Crime Against the Country to read this.

He put his arm around my shoulder and kissed the top of my head.

"Together," he said, "we're remarkable."

We waited for midday, when the university shut down until the hottest part of the afternoon had passed, and then quickly posted the fliers on the entrances to the main buildings on campus. Isaac signed each one after we had taped it to the door: "The Paper Revolution Has Begun."

When we finished, I suggested we go home. I still thought like someone afraid of ruining his chances of becoming a student.

Isaac shook his head no. "They'll be gone by the end of the day, and we'll have missed out on all the fun."

Over the course of that afternoon, we stood outside of every building, Isaac right next to the doors, me a few feet behind him. It was better than we had hoped. A small rotating crowd of students hovered around each entrance. At one point someone tried to take one of the fliers down, but he was quickly pushed to the back of the crowd.

The next morning, when we returned to campus, the fliers and the paper revolution were all the students could talk about.

HELEN

I knew my time with Isaac was temporary. His visa granted him one year, and we never discussed the possibility of extending it. I did, despite my best efforts to stay grounded, sometimes imagine that one day we'd drive together to City Hall, nicely dressed, carrying simple silver bands picked up from the town's largest general store in our pockets, so that we could declare our marriage in front of a judge, in the hope that by doing so we would be able to make something permanent, a shared life which, as the saying goes, no man or woman could tear asunder. I imagined us living on a large farm, far away from any town and family, with only chickens and acres of corn for company.

"How would you feel about living on a farm?" I asked him.

"That depends. Are you there with me?"

"Maybe if you were good, I'd come visit you on the weekends."

When it came to more domestic fantasies, however, we fell apart. The distance between what we had and what we wanted was too obvious if we dreamed close to home.

I remember taking him to the post office once so he could mail a letter to his mother. While we stood in line to buy stamps, I asked him what her name was. He looked up as if he no longer knew the answer to that question, or had lost the right to answer it.

"Her name doesn't matter," he said. "Everyone only calls her Imaye. It means 'Mother.' "

When we reached the teller, Isaac handed me the envelope. He was shy speaking in front of strangers, so I was the one who asked how many stamps were needed to mail the letter. While we waited, I tried to pronounce her name the same way he had. I said out loud: "Im-e-ya . . . Im-a-yu."

"Not even close," he said.

He pronounced it once more so I could hear how far off I was, and finally, after failing two more times, I laughed and said, "Forget it. When we meet, I'll just call her Mother."

He became silent. What I had said bothered him. I didn't know him well enough yet to understand why, but I felt the distance expanding between us. We paid for the stamps and left the post office, and it wasn't until we were alone in the car that he told me what he was thinking.

"It doesn't do us any good to talk about things that will never happen," he said.

I promised myself I would never ask him about his family again, and by and large I stayed true to that. I thought as well, however, that if we couldn't have a future, I could at least try to make the most of our present. We were running out of errands and chores to complete, and it was time, I told him, we moved on to something else.

"We're going to have to find other things to do," I said, "except go to the grocery store."

"What would you like?"

I thought of all the possible options open to us. I thought of what normal couples did. They went to the movies, dinner. They invited friends over on the weekend. They had beach vacations. I knew we couldn't get away with any of that, so I told Isaac, "I don't know. But I'll come up with something."

I decided over breakfast with my mother that certain risks had to be taken if Isaac and I were going to have any sort of life together. I didn't make this decision lightly. She asked me that morning, while setting the table, "Do you have a new friend, Helen?" She was dependent on gentle phrasing; that was the register we carried on all our conversations in: "Would you like to help me with the shopping this weekend, Helen? Do you think it's time we changed the curtains in the living room, Helen?"

I always responded in kind.

"No one that I know of," I said. "But I promise to keep looking."

The last time she had asked that question was shortly after I began working with David. I spoke of him often around the house, and if there was anyone I spent the weekends and evenings with, it was him. She asked me repeatedly if David was a special friend—a hope abruptly relinquished once she met him. Telling her about Isaac wouldn't have brought her any comfort.

David was the only one who had suspected, and even he was quietly alarmed by the suggestion.

When we were alone, in his office, he had said, "I hope you know what you're doing with your Dickens." It wasn't a reproach; I had the feeling he found saying those words embarrassing. I nodded and tried to make it all seem lighthearted.

"Of course I know," I said. "I'm a professional at this."

We weren't divided like the South and had nothing to do with any of the large cities in the North. We were exactly what geography had made us: middle of the road, never bitterly segregated, but with lines dividing black from white all over town, whether in neighborhoods, churches, schools, or parks. We lived semi-peacefully apart, like a married couple in separate wings of a large house. That was the image I had in mind during breakfast when I decided something different had to be done. Change! It seemed to be everywhere except Laurel.

I set my sights low. Incremental progress was my philosophy. We didn't have to be heroes. There had been enough of those already, and in many ways, I reasoned, Isaac and I had already picked up the fight; we just hadn't known that was what we were doing. I made a list of all the places we had gone to in the three months since we'd met: the grocery store, the mall, post office, bank, Goodwill. I thought of them while sitting at my desk and tried to remember if any obvious signs of affection had passed between us. I came up with a crude value system to measure each trip by.

1) Shopping for food: After sex and children, what could be more intimate in America than choosing what kind of meat to cook? The grocery store was the first place in our town that I knew for certain we had conquered. We went once, sometimes twice a week. We laughed in the aisles, took turns pushing the cart. I gave him cooking lessons at the meat counter. Those were all important victories.

2) The post office: I had to admit that had been a terrible loss, and because it was a government office I felt I had to weigh the defeat a bit more. One post-office defeat was the equivalent of two grocery-store victories. Mail was dangerous, personal letters especially. They pointed to great distances and old, mysterious lives I knew nothing about. There were tellers instead of clerks, forms that had to be filled. It would be difficult, if not impossible, to win in a place like that.

3) Anything else that was related to shopping: furniture, plates, cutlery—we had chosen all that together, right under the skeptical eye of the clerks. Had Isaac and I

touched each other once, I would have said we dealt an important blow against segregation, but I had to be honest. I knew we had never touched except by accident, so I had to temper the victory with the knowledge that we could have done better.

What I needed next were new targets. The first one that came to mind was the most obvious, and I couldn't believe I hadn't thought of it before. A week after our defeat at the post office, I called Isaac from my office and said I wanted to take him out to lunch.

"To lunch?"

"Yes," I said, "for lunch. I'm tired of eating at my desk alone."

I chose the same diner my father had gone to every morning, and where as a child I had joined him on Saturday afternoons. It was the only place in Laurel that I associated exclusively with him. I had been going there for years, on my own and with friends and co-workers, but those other occasions were mere intrusions on the central event, a semi-regular father-daughter lunch that had lasted for two years and that had ended in one of those booths with my father promising to visit every week once he moved out. A month went by before I saw him again. I stopped worrying, and then, with more time, caring if he returned. Gradually, my memories of him were distilled into a single fluid image of a man confined to a booth, or counter, with thick sideburns and occasionally a soft mustache that moved when he spoke, which wasn't often.

The diner was never officially segregated, but I couldn't remember anyone who wasn't white eating there, either. In this case it was etiquette, and not a sign, that served as the cover for our division. Before I left to pick up Isaac, I wrote down on a piece of paper in case I forgot it later: "We have every right to be here."

We arrived shortly after noon, when I knew the restaurant would be crowded. Isaac said he could meet me there, but I insisted on picking him up so everyone could see us walk in together. The lunch counter was already full. Of the half-dozen men sitting there, I knew three by name and the others were familiar. Bill, whose chest and forearms were known throughout Laurel for the strong black hair that sprouted from them, was leaning over the counter smiling halfheartedly at everyone who came and left. My father used to tell me to be careful with my food when Bill stood over us. "He sheds," he told me, "like a dog."

In the scripted version that had played in my head during the five-minute drive from Isaac's apartment to the restaurant, the entire diner fell silent as soon as we entered. All eyes turned toward us, and we ignored them. We didn't hold hands—that would have been too provocative—but we did pause to look at each other with what I thought of as an abundance of affection. In the version we lived, no one stopped talking. Bill saw me as soon as I walked in and pointed to a table in the middle of the diner. Isaac followed me, but I was so focused on making it to the table that I never stopped to notice if anyone was staring at him. We took our seats. When I picked up my menu as a cover so I could look around the room, I realized no one had noticed yet how remarkable we were.

Isaac saw my gaze wandering. "Why are we here?" he asked me.

I looked around the room again. I thought I saw Bill and two of the men at the counter staring in our general direction.

"No particular reason," I told him. "I just wanted to get out."

I asked Isaac what he had done all day.

"I was at the library," he said.

He described the book on contemporary American architecture he had been reading. I told him twice that it sounded very interesting. "Fascinating," I said, "what they can build these days." Chitchat. Simple conversation. When Isaac put his hand on the table, I took his pinky and index finger in mine. I held them for two, maybe three seconds while looking at the menu. I used a strand of loose hair as an excuse to let go.

Our waitress came and took our order. I ordered the fried chicken; Isaac pointed to the Denver omelet and let me order for him.

After our waitress left, I turned my attention back to the counter. I wanted to tell Isaac what my father had said about Bill, but he was no longer there; with him gone, the men at the counter stopped pretending they weren't staring at us.

I tried to ignore them, but then our waitress came back empty-handed, and I felt certain that if I looked over again at them I'd see them smiling. She was young, fresh out of high school. Had I been younger, I would have known who she was. She had a kind, round face and wore her dark-brown hair in a bun. She leaned over and whispered to us, "Bill wants to know if you would like to take your food with you." She was doing her best to be kind.

Isaac understood immediately what was happening, and, in the same breath, knew how to respond. Before I could answer, he told her, "No. We would rather eat here"—polite yet determined. She nodded her head; she had no idea what else she could do. Isaac pursed his lips and waited until she had returned to the kitchen before turning his attention to me.

"Do you come here frequently?" he asked.

I nodded yes, then changed my mind and said, "No, not really."

"Which one is it?"

"I used to come here when I was younger," I said, "but I don't that often anymore." It was true: the diner was a few blocks away from my office, but I went there once a month, at most.

"We should go," I said.

Isaac hadn't stopped staring at me since the waitress left. I was tempted to confess my reasons for bringing him, but I realized I didn't have to. The best intentions didn't change what was obvious: I should have known better.

"I'm not going to run," he said. "I'm going to eat my lunch."

Briefly, I felt bold again. I saw myself adding this lunch to my column of victories once I returned to the office. If we made it through this, then perhaps there was nothing in the world that we couldn't conquer, from post offices to movie theaters and the all-too-perilous family dinner at home. I was imagining what my mother would say if Isaac were to show up one Sunday evening, when his lunch arrived. The same waitress brought it, although this time she didn't look at either of us. Her embarrassment was evident. Isaac's omelet was on a stack of thin paper plates barely large enough to hold the food. A plastic fork and knife had been wrapped in a napkin and placed on top, a strangely delicate touch that she must have been responsible for. He unwrapped the knife and fork and placed the palm-sized napkin on his lap.

"Do you mind if I start? I hate eggs when they're cold."

He spoke so calmly I assumed he was joking, and I suppose to some degree he was. I tried to laugh—ha-ha—but then he cut his omelet into seven even pieces before taking the first bite. He chewed slowly. With every bite I was reminded that we were no longer, if ever, on the same side.

He had finished his omelet by the time my order arrived on the standard cream-colored plates used for everyone other than

Isaac. The waitress tried to walk away quickly, but I grabbed her wrist and told her I wanted to cancel my order. "Tell Bill that I don't want to eat here."

The poor child—she was struggling not to cry. We didn't make it any easier on her.

"Leave the plate," Isaac said to her. "We're going to stay and eat it."

She hurried back to the kitchen. I stared at the plate of chicken and mashed potatoes and blinked twice, childishly hoping I could make it vanish.

"Please," I said to him, "let's leave now."

He shook his head no.

"Not until we both finish our lunch," he said. "That's what you wanted, isn't it?"

If that was his way of settling the score, then I thought I could play along just as well. For the next ten minutes, I slowly took my food apart. With my first halfhearted stab into the chicken, all the momentum was gone; there was nothing we could change. I felt a regression back to my mother's kitchen table, where I had spent many nights and afternoons laboring to finish a meal that my father had never shown up for and that my mother had refused. I had always known that there was something cruel in her insistence that I eat every bite on my plate while my father's food grew cold next to me. She needed a victim besides herself, and when I finally looked up at Isaac after a few minutes and saw him smiling at me, I knew there was something slightly cruel lurking in his gaze.

I was too busy creating a new story to linger on that thought. In this story, Isaac and I were still heroes. The fact that we chose to sit there and linger when every part of me wanted to run was proof of the sacrifices we were willing to make.

When we left the restaurant and were back in the car, he said to me, "Now you know. This is how they break you, slowly, in pieces."

ISAAC

Isaac wanted to celebrate the paper revolution's first victory. "Very soon," he said, "the whole campus will know who we are. After that we'll be famous." We felt that we were getting somewhere, that we were more than just idle spectators of campus life and more than just friends. We formed a team, and our opposition was anyone who wasn't us.

Isaac suggested I choose a poet's name. "You're no longer just the Professor," he said. "It's time you moved on to something new. Choose someone famous, but not too famous."

I chose Langston.

"He's a poet?" he asked me.

"Yes," I told him, "a great one," although I had never read anything by him, and wasn't even certain that he was a poet. I knew that he had attended that conference of writers at the university, and that I had instantly felt attached to his name.

To celebrate our rise, Isaac suggested we go to the Café Flamingo, which was then the most popular of all the cafés that sat along the winding, tree-lined road leading up to the campus. The students who spent time in those cafés had a reputation for ordering lavishly. They commanded pastries, teas, and coffee like mini-sovereigns and then later fought over who would pay. Normally, Isaac and I would have been embarrassed to sit in one of those cafés for hours with only enough money to order tea, but Isaac was feeling victorious, and there was nothing that could shame him.

"That's where we belong," he said, "in one of those expensive cafés with the rest of the students. Years from now, they will say, 'That is where Isaac and Langston the Poet Professor met.'"

The owners of the Café Flamingo were rumored to be multiple things: Lebanese businessmen; distant cousins of the president, or one of his close allies. No one knew for sure, and it was better to believe that the café, and those who dined there, were in proximity to some form of power. The truth, as I learned later, was more simple and complex. The café had been opened by a French-American couple who fled the country after independence. The two middle-aged African women who worked there day in and day out were not the help, but the wives of the two brothers who had legally claimed the café as their own after its abandonment, and who for years had run the place as if it were their own. They did so, however, not as businessmen but as loyal friends and followers of a young man who had just returned to the capital after years of exile in England.

On the afternoon when Isaac and I decided to stop at the Flamingo, a pair of the marabou storks that hung lazily around the city were perched on the ground just in front of the café, staring at the four plastic flamingos that had been nailed into the dirt just outside the front door. They stretched their wings and cast their shadows over the plastic birds, and when nothing happened they began to fly slowly away. Those birds were harmless, but their elongated, pointed beaks suggested nature or time had denuded them; their ugly bald heads made them look like masters of prey. One of the students sitting outside on the plastic lawn chairs threw a spoon in their direction, and you could see, even though they were already almost a foot in the air, that they were afraid. They flapped their wings faster until they found refuge on the roof of a building across the street.

Whether any of the students noticed Isaac and me take our seats outside is hard to say. We aroused only the mildest curiosity. Had we walked off, no one would have thought of us again, but Isaac didn't want it to be that way, and so it wasn't. He chose a table next to a group of boys who had their wide, butterfly-collared shirts exposed to reveal the gold underneath. Two spoke with genuine English accents, different in register from the fraudulent ones often heard around the campus. All of them wore freshly polished shoes.

"This place is full of Alexes," I said to him.

"I know," he said. "That's why we came here."

Isaac clapped loudly to get the waitress's attention. The boys stopped their discussion and turned toward him. They immediately saw us for the poor village boys that we were.

They started laughing at us in unison. A boy in a blue-and-white shirt stood and began to clap slowly while looking directly at us. The rest followed: some stood, a few sat, but all of them except one man were clapping and mocking us. The students sitting inside looked out the window to watch. Even though they didn't know why, I'm sure they understood we were being humiliated.

Poor Isaac. He was outsized and outnumbered, but I didn't know him well enough to understand that this made no difference to him.

"Don't get up," he said. "I know how to handle this."

And so I sat while he made his way toward them. It was a slower, more tempered version of his usual lope. He paused mid-stride, bent down, and briefly grazed the ground with his right hand. No one other than me noticed he had picked something up. When he was a few meters away from the boys, who were applauding and looking directly at him as if he were merely the shell of a man, the form without the beating heart, he turned back to see if I was watching. I was; I had worked hard not to turn away.

Isaac took two more long strides, during which he aimed, wound his arm, and released the rock he had been carrying into the mouth of the boy in the blue-and-white shirt. The applause stopped in time to hear the bones in the boy's jaw crack.

Isaac was taken down quickly. He held his ground as three, maybe four boys roughly the same size as him charged. I kept my eyes focused on him long enough to know that he made no attempt to run, and then I stopped looking. He was punched and kicked for several minutes. I heard the blows land. The beating would have lasted much longer had those boys not been ordered to stop by the older man who had been sitting near, but not exactly with them. When I turned back, the man had his arm around two of their shoulders and was walking them out of the café.

Isaac was still conscious, bleeding from his mouth and nose. His face and arms seemed to be swelling as I knelt next to his head.

"What should I do?" I asked him.

He tried to laugh, but his lungs refused.

"This is nothing," he said. "Go home and pretend this never happened."

One of the women who worked in the café and two men who took orders from her came to attend to him. She pressed into his ribs, chest, and stomach and placed a damp rag over his forehead. She gestured up with her hand and the men lifted Isaac slowly from his waist and shoulder.

I tried to follow them into the café but Isaac continued to mumble with what little breath he had that I should go home. I stopped once we reached the door. I was standing next to Isaac's feet. One step farther back and I wouldn't have heard him say, "We need you on campus."

Two weeks passed before I saw Isaac again. I searched for him on campus and in our neighborhood, retracing the routes he was most likely to take. I had only a general sense of where his house should have been, so I wandered through the most obscure corners of our slum in the hope that I might hear his voice out of a window, or see his face in a crowd. At the end of the first week, I began to worry that his injuries were worse than I thought. Later, I felt certain that he had been brought into the café so he could be discreetly finished off, and there was always the fear, present from the beginning, that Isaac had been rounded up and thrown into a prison on a whim, or because of what he had done, and if that was true it was unlikely I would ever see him again.

Near the end of the second week, I thought I saw him lying on a mattress on the floor of a one-room home, naked except for a thin white blanket draped over his waist. I whispered through the open window, "Isaac, Isaac." When the arm moved, I saw that it wasn't Isaac. The boy was roughly our age and the same height and weight as Isaac, but with a deformed palate that must have made it hard for him to speak. He looked at me and waved. I waved back. I was so grateful that someone had actually noticed me that I stood there waving for another minute, perhaps much longer. Before Isaac, I had always been content to cast myself as the outsider, because only by such measures, I thought, could you break from the grips of the family and tribe around which you were supposed to order your life. I had ventured far away from home to live up to that idea without understanding that, inevitably, something had to be paid for it. Every day following Isaac's absence, I was reminded that without him I made an impact on no one. I was seen, and perhaps occasionally heard, strictly by strangers, and always in passing. I was a much poorer man for this than I had ever thought.

Isaac made a dramatic return to campus on a Monday afternoon. He looked heroic as he walked through the front gates with dark bruises beneath both eyes, a gash across his pointed chin, and a patch of scabs across the right side of his face. He limped gracefully but with force, as if trying to show the damage wasn't permanent. I watched as every head turned toward him. I knew the injuries were genuine, but still I thought, You're doing a wonderful job, Isaac. By the time he reached me, there were pockets of students all across the main lawn whispering about him.

Had I not been so uncertain as to where I stood with Isaac, I would have made more of his return. I would have told him that it was good to see him again, that he had been missed.

"So—you're finally back," I said. I couldn't decide if I should hold out my hand.

"Yes," he said. "I knew this place would be empty without me."

And we left it there. I followed Isaac toward the center of the campus—to the large, open space where most of the students gathered. When we reached the southwest corner of the square, a spot normally occupied by the only two Angolans on campus, we stopped. Isaac didn't acknowledge it, but it was obvious he was feeling tired.

"We should sit," he said.

"There's a bench over there." I pointed to a spot far from the center but covered in shade.

"Too far," Isaac said, and it was then that I caught the distinct wheezing in his breath. He had carried his limp far enough. He leaned gently backward against a young tree that bent slightly against his weight. He eased his way onto the ground and pulled his knees up to his chest.

Throughout the morning, every person who passed us stared at Isaac. There were brutally broken bodies begging on street corners across the city, and most of us hardly noticed them. People stared at Isaac because they assumed he was a student at the university, and therefore they thought they knew how he had earned his injuries. Several days earlier, a large crowd had marched along one of the main boulevards leading up to the presidential palace, demanding some sort of reform. They were allowed to get within a hundred yards of the palace before the tear gas and clubs came out. The first time I heard Isaac connected to that protest was when a young woman walked past us and, without breaking her stride, said, "Our country needs more boys like you." Many other students waved or said hello to him—even the militant Rhodesians, who didn't trust anybody.

"You've become very popular," I said, "and you haven't even been around."

"I know," Isaac said. "It's a shame. I should have had myself beaten earlier. I could have been president by now."

I didn't judge him for letting that misconception spread, but only because I believed the timing of his return was a coincidence.

Isaac offered little about where he had been and what had happened since the fight at the café. When I asked him, he told me those things didn't matter. "It's over," he said. "I'm here now." Because I was ashamed for having left him, I was happy to settle for that as an answer.

· · ·

The weeks after that were calm around the university. One semester ended and a new one began, but for Isaac and me the difference was negligible. We returned to the university in January as if nothing had changed, which was true as long as we remained focused solely on our second lives on campus. There were rumors and a few sparely written stories in the English-language newspapers about more arrests and violence on the edges of the city, which I read and then ignored, as if they were dispatches from a foreign country. Isaac and I continued to spend our days in the center of campus, no longer relegated to the margins, where I felt more comfortable. The attention cast toward Isaac waned but never vanished. It was understood that Isaac could always be found in the same spot, even if no one had yet tried to seek him out. When I suggested to Isaac that we find a quieter, less obvious corner of the campus, he insisted he couldn't do it. "We're becoming known," he said, "Why would we quit now?"

Each day at dusk we made our way back home. Isaac was still limping, although less noticeably. Walking required his concentration, but I suspected he had to remember to struggle. If he was lying about his injury, I was hardly ready to hold him accountable. His wounds had gotten him somewhere. He was a figure, even if without a name, and I understood his desire to hold on to that until another step on the university's social ladder had been mounted. Once that was done, I knew he would give up the limp and the bandages; fortunately, he would have the scars. I imagined him pointing to an old wound on his hand or face, and saying, "This one came from the police." Or, "This one I can't remember anymore. I have so many on my body."

HELEN

What I feared most for Isaac and me happened that afternoon in the diner. It seemed impossible now for us to move forward, and I assumed after that lunch that if there was any relationship left it would live on in the strictest privacy, late at night and exclusively in his apartment, with all the blinds closed and the lights off. Whatever warmth and affection we had would quickly burn out, until, eventually, we stopped speaking and became bitter strangers. I returned to the office that afternoon with a weight in the center of my chest. I spent hours trying to shake it. I went to the bathroom repeatedly. I drank cup after cup of water. When David asked me how I was feeling, I nearly choked trying to answer him.

"I think I'm coming down with a cold," I said.

He looked me up and down. He claimed to always know when someone was lying to him, "No, you're not. But go home anyway."

I stayed in my bedroom all evening. My mother came to the door twice and asked if I wanted some tea, and then, later, soup. I felt the limits of my life every time she knocked. I fell asleep promising myself greater independence—a home, and then a life, and someday soon a family of my own.

. . .

I made it almost two weeks before I called on Isaac. A part of me hoped that, given enough time, he might begin to forget what I looked like, that my chin and nose and eyes might begin to blur with the images of a million other women, and that when that happened the pieces of me that I thought mattered the most to him would be restored. I prepared myself as well for the possibility that we would never recover. I looked in the classified section of the newspaper for an apartment in a different town, a relic of the Westerns I had watched with my father. I checked off the vacancies while whispering to myself, "This town isn't big enough for the both of us."

I shared hints of my plan with my mother, without revealing the reason behind it.

"I think it's time I found a place of my own," I said.

She sipped her tea and waited until she had placed her cup back on the saucer to respond.

"Why would you ever want to do that, Helen? Don't you think we're doing well together?"

I was the sole long-term relationship she had. She went to church on Sundays and spent one or two afternoons a week having tea at someone's house, but those were only the rituals of life, performed faithfully as a substitute for the real thing. Finally, I was worried about becoming her.

I decided on Thursday, when the second week of not seeing each other was almost over, that I would drop by Isaac's house. I was going to make a joke, something along the lines of "Are you hungry? I know a great little diner that has the best omelets in town." We'd laugh and then fall into each other's arms, and, in the weeks afterward, find ways of mocking what had happened until it eventually became one of those stories that couples use to remind themselves of the obstacles they had overcome and the distance they had traveled. Isaac never gave me that chance, however. He came unannounced to my office early Friday morning, and I knew when I saw him sitting with his legs crossed and a tabloid magazine that was at least two years old spread across his lap that it wasn't an accident that he had come to me first. He knew, whether by instinct or by careful thought, that I was one or two days away from doing the same, and that, had I been able to do so, some of the power in our relationship might have tipped in my favor.

I'd never felt afraid of him before, but seeing him in that chair that morning I was reminded of how little I knew about him, and for a few seconds I considered turning around and running away. I told myself I was worried about what my coworkers would think if they came through the door and saw us so awkwardly arranged, that there was something valid to that logic made it easier to believe that was the real reason I found it hard to stand there.

I tried my best to give off an air of professional detachment.

"I'm sorry," I said. "Did we have an appointment scheduled for today?"

If David had heard me, he would have said I was a terrible actress. My attempt at sounding detached was a bad cliché of the wounded-lover role I was trying so hard to avoid.

"No," Isaac said. "We did not have an appointment scheduled for today. I came for personal reasons."

Who speaks like that? I wanted to yell this at him until he gave me an honest answer. It wasn't just his words but the tone that came with them. If he sounded like a character from Dickens, it was because he had decided that was what proper English sounded like. I didn't hear his real voice until the very end of our relationship, in the months just before he was supposed to leave. It began with a slip—he called me "love" instead of Helen. "Love," he said, "come here," and he extended his arms to me, knowing I would meet him. He rarely ever called me Helen again. Instead of asking if I wanted to stay the night, he'd simply say, "So what now, love?" while squeezing my hand or pressing his body against mine.

But before getting to that point, I had to convince myself that whatever Isaac said next was true. When he said, "I came here because I was concerned about you. I wanted to make sure you were all right," I focused strictly on the words; despite their restraint, they were enough to move me. He didn't say that he missed me or cared about me; I added that for him. I told myself the only reason he hadn't said as much was that he lacked the confidence to do so, not the heart.

"Are you happy to see me?" he asked. "Should I have not come?"

"Of course I'm happy," I told him.

And I genuinely was.

Isaac left the office immediately afterward. He looked to make sure no one was watching before kissing me as softly as possible on the cheek. I wished he'd had an old bowler hat he could have put on before walking out the door, something to match the antiquated way we had made up. For the next two weeks, I left work early and went to his apartment. In the beginning, we hardly talked before moving to the bedroom. The first two times, he acted as if he was surprised I had come at all.

"You're here," he said.

"I got lost on my way home," I told him.

"Follow me," he said. "I have a map somewhere in my bedroom."

We needed disguises. One day it was a map; the next, I pretended I had come in search of a glass of water.

"Water?" he said.

"Tomorrow I promise to do better."

We didn't know where all the cracks and fault lines between us lay, and so we said little, in order to avoid them. Once we were in the bedroom, we rushed through our clothes. Kissing was an afterthought. It wasn't until he was inside me that I felt I could look at him closely. We spent hours in bed each night, testing the range of what could be said. We'd fall asleep, and then one of us would wake up and immediately climb on top of the other, as if desperately trying to make a point that hadn't yet been touched upon or that needed repeating. By the time I left, it was always well after midnight—six to eight hours would have passed, during which I might have said no more than a few hundred words, not one of which had any special meaning. Once I returned home, on the way up to my bedroom, I'd stop outside my mother's room, at the opposite end of the long hallway lined with pictures taken more than two decades ago. Even before they separated, the only thing my parents had that resembled a relationship was the fact that they slept in the same bed. I remembered trying to sleep with them as a child and finding that I felt more alone lying between them than I did in my own room.

I hadn't stood outside their bedroom door since I was a teenager, trying to sneak out of the house. I used to press my ear against the door and count to fifty before deciding it was safe to go. Gradually, that number was whittled down to thirty, and then ten, until I was finally certain that I would never hear anything coming out of that room.

The first five nights I came home late from Isaac's apartment, I found myself pitying my mother for the cold and virtually barren life she had shared with my father. I thought the kindest thing I could do for her would be to crawl into her bed and press my body against hers, so she would know how much comfort could be found in being held while you slept. If I did this, maybe some trace of that affection would linger on in her room after I left.

As I said, though, those feelings only lasted for five nights. By the sixth, I couldn't remember what had made me carry on like that. I left Isaac's apartment knowing that we were sleeping with each other not to draw closer but to try and rid ourselves of a desire we both thought we would be better off without. After he came, I'd try to get him back inside me, and when that failed, I told him, "Don't sleep. I can wait." I left thinking I had had enough of him, only to realize, before reaching home, that I felt emptier now than I had before I saw him.

I still stopped outside my mother's bedroom that night, and every night after for the next week, but it wasn't out of pity. Each time I stood in front of the door, I wanted to throw it open so I could stand at the foot of her bed and, as she dragged herself out of sleep, tell her in intimate detail how I'd spent my evening with Isaac, from the time I walked into his apartment and silently undressed in his bedroom, until the moment I left while he was sleeping, or at least pretending to. And if when I finished she asked why I was telling her this, I'd say, "So you can see how much we resemble one another."

ISAAC

It wasn't long before students began to join Isaac and me at our tree in the center of campus. They had heard rumors about Isaac and knew nothing about me, but regardless our daily vigil on the grass had made us familiar, comforting figures to gather around. We had no obvious politics, and, compared with many of the other students, who squatted on the grass under banners of Lenin and maps of a borderless Africa, we seemed innocent, if not harmless. The only marker we had to distinguish us was a sign that Isaac posted on the tree behind us every day we were there: "What Crimes Against the Country have you committed today?"

The sign, as he saw it, was an invitation for the entire campus to join our paper revolution, since, according to him, "everyone has a crime to confess."

On either side of us were two opposing camps of student communists. Each day they unfurled signs announcing the People's Revolution and the Communist Utopia. Their portraits of Marx and Lenin grew larger every week. They yelled insults at each other from their separate camps—rarely in English, the language of the capitalists.

"You know what they fight over?" Isaac said. "Posters—who has the bigger flag."

Isaac claimed that, unlike the other student radicals and revolutionaries, he had no agenda. "We are a true democracy," he said. "The paper revolution is for everyone."

I assumed that the story of our paper revolution was already forgotten, and that Isaac's crude sign was a poor attempt to recapture some of the glory of that afternoon. The day Isaac hung his sign, however, students came. Whether it was out of curiosity or boredom didn't matter. Even the ones who knew nothing about him did exactly what he wanted: they played the game; they sat down and stayed long enough to confess.

The first students who came to Isaac were cousins. Their names were Patience and Hope, and they were dressed in matching pleated gray skirts that took the risk of being cut almost an inch above the knee.

"Sit," he told them, and then he gestured with his hand toward me. "This is my friend Langston the Professor, the future Emperor of Ethiopia." Before they had the time to question what they were doing, he said, "Now, tell me, what crimes against our country have you committed today?"

Neither was timid, and Isaac was perfectly at ease; I was the one who, in the company of women my own age, wanted to run.

Patience, whose mouth bristled with clean, hard white teeth, spoke first. "Does sitting here count as a crime?" she asked.

Isaac smiled. "Yes," he said, "it definitely does."

He turned to Hope, who was leaning against her cousin. "And you," he said. "If you're related, then that makes you guilty as well."

They laughed. They had come to be amused, and Isaac had charmed them. He didn't try for more than that. After they had played their role, he asked where they were from and what they were studying. Both were majoring in economics; they were born and raised in the capital.

"Economics," Isaac said, "that's very good," but I knew that, like me, he had only a vague understanding of what that meant: money, who had it and who didn't. As Patience and Hope walked away, Isaac told them not to forget to say goodbye to the future emperor. Only Patience acknowledged me: "Goodbye, Emperor," she said. By the time I thought to respond, she was too far away to hear me. Isaac watched me follow her with my eyes.

"Don't worry," he said. "She'll be back."

Patience and Hope were just the beginning. More students came and introduced themselves to Isaac so he could ask them what crimes they had committed that day. One boy confessed to stealing money from his father, to which Isaac responded: "Stealing is not a crime in this country. Not stealing, however, is a terrible thing." All the boys and girls close enough to hear that made sure everyone saw them laugh. When they were gone, Isaac whispered to me: "Did you see who laughed the hardest?" I hadn't, and I doubt he had, either, but I knew the answer.

"The boys with the polished shoes," I said.

"That's right. It was Alex."

If students didn't know what to say, he adjusted the rules of his game. He helped them invent their crimes. He borrowed from the president's daily radio broadcasts, which for months had been long, rambling diatribes against all the enemies of the country, from the Europeans and Americans to the Africans who were secretly working with them.

"Have you ever been an imperialist?" he asked them. "Have you ever tried to colonize a country?" "Do you listen to British Radio?" "Do you know who the Queen of England is?" "Have you ever been friends with a European?" "Have you ever wanted to go to America?"

Over the course of a few weeks, Isaac's confessions drew hundreds of students, and of those, a few dozen returned consistently. On most days, those of us gathered under the tree did so simply to be in the company of others. There was comfort, even a certain amount of joy, in finding one another in the grass and in seeing others join us. We were two, then five and ten, sometimes as many as twenty. Most of us didn't know one another's names or ages or reasons for being there, and that was fine, because silence isn't the same when it's shared. Its sad and lonely sides are shunted off. We were content just to be there, and had nothing else ever come out of it, I'm certain I would have regarded those moments as some of the most memorable of my life.

The protests that had begun at the start of the semester turned violent at the same time Isaac's confessions were making him a celebrity on campus. When we returned home one evening, we heard how, in another shanty village that neither of us had ever been to, tires had been cast around the necks of four soldiers who had come to arrest someone. After a few minutes of watching the soldiers struggle to free themselves, someone doused the tires with gasoline and set them ablaze. The smell and their cries were said to have been so strong that no one stayed to watch them die; they were left to smolder for almost an hour, with the extra shame of having no one there to witness their torture. The next day, the neighborhood was cordoned off, and for twenty-four hours no one who lived there was allowed to leave. A few days later, several people were shot while walking too close to the palace gates as part of a supposed plot to kill the president. The proof came in the arrests of the dead people's family and friends, who filled in the script when they confessed to the conspiracy that had been invented for them. And so, even though our neighborhood was quiet, everyone who lived around us felt vulnerable. If tomorrow it was decided that your neighbor, whom you had known your whole life, was trying to undermine the government, then the only thing you could say was "Yes, I had suspected that might be possible all along."

Isaac and I did our best to ignore what was happening. While we were walking home from the campus, I asked what he thought about the soldiers who had been burned; rather than respond, he took my wrist and asked if I was making any progress with Patience, who for the past four days had joined our crowd for an hour after lunch.

"I'm taking my time," I told him.

"Maybe you should try for Hope instead."

We spent the rest of our walk making crude, childish jokes about which was better, patience or hope. We should have been too old to talk like that, but we were at heart village boys, ignorant and immature about love in any form. Isaac and I never talked about the old relationships we may have had, and we never mentioned our desire for love or sex, which could be bought easily in almost every neighborhood in the capital. We avoided such conversations for the same reasons we avoided talking about the dead soldiers, the heavily armed patrols, and the pickup trucks that now sat, day and night, filled with bored, armed men, on the edges of every poor neighborhood in the capital. We were afraid of what would come next.

Up on the hill where the university and the neighborhoods that bordered it sat, little had changed. Isaac took down his sign in March. "I think it's gone on long enough," he said. He had earned the respect of the communists on both sides of us. Students waved or said hello as they passed. When he took down the sign, I asked if he knew what he was going to do next.

"I do."

· · ·

He leaned against his tree and crossed his legs as if preparing to nap. "I'm going to enjoy this for as long as it lasts."

The hours we spent on campus followed us home at the end of the day. For weeks we were only visitors in our real lives, and even then we were terrible tourists, purposefully blind to the plainclothesmen who watched all the houses with notebooks in their hands, deaf to the evening shouts around us. I knew it wouldn't last long. My landlord, Thomas, came to my room one evening and told me to pay attention at night, especially when I was supposed to be sleeping. "Rest in the day," he said. "Keep your eyes open at night. I tell this to everyone." But I knew it was me he was worried about. I was a foreigner. I had no ties to any of the local or even distant tribes. I played on the grass in the afternoon with Isaac, and then worried late at night. It was always in times of trouble that those on the outside suffered most, and though I never shared any of my fears with Isaac, I was terrified someone would realize that if I was killed or injured, if I abruptly disappeared, there would be no one to answer to. I imagined my neighbors and Thomas—who when drunk said I was like a son to him, though we knew little about each other—pointing to my room and saying, "Take him. He's behind the trouble. And no one will know."

As it turned out, it was Isaac who was cast out into the street first. Not long after the soldiers were burned, the friends of his father whom he had been living with told him they could no longer afford to keep him there.

"They told me they don't have enough space for another person," he said. That was on the first night of his homelessness, when he came and knocked on the walls outside my room sometime after midnight, looking for a place to sleep. Because it was night, Isaac knew better than to say more, in case someone was listening or I turned out to be the type that was easily frightened. Isaac made a bed on the floor out of the clothes he had brought with him. One of us often fell asleep for a half-hour or less while on campus. Whoever was awake sat guard; in most cases, I was the one who slept. Those brief naps had become the best sleep I got, because it was daytime and because I knew Isaac was next to me and wouldn't leave unless I awoke. I turned onto my side so I could see his outline on the floor.

"I know you're tired," he said. "Don't worry. Nothing is going to happen. Get some sleep."

I tried to sound as confident as he did. "I'm not worried," I said, but it was obvious I was scared and had been for many days.

"You're an emperor," he told me. "King of kings. No harm can come to you."

I listened to him breathe. I counted his breaths. I doubt I made it to a hundred before I was asleep. I didn't wake up until late the next morning, and by then he was gone.

A notice was published in all the newspapers that morning, warning people not to gather in large numbers. It took the top spot on every front page, under headlines such as "Government Warns of Increasing Risks in Public Gatherings." The risks were never named, but in case people failed to understand the story's true intent, there was a quote from the army declaring, "Our heightened security measures would make it unwise for those looking to disturb the peace and tranquility of our city to show their faces outside." Had the article simply stated what its authors knew to be true, something along the lines of "Mass arrests and torture have been planned" or, more simply, "Leave now," a lot of time and an unknown number of lives could have been saved. Instead, there were several days of random beatings and arrests of young men across the capital before a mass retreat indoors began. By the end of the week, wedding parties were being held inside; the few open fields used for football games sat empty; funerals were no longer accompanied by long lines of mourners who were unafraid to wail and rend their garments in public.

When I saw Isaac on campus again, I asked him where he was living. He told me that he was staying with someone far away from our neighborhood and that I shouldn't worry. "I have friends who have given me a place," he said.

I went to campus daily, to see him but also simply to breathe easier, to walk, sit, and read without fear. I knew that this wouldn't be true for much longer; the noose cast over the city would find its way up the hill, regardless of how many ministers' children were at the university. I'm sure Isaac knew that, too, and why, in the days following the headlines, the number of students who gathered around him began to grow rapidly. The police who patrolled the campus had taken note of our numbers and begun to linger around the edge of our group. They looked nervous, suspicious as they circled us with their batons slung over their backs. Someone from inside our circle noted out loud for all to hear, including the guards standing near us: "There is nothing more restless than men in power."

Our gathering was broken up on a Friday afternoon at the start of April, after all the classes had ended. Our numbers that

Friday were no larger than they had been the week before: we were twenty or thirty at most. The only difference was that we huddled closer together. When four campus guards in their shabby blue uniforms, wielding their worn wooden nightsticks, surrounded us, more than a minute must have passed before any of us thought to run. We felt safe the closer we were to one another, and each of us was reluctant to give that up.

The guards waited until they were certain they had our attention before they began to swing. To their credit, they aimed for the padded parts of our bodies, and all the women who were with us were left alone. Imagine four angry mothers trying to paddle a classroom of running children and you have a sense of what that afternoon looked like. We ran, but often enough circled back to pick up a book that had been left on the grass, or to grab someone's arm to lead him away while a guard chased after him, swinging mildly at his back.

The only one among us who didn't run was Isaac. When I looked for him, he was just standing up, his arms at his sides so his entire body was fully exposed. A few minutes passed before one of the guards noticed him. He was the perfect image of defiance, with his arms folded over his chest and his legs slightly spread apart. They're going to bash his head in, I thought. Seconds later came the crack of wood meeting bone.

The guards left Isaac where he fell. When I came back, ten minutes later, he was already gone. I walked to the tree where I had last seen him and searched the grass for proof that he had been there—an impression of a body pressed into the grass, a few flecks of blood—but there was nothing. I waited for one hour, and then two, knowing he wouldn't return, but hoping that perhaps he might see me and know that this time I hadn't abandoned him. I had tried my best to stand ground; failing that, I became a one-man vigil.

I waited each night for Isaac to knock on my window; I would have taken him in without hesitation, but I was afraid as well that he would ask. Every day, new checkpoints were erected in the city, and within days it was impossible to penetrate the cluster of shacks that ringed our neighborhood and the two surrounding it without showing your official ID. Every coming and going, except those through obscure back routes that wound through half-burnt piles of trash and open latrine pits, eventually had a checkpoint where young men logged into notebooks the names and occupations of everyone who passed. No bureaucracy in the country until then had ever worked properly. Years could be lost in search of a birth certificate, driver's license, or passport. It was easy to be invisible in a city that had clearly stretched its limits and was bursting at its seams. The daily records of names, entries, and departures signaled the end of that.

I assumed Isaac had chosen to keep his distance. I imagined that, after recovering on a bed in a stranger's apartment, he had walked to our neighborhood and taken note of the checkpoints and the blue-and-gray fatigues of the presidential guard. Then he would turn his head in the other direction, to hide the bruises that covered his face, and walk farther and farther north, past the last of the slums, until he reached a corner of the city that was barely inhabited and that until a few years earlier had been a village of a dozen thatch-roofed huts. If I wanted to believe that, then I could also just as easily imagine Isaac walking until he had abandoned the city altogether, stopping after he had traveled well beyond the reach of the president's powers, to a village that had been touched slightly by the British and not at all by the new government. I'd be lying if I didn't admit this was exactly what I hoped Isaac had done, as much for his sake as mine. Each day I didn't hear from him, I was more convinced he was lost to me. I didn't have the heart or courage to imagine him in prison, much less dead; I thought of him simply as lost, one of the millions across the world who one day vanished and could therefore rise again.

When I returned to campus, after a week, it was obvious that the days of banners, posters, and speeches were over. I knew, as soon as I passed through the front gates of the university and saw at least a hundred students sitting shoulder to shoulder, back to back, on the same grounds where Isaac and I had often sat, that the only thing left of the campus I had known was the buildings. The students had conquered that piece of land, and their huddled mass was proof of the lengths to which they were willing to go to defend it. Something was smoldering along the edges of the circle, but it was impossible to tell what had been burned from my angle; there were too many soldiers and police for me to take in the entire scene. The best thing for me was to turn around and exit through the front gates; this was not my fight and not why I had come here. Had I left, though, I could never have confirmed the suspicion I had had from the moment I entered the campus that somewhere in that crowd, not on the edges but certainly in the very center, I'd find Isaac, smiling, looking happier than I had ever seen him before.

HELEN

I didn't know how long Isaac and I could continue to sleep together while barely speaking. Our silence had begun as the easiest way to avoid any further damage, and had turned into a source of pain in itself. If I asked Isaac how his day had been, he never responded with more than a six-word answer: "It was fine," "It was nothing special," "I read most of the day." I filled in some of the empty spaces with trivial stories about my day—the gas-station attendant who took fifteen minutes to fill my tank, the ongoing feud between Denise and David in the office—when what I really wanted was to ask him, "What are you thinking? What goes through your mind when I show up at your apartment each evening?" I was too afraid of the answer to do that. Isaac was too kind to say anything cruel, but he wasn't above remaining silent, and so I avoided the short but difficult questions I needed answers to. I saw our cowardice and didn't know how to make it stop.

I did my best to avoid David at work: he would see the darkening half-circles under my eyes and without any effort extract a confession from me. I arrived at work later than normal, when I knew he was locked in his office, and left early in the afternoon for what I claimed to be home visits. I drove along the outskirts of

our town, close to where Isaac lived, and where many of my clients did as well. I parked near churches and playgrounds and slept
with the windows rolled up and doors locked. I managed to keep
that going for a week before David left a note on my desk that
said, "I see you," with an arrow pointing to his office. Sharon and
Denise had already left for the day, and normally those were my
favorite hours in the office. David would emerge from the back
and, left to ourselves, we'd roll two chairs into the middle of the
office and run through the increasingly diminishing parts of our
lives that had nothing to do with work. David had come to our
town for college from an even smaller town at the very southern
tip of the state and, unlike most who moved here, never left. We
bonded over our entrapment.

"This was the biggest city I had ever been in," he had told me. "I
was afraid of coming here: all those people, and hardly any cows.
I didn't think I would ever get used to it. And then I was afraid
of what would happen to me if I left." That was eighteen years
ago. Since then, David had bought a house near the university.
Every year, he made it a touch nicer. He stripped and repainted
the exterior, added a large brass handle to the front door, new
railings on the porch, and, finally, a hedge fence around what had
been a barren front yard. Such attentions by a middle-aged single
man didn't go unnoticed. I knew the rumors, and David did as
well. We joked occasionally about getting married.

"My mother would be happy," I said.

"Mine would probably die from a heart attack. The relief
would be too much for her."

"I'd have to quit my job."

David shook his head.

"No, no, no," he said. "You can keep the job. That way we don't
have to talk to each other at home, like a real married couple."

When I walked into David's office, he was hanging up the

phone. In his college photos, he was skinny to the point of look-ing malnourished. The job had filled him in. Since he became the director, he rarely had to leave the office anymore. "I get fatter every day I come in here," he said, and now he barely fit comfort-ably behind his desk, all his girth gathered around his midsection like an inner tube that I imagined him someday slipping out of.

"You wanted to see me," I said.

He shrugged his shoulders. "What gave you that impression?"

I took the note he had taped to my desk and slapped it onto my forehead.

"Just a hunch," I said.

He scratched his head. Looked up at the ceiling.

"I remember now," he said. "I wanted to ask you if you were ever going to come back to work."

"I'm here every day," I said.

He looked down at his tie.

"I saw you sleeping in your car yesterday afternoon. You didn't notice I was in my car when you left the office, so I followed you. I thought you were going to see your Dickens, but instead you just pulled onto the side of the road and fell asleep. I stayed parked behind you for over an hour. I was worried someone would rob you. That's not the neighborhood for someone like you to fall asleep in."

I was too ashamed to be angry. I was on the verge of apologiz-ing, and once I did I imagined I would confess the entire story of my relationship with Isaac. I just had one question to ask him before doing so:

"Why did you follow me?"

"I told you," he said.

"No. You said you thought I was going to see my Dickens. But that doesn't explain why you followed me."

He finally looked up. I had caught him in something better than a lie.

"Why I would follow you?"

He repeated the question, although this time he was posing it only to himself. I saw a smirk pass over his face as he tried to answer it.

"Why would I follow you? You of all people, Helen, should be able to guess an answer to that."

David and I had that conversation on a Friday. Before leaving, I told him that I would try not to disappear from the office again. He kissed me goodbye on the forehead.

"Don't try too hard," he said.

I didn't see Isaac that evening or over the weekend. On Monday, I came into the office early and spent four hours on the phone, checking in on old clients, and the next three hours writing reports on the conversations I'd just had. I left the office an hour early. Before doing so, I knocked on David's door.

"Just in case you have any ideas in your head," I told him, "I'm leaving early. I'm going to go have a talk with Mr. Dickens, if you want to follow me."

"That sounds better than watching you sleep in your car," he said.

I had a list of ultimatums and rules for Isaac, only one of which really mattered: we had to talk to each other and not just about small, petty things but a real conversation with depth and insight. Before I rang the doorbell, I told myself I was going to leave if we didn't say something important. I rang the bell twice. I waited for several minutes before being convinced he wasn't home. The same was true the next day. It took me one more day to start worrying that he would never return. If that was true, as long as he wasn't dead or seriously injured, then I also thought that maybe for once fate was doing me a favor.

I rarely called Isaac before coming over. I had my own key to the apartment in case he ever locked himself out, but I had never used it. When I arrived on Wednesday, it was a few minutes after 6 p.m. The streetlights had already come on. I didn't expect Isaac to answer when I knocked—I knew he wasn't home—but I did so anyway, out of a sense of decorum, because even if you had keys it was still rude just to walk into someone's home. He didn't answer, and I heard nothing when I pressed my ear to the door. I took the spare keys and pretended to struggle with the lock.

I followed the same routine after I entered. I couldn't shake the idea that maybe Isaac was watching me from a corner to test my loyalty to the pattern we'd created. I poured myself a glass of water and drank it while standing in the kitchen. I moved to the bedroom, and though Isaac was gone, I still undressed, crawled into the bed, and quickly pulled the sheets over me. I had spent hours in that bed but had never slept in it. Once or twice I'd slipped into a semi–dream state, but without ever forgetting where I was or that Isaac was lying next to me. When completely exhausted, I'd fought off sleep by thinking of things to worry about. I'd imagine myself pregnant. I'd think of what would happen if someone I knew drove by and saw my car parked outside. I'd think, What if there was a fire in the building right now and I had to run out with hardly any clothes on? If anything kept me awake, it was the silly delight I took in imagining all the different ways my life, as I knew it, might crumble.

It was glorious lying in Isaac's bed alone. The sheets smelled faintly like the baby oil he slathered on himself after each shower. I lay on my stomach, my arms outstretched, my finger caressing the carpet just a few inches beneath them. I wished it were always like this. Isaac was so much easier to be with when only the ghost of him was around, and I remember thinking that if he were dead or never came back I'd probably learn to care for him more than if he were to walk through that door right then and never leave. I was tired. For two weeks I hadn't slept more than five hours a night. I happily closed my eyes and slept.

When I woke up, hours later, the apartment was completely dark—the shades in the bedroom were drawn, so not even the street lamps could be seen. It was after midnight, roughly the same time I always went home. I was more worried about staying too long than I was about Isaac's absence. I knew his life was full of secrets, starting with the visa that had brought him here, and it was natural to assume that his sudden disappearance was another secret I'd probably never have access to. I didn't have to think of anything grand to find that secrecy appealing. In a life of small-town wonders, a man with a passport that had been stamped several times was already extraordinary, and Isaac, by those measures, was remarkable. The more mystery I could attach to him, the more exceptional he became. When David later asked if I didn't have my doubts about who Isaac claimed to be, I tried to explain to him that I'd always had my doubts, and that I tried my best to protect them. The last thing I wanted was to bring Isaac down to earth, to find out that he was just an ordinary exchange student who'd come to America. I wanted him far removed from life as I knew it, for as long and in as many ways as possible. This made it easier to tolerate, if not forgive, almost anything he did.

When I left work the following day, I drove straight to Isaac's apartment. I didn't expect to find him at home, but I was anxious nonetheless. I knew I could do whatever I wanted in that apartment. I could rummage through the closets and drawers, and this time, if anything made me nervous, it was that I was certain I was going to do so.

When I walked into the apartment, I had the feeling Isaac was gone for good. Though I didn't imagine him dead, his presence was just as remote. There was no routine to follow, and a part of me wished I had brought a change of clothes to spend the night in.

I lingered around the kitchen and living room, dragging my finger along the counter and over the coffee table, searching for dust. Isaac's apartment was always clean. Each time I came over, the place was immaculate, as if nothing had been touched since I was last there. He had the type of kitchen my mother would have been proud of: free of dust, without a hint of grease on the counters, in the sink, or on the stove. I didn't like it. The longer I stood in the kitchen, the more uncomfortable I became. I had the sensation that, just by standing there for more than a few minutes, I was violating if not ruining it with my fingerprints and the dirt attached to my clothes and bag. Whether Isaac intended to or not, he had made it impossible to live in that apartment. We had filled it together—there was a gray couch in the living room, a small television set, plates and bowls and silverware in the kitchen, and lamps throughout—but the place felt emptier than if there had there been nothing inside it.

Life! That's what was missing. Where were the pictures and stacks of unopened junk mail, the lone sock under the bed, the fingernail clippings on the bathroom floor, the soap stains on the sink, or the early traces of mildew on the shower curtains? I thought I was going to search for intimate details about Isaac, but instead I roamed the apartment for an hour looking for proof he existed. When I was finished, what did I come up with? A carton of eggs and a stick of butter in the refrigerator; a letter that Isaac had begun one month earlier that had only a date and the words "My dear friend," which had fallen behind his pillow, a bottle of baby oil and two unopened rolls of toilet paper in the bathroom. I thought that perhaps Isaac was just covering his tracks, or that he knew when he left he wasn't coming back, but this would have meant that there had been some hint of life to cover; no one who saw that apartment could have believed that a man had lived there every day for months.

That apartment was the only place Isaac and I had. Its emptiness felt personal. I could picture him scrubbing away any trace of me each time I left.

Before I understood all the reasons why I never wanted to be like my mother, I was deliberately terrible in the kitchen. I burned everything she asked me to watch and had a habit of dropping plates and glasses. I ruined the domestic chores dear to her because they were the only things in her life she could control. What had been semiconscious rebellion when I was a teenager had become second nature in my adulthood; anything I touched in the kitchen was destined to come out wrong. I had never cooked or eaten inside of Isaac's apartment, but I was suddenly determined to do so. I thought of it not as trying to leave my mark but, rather, as trying to leave an impression on the place, a fingerprint that couldn't be easily removed. I took the eggs out of the refrigerator, hoping not to burn them. I cracked all twelve into a bowl and then spent several more minutes fishing out the bits of shell that had fallen inside. I tried to beat them like my mother had shown me, with the bowl tilted at a slight angle, but it was too shallow, and I had gotten carried away and whisked too briskly. By the time I was finished, there was at least one egg's worth of yolk on the floor and on my shirt. I saw the mess I had made, and felt a bit of relief. Life is messy, I told myself. There should be a bumper sticker that reads, "You can't live without breaking some eggs," or, "Don't worry about the yolk on the floor." And another one just for Isaac: "A man can't live on eggs alone."

Though I had begun recklessly, I was determined to make

something that resembled a proper meal. I scrambled the eggs in three batches, with ample amounts of butter that turned them to a pale shade of yellow, a color that would have been perfect for the kitchen walls. I put the eggs in a wooden salad bowl that I had bought for twenty-five cents. I thought the brown and yellow shades would complement one another, and I was right: they made an elegant pair. I set the bowl in the center of the dining-room table and then stepped back so I could judge its effects clearly. I had no intention of eating those eggs; I hated eggs. The only thing I was interested in was how they looked and what kind of effect they had on the room. A trail of steam rose from them. I admired that—it added a bit of domestic charm to the scene—but it wasn't enough.

I dressed the table for two as best I could, with knives and forks on either side of the plates, and glasses on the top right-hand corner. Playing house was the last thing I would have done as a child—my mother did that for the two of us—but now that it was my turn I was surprised how much pleasure it brought me. If I had built a small wooden home in the middle of a forest, I'm sure I would have felt a similar sense of victory. However temporary it may have been, that table and those eggs brought life to the apartment. If I could do it once, I was certain that when Isaac came back, and the time was right, I'd be able to do it again.

I began to think of my work differently after that night. I was a social worker, but I hadn't really thought of myself as one for years. If I was honest in describing what I did, I would have said I was a caretaker: I dispensed bandages to bleeding souls and broken hearts. Lives that had fallen apart or never really begun were sent to me, and I treated them as quickly as I could. I searched for the cheapest nursing homes for the elderly and requested food stamps and sometimes housing subsidies for any woman who could convince me that she and her children had no food and nowhere to go. Recently returned veterans were supposed to have been assigned to David, since he was the man in the office, but after two soldiers mocked him (for what he never said), he claimed he no longer had the time or energy for such hard cases, so I took on most of them as well, arranging trips to the hospital and sometimes to the movies for those who couldn't walk. I knew everyone who came to me had suffered some form of ruin. Whether it was poverty, age, or war didn't matter; they all suffered the same. My first day at the job, David gave me a passionate and I believe genuinely heartfelt speech about the shattered lives I'd be working with. "We are here to change people's lives," he said. "I firmly believe that, after everything we went through in the last decade, we are on the verge of making a great society."

I remember that my eyes brimmed with tears when he said that last part.

Disappointments, I knew, were to be expected. A client cried for an hour after I told her the housing subsidy had run out, and my eyes never fluttered. Others lied to me about their poverty. My black clients accused me of being racist, and my white clients said I'd treat them better if they were niggers. I bore that easily. It weighed on me, but not in the corners that counted. It wasn't until an entire year had passed and I was asked to make a list of all my successes that my faith began to give. I only had vague memories of the 154 people who had been assigned to me. After a year, most of the clients were wiped off our list to clear the slate for the hundreds more waiting.

I gradually gave up trying to change anyone's life. I was twenty-six at the end of my first year, but felt much older. When fall came, I suddenly found myself crippled with nostalgia. I wanted to be a child again, or, at the very least, crawl my way back in time a few years. I canceled my plans to move out of my mother's house. When I told her I wasn't ready to leave home yet, she made an awkward gesture toward me with me her hands. They fluttered, or flapped; I don't think either description alone is accurate. Whether her hands were fishes or birds, they were trying to speak for her. When they were close enough, they latched on to my elbows, and squeezed hard, as if trying to break through the flesh.

I began to spend more time with her in the kitchen and in the living room. She had an empty home that she tried her best to care for, and I had the lives of strangers that I was hopelessly trying to clean up after. I thought I would be fine as long as that was all we had in common.

The only thing that had changed between that time and Isaac's arrival four years later was that I no longer missed the restless anticipation I'd experienced during my childhood and the surges of joy and sadness that came with it. I didn't feel troubled when the seasons changed. My heart beat the same in winter as it did in spring, because I knew what was around the corner. If I saw a group of students from my old high school walking home at the end of the day, I felt something close to pity for them: no one had told them yet how ordinary and predictable their lives were going to be. I had, in other words, accepted the measured composure of adulthood. I saved money. I bought a used car from a friend of my father's. I slept with several men, just to see if I could. Isaac was the first break I'd had from that routine. Our relationship had upended my private life while leaving the bulk of my days relatively the same. It wasn't until I left his apartment with the table set and the eggs tossed into the trash that the rest began to change.

As I drove back home, I had the idea that when I went to work the next day I was going to do everything differently. I'm going to start making homes, is what I told myself in the car, though I wasn't sure what I meant.

The morning after leaving Isaac's apartment, I planned to stop by the homes of four of my clients. The only one I visited was Rose. Her real name was Agnes, but after her husband died five years before, she decided she wanted to be called Rose. She was eighty-one. She lived on far too little and made up the difference with jars of spare change, a table overflowing with coupons, and church-donated canned food. She lived in a one-bedroom home I helped her find after she could no longer afford the property tax on the house she and her husband had owned. She had been on my list for eight months, and this was only the third time I came to see her. I showed up with a dozen plastic yellow and red roses tied together with a bit of rope. The loneliness of old age had taught her to be excessively grateful for any human presence, however fleeting.

"Flowers," she said. "How lovely."

She didn't take the bouquet from me. She had me place it in her hands, as if the flowers were real and fragile, and then she embraced them against her chest as if they had come to her seeking comfort and she was the only person in the world who could provide it. I helped Rose arrange the flowers on her coffee table. She didn't have any vases, so I used the tallest glass I could find and filled the bottom third with water. I looked around the house for signs of emptiness.

"Would you like to have some pictures on your wall?" I asked her.

"I used to have so many pictures in my house," she said. "There were pictures of every place my husband and I had been to: New York, Boston, Chicago, Detroit."

For the next three hours, I sat with her as she told me about staying at the Knickerbocker Hotel in Chicago at the same time as

Al Capone, and then the Warwick in New York, which was a disappointment after all the glamorous stories she had heard. I only half listened. As she spoke, I was also trying to see if her stories filled that apartment in any meaningful way, if they could take up space, like a trinket picked up in an airport that sat on a mantelpiece, yet somehow more substantial than that. If listening to her talk for ten more hours would have answered this question, I would have stayed; there was so much emptiness in life that had to be filled, and I was just seeing it. Rose, however, was getting tired. She was starting to fall asleep as she talked, which was fine. She was happy and maybe at peace, and I felt certain that, even if I didn't understand how to fill all those holes, I was finally on to something.

ISAAC

Despite the crowd and smoke, I noticed immediately how well Isaac had healed. He had one scar above his right eye, but even if his face had been covered in bruises, he would have looked better than ever. His clothes were new, his hair had been recently cut, and he had the vague glow of someone who had easy access to running water.

As soon as he saw me he gestured for me to join him, as if inviting me into a circle of friends at a party where I was the stranger. That simple wave of the hand was all it took. I began walking to him before he had time to put his arm down. I walked past the soldiers, who formed a loose perimeter around the students, and never once did I feel afraid. Even at that early stage, the power in numbers was staggering. The crowd parted to let me through; I turned back once so I could see it close ranks behind me. It wasn't how I had imagined it, but once Isaac put his arm around me, and boys I had never met slapped me on the back, I became a student at the university.

During the thirty-six hours the grounds were occupied, not one sign went up. We had no chants, and the few songs we sang were those that had been popular in the years just before independence. The revolutionary songs from the late 1950s and 1960s were everyone's favorites, the songs of our parents and of our childhood, which we might have scorned at one time, but which we sang throughout the night to keep from falling asleep. The generation before us had had their revolution, and look what they had done with it. Over the course of the evening, I heard more than one student say that we were going to finish what our parents had started. There was the standard talk of a new African utopia, of a borderless and free continent. The students from the two opposing communist camps had their arms draped around one another, and at various times draped around Isaac and me as well.

"Look how happy they are," Isaac whispered to me. I zoomed in on the boys at the end of the chain. They had the clothes and hair that came with privilege, but what I noticed most was the sheer, unrestrained joy that was on all their faces. They seemed incapable of closing their mouths.

It wasn't until the first traces of sunlight began to emerge that I finally thought to ask Isaac what had happened to bring so many students together like this. None had left, but it was easy to see their resolve weakening. The songs had ended in the middle of the night, and everywhere I turned I saw eyes blighted not just by fatigue but by doubt. The party had gone on long enough for them, and what they sought wasn't a renewal of their convictions, but a quick and, they hoped, painless exit from them. Isaac was one of the few who showed no signs of wear; it was, after all, his party to begin with.

Before I could think about what I wanted to say to him, I found myself looking up, along with Isaac and the two other boys nearest us, at the trail of smoke that had already peaked and was beginning to make its descent. The one thought I remember clearly before the canister burst several feet short of us was "I wonder if Isaac is going to tell us to run." We were among the few who had seen tear gas fired before and knew how to respond. Long before the massing of soldiers around our slum, most protests in the poorest neighborhoods ended this way.

Isaac and I were the only two who moved deliberately in the opposite direction of the wind; the rest of the students simply ran, not knowing what they were up against or what to expect. Isaac had no intention of leading any of them to safety, and so dozens ran with eyes closed through the smoke, running first into one another and then, eventually, into the soldiers, who had pulled out their batons and were whipping the blind as they stumbled out of the mist. Isaac and I held our breath and were clear of the crowd in a few minutes. I followed him through a side door in one of the buildings, maybe the only door near us that wasn't locked. We climbed to the second floor and, for the second time, I found myself in a classroom at the university—a science lab of six long tables and metal stools that looked directly onto the circle we had just left. From there we watched soldiers dressed in riot gear leisurely whip their way through the crowd. From the students left lying on the ground, a handful of boys were dragged away; two had been standing next to Isaac; both had given long, rambling speeches the previous evening and undoubtedly made targets of themselves as a result.

I waited for Isaac to speak. I expected to him say something about how tragic and terrible it was to see the boys we had just spent the night with beaten and taken away like that; those boys would have expected at least as much from us, but whatever pity I tried to find for them was forced, and I knew the same would have been true for Isaac, who, like me, felt almost grateful to the uniformed men for leveling the differences between our lives in the slums and those on the campus, with each blow they struck.

"It's about time," Isaac said. "I was beginning to think they'd never come. I was almost afraid they'd run out of gas."

"I don't think that's possible," I said. "At least, not anymore."

I followed him to the windows.

"I heard there was a tank in our neighborhood."

"No tanks," I said. "At least not near us."

"They'll come," he said. "It's not even a question anymore."

He spoke with the certainty of someone who'd drawn the battle plans himself.

"Where have you been sleeping?" I asked him.

"For the past two days, here."

"On campus."

"In this room. Under the table all the way in the back." Isaac walked to the cupboards that lined one of the walls and pulled from one a thin roll-away mattress and a duffel bag full of clothes so I could see how he'd been living.

"No one uses this room. The lights don't even work anymore. There are a dozen others like it on campus, but I have a key to this one."

"Why this room?"

"Because," he said, "haven't you noticed, it has the best view."

That was all Isaac would tell me about how far in advance the protest had been planned. He wanted me to know that it wasn't an accident, and that if anyone was at the center, it was him. Nothing he said hinted that there were others behind him, but it was clear that he wasn't alone. The most visible mark of our poverty had always been the state of our clothes; the few pants and shirts we both had were used to begin with, and since we rarely had the means to have them washed, they were that much the worse for wear. The clothes in that duffel bag and the ones Isaac was wearing, however, had never been touched; a set of white-and-blue shirts were neatly stacked in one corner of the bag, with a set of identical khaki pants like the ones Isaac was wearing next to them; it was the standard uniform for many of the boys at the university. I saw the clothes only briefly, but Isaac knew that their impression on me would last, and that when I left him I would do so wondering who had lavished such attention on him.

We spent the rest of the morning and the afternoon in the abandoned science lab. "You have to wait until it's safe to leave," he told me. "No one can see you walk out."

If he hadn't said that, I would have asked to stay longer anyway. I felt safe in that room, because Isaac was there and because I had always believed that one of the hidden benefits of being a student at the university was that it gave you a vantage point from which you could gaze upon the world without being injured. I watched the smoke disappear and the soldiers and police pick through the remains left behind by the students. I saw them gather coats, sweaters, and school bags; a red purse was lifted from the ground by one of the soldiers with the barrel of his gun and was swung in circles so the others could see his find. There were maybe a dozen students too injured to move; most sat slumped against trees, and a few lay flat on the ground. I didn't expect anyone to tend to them, but I stared at them for over an hour just to make sure. The last student who was taken away was a young girl in a black skirt that was cut just above her knees. I told myself she was too short, and her skin the wrong shade of black, to be Patience. The men who carried her away were in uniform. She was the only one I felt genuine, unrestrained pity for: unlike that of the others, her suffering had just begun.

By noon, the campus was completely abandoned except for a few soldiers who patrolled with their guns slung over their backs.

"Did you ever study any science?" Isaac asked me.

I lied and said, "A little in high school."

Isaac did the same. "Me, too."

He walked to the large wooden cabinet that stood alone in the back of the room and removed the lock.

"Don't worry," he said. "I wasn't the one who broke it."

The cabinet had once held all the necessary supplies a classroom full of science students would have needed, but the only items left were a pair of plastic goggles and a single row of beakers and test tubes, many of which were slightly cracked and all of which were stained. Isaac took everything out and arranged it on one of the long black tables.

"What do you think we'd need," he asked, "to make a bomb?"

"Depends what kind," I said.

"Something simple."

Hanging on one of the walls was a large laminated chart headed "Periodic Table." I knew just enough about it to understand that the element in one box combined with the element in another lay at the heart of much of what I saw and touched every day. There had been a young white American teacher in my high school—if I remember correctly, Rich was his name. He had brought one of those charts with him from America, and every day he asked us to pass it around from one person to another so, he said, we could all "feel like we had the world in our hands." Because he was white and came from America, we took what he said seriously but at the same time believed he was crazy. "Africa is where America sends its crazy people" was the common refrain among us, and we always laughed with each variation of that thought. Each of us knew that, more likely than not, what Rich said was true, and that by extension our ignorance was so vast as to be unfathomable; the only power we had was to make a mockery of what he said.

I took the chart down, and as soon as I laid it on the table I began to strip it of all its meaning.

"We need a bit of Pb, and Fe, and Zr," I said. I didn't pretend to know the proper names of any of the elements, and if someone had come along then and tried to tell me, I would have said he had no idea what he was talking about. This was my world, and in this reality I was the one who dictated the terms, and according to me anything Isaac and I wanted could be made into a bomb.

Isaac made for the blackboard; there was no chalk to write with, so he pulled a marker from his pocket and wrote everything I said on the board in immaculate script, so clean that no one would have to guess what the letters were. He made his own additions to everything I said. He threw in plus signs, added parentheses and even fractions as he saw fit. By the time we were finished, half of the board was almost completely full of equations that only we could decipher.

We pretended we were making a bomb; I won't try to dismiss the subtext of violence that came with that, but there was also a naïveté and childishness behind our imagining as well. It was as close as we could come to claiming innocence—for what happened that morning, and for what would surely come next.

I left Isaac late that night. We spent hours in the dark rather than light any candles, out of fear that someone might see our shadows in the windows; the only light we had came from the thin sliver of a moon, which by the time I left was barely visible. Even then, just to be careful, Isaac had insisted that we pass the entire evening sitting under the desks so that neither of us could accidentally stand up or stretch an arm just high enough to be seen by someone watching from the building opposite us. When Isaac gave me instructions for leaving, he had his knees curled up to his chest and both arms wrapped around his legs, as if he were trying to remind his body that even if it wanted to leave as well, it didn't have the right to.

"You should run when you leave the campus," he told me. "Don't stop running until you're far away, when you can get off the main roads. They can't patrol the side streets in those jeeps—the roads are too bad—and if you see one, you can outrun it. If you get stopped before then, tell them you were at the Churchill hotel—a lot of soldiers go to see the girls there. And then tell them that all you have left now is ten pounds."

Isaac handed me the money along with a little loose change from his pocket. Two weeks ago, that would have been a fortune for both of us.

"You won't even have to offer them the money. They'll just take it, and as soon as they do, start walking away. Don't look back, and don't say anything to them. Wait until you get to a small road, and then, once you turn the corner, run—and this time don't stop until you're home. I'd tell you to stay here, but I have to leave early in the morning, and there'll be problems if you're here alone.

"No one knows who you are, and from now on, if anyone asks, give them a name that's easy to remember. Tell them it's John, or William."

I listened to Isaac's instructions, but I can't say that I really believed anything he said until I had left him and was standing alone in the middle of the campus, a few feet from the tear-gas canisters deliberately left behind by the guards. Until then, I had had the distinct feeling that he was playing a role that had been cast for him, and that the same was happening to me. I kept thinking that any moment now Isaac was going to say "Stop," and the lights in the classroom were going to come on, and we would both be able to stand up and walk away.

I would have embarrassed him had I asked him to come with me, and so the only thing I said to him before leaving was "Are you going to be okay here?"

"Of course I am," he told me. "I have everything planned out."

I left just as Isaac told me to. As soon as I opened the door and touched ground, I ran, promising myself I wouldn't stop even if I felt safe. On the other side of the campus gates were two jeeps facing in opposite directions. I saw them while I still had time to turn around, but where would I have gone? As frightened as I was, I also felt relief, knowing that whatever path I cut across the city, even if it led to prison, I would be the one who chose it. And so I didn't hesitate at the gates, and it wasn't until I was at the very bottom of the hill that the university was built on that I turned to see if I was being pursued. The only other creature on the street was a stray dog with an injured hip that forced it to run crooked. The jeeps hadn't moved; though at the time I credited it to my good fortune and courage, I later learned it had nothing to do with either.

For the next several days, I hardly left my room. My landlord, Thomas, came by twice a day to see if I was ill, but it was obvious he was worried that maybe I was being hunted. I heard him whispering rather than shouting to his friends, and his shadow seemed to be permanently fixed outside my one window. I left once every afternoon so I could walk to one of the main avenues to read the newspaper headlines that were spread across the sidewalk on all the busy streets across the capital. If you had the money, you could pay a few cents to read one of the papers in private before laying it down again. One paper might have been skimmed a dozen times before someone finally paid half-price to take it home, granting everybody, even the poorest among us, just enough information to take a position, however misinformed.

For three days, nothing about what happened at the university appeared in the news, not even in the government papers that used any hint of violence as proof of the growing threat against the nation and its president. The headlines in all five papers consisted solely of the great achievements and advancements that were being made across the country. A school and a health clinic opening in the remote southern corner of the country was front-page news one day; the next, all five papers had full-page photos of the president meeting other heads of state in Yugoslavia. Finally, on the fourth day, one of the papers ran at the bottom of the front page an article titled: "Government Warns Against Growing Foreign Terrorist Threat to Our Nation."

I had kept in my pocket enough spare change to buy a paper on the day a story like that appeared, but as I stood among the crowd of ten to fifteen men, all craning their necks to see the headlines, I began to think that was exactly what someone was waiting for. I was the only obvious foreigner, and I could imagine how the men there might look at me if I were to buy that particular paper. I had been at the intersection dozens of times before, but only now did I notice the pair of traffic officers standing in the middle of the road; they were watching the traffic more than guiding it. On the other corner were two men in suits with sunglasses on, and I began to suspect they were always there, and not for pleasure, but because they had been assigned to watch from that post. Even the man selling the newspaper suddenly struck me as odd. There was nothing special about him—he was maybe a decade older than me, had his hair cut close, and was dressed in matching pants and shirt, either beige or blue. He had one of the best spots in the city to sell papers from, with crowds constant on all four corners and not one other vendor anywhere near him to compete against. I wasn't convinced that selling newspapers was merely a cover, but once I saw the possibility that it was, I could no longer dismiss it outright.

I took the change out of my pocket and pointed to the paper that was officially published by the government, which included at the top of every issue a portrait of the president in full military dress. I tucked it under my arm and walked slowly toward a café on the other corner. I thought of taking a seat at one of the tables outside, but I felt that the men already sitting there were also watching me. I couldn't tell, though, if it was me or the paper they were staring at, and so I abruptly turned and headed south, down a road that I had been on once before.

Several schools must have let out just then; the sidewalks and street were full of children in either blue-and-white or red-and-white uniforms. A remarkable sight, they blotted out everything that surrounded them as they moved back and forth, in circles, in swarms. I felt safe following them—not because I believed nothing bad could happen in their presence, but because I felt invisible in their midst. I can remember the dust rising from the sides of the road, which hadn't been paved, and the sounds of hundreds of sandals clapping against heels.

At some point early in that walk, I stopped worrying about who might or might not have been watching me. I went back to taking my innocence for granted; the newspaper under my arm, which I had carefully folded to make sure its distinctive red-and-white banner was clearly visible, meant no more to me than the dust on my shoes; to be honest, I had forgotten why I had bought it.

Had I not been so enamored by the scene in front of me, I would have noticed the two men following me before they were in shouting range. I didn't turn to face them until I heard them yell in English, "Stop," over and over. I didn't understand what they said next, except when they spat on the ground after saying the president's name, or what their anger had to do with me, until they stepped closer and one grabbed the newspaper from under my arm and threw it to the ground. I had never been in that neighborhood before; I didn't know its rules or recent history. Many young men from there had recently disappeared, and there was nothing but hatred for the government and anyone who favored it. The paper you read was more than enough to determine which side you fell on; in my case, I was never given the chance to explain why I was carrying it, and even if I had, who would have believed me.

My memory of what happened after the paper was taken has never returned; if parts ever did start to emerge, I would do whatever was necessary to keep them buried. There's a coin-sized circle in the back of my head where no hair will ever grow again, along with three thin, distinct scar lines along the right side of my scalp. And though I don't remember this, I was later told that at least an hour passed before anyone sought help for me, and so I also have, whether I want to or not, a clear image of all those children walking and laughing as they stepped over me on their way home.

When I regained consciousness two days later, I was in a hospital run by a Catholic charity, in a large white room with forty other bodies around me and the stench of ammonia and decay mixed together. I had never seen African nuns before, but there they were, all of them the same shade of black, in sparkling white dresses with blue veils covering their hair. None of them were in the room when I first woke up, and in my confusion I screamed, not out of fear or pain, but I think simply to hear my own voice and to know that I was alive.

Later that afternoon, Isaac came to see me. I was so relieved not to be alone that I didn't question how he had known I was there. He handed me a black palm-sized notebook. "Something for you to write in until you can leave here," he said.

He pulled a chair next to the bed, and finally took off his sunglasses. "So, my friend. Now you know what it feels like."

I knew what he meant by that, but it wasn't true, at least not yet. The men who beat me were driven as much by fear as hate. They had lashed out blindly and left me for dead. Isaac had yet to feel that distinct version of violence, and because I was certain that soon enough he would, and that odds were when he did he wouldn't survive, I didn't bother to point out the difference. He offered me his hand as he bent down to kiss my forehead—a gesture that was intended to say that there was more between us now than just friendship. I gripped his hand just as tightly, and even lifted my head to his lips to make sure that he understood that I felt exactly the same way.

HELEN

It's possible that if Isaac had never returned I might have gone on to live a perfectly reasonable, happy life. I would have spent my days with women like Rose, kind, decent old women who, though alone and poor at the end of their lives, were above any cheap, easy pity. Through them and maybe a few dozen others whose lives I managed to make less alone, at least briefly, I could say that I had found a purpose, until, eventually, one day, the tables were turned and it was my turn to play the role of the aged host for the young women assigned to look after me. Isaac came back exactly three weeks after he had left, and when he did, he shut the doors to that world behind him. I visited Rose two more times, and each time stayed less than an hour and was so occupied with my own thoughts that I barely heard a word she said. When I think of Isaac's return now, I imagine myself sitting in a semi-barren living room with all the windows open, a faint breeze barely rocking the white curtains, when a sudden explosion shatters the windows and blows the curtains apart—my own private little blast, which I was too stupid not to be afraid of.

Isaac returned bearing gifts, not of apology or remorse but of America, which he said he had finally discovered, and was eager to tell me about. His first morning back, he took a bus to my office and left with the secretary a package that had my name on it. I opened it at my desk and found a box filled with cheap plastic souvenirs, each individually wrapped in a thin sheet of white paper. There was a palm-sized Statue of Liberty and Empire State Building, along with even smaller replicas of the White House, Lincoln Memorial, and Golden Gate Bridge, and a typed letter at the bottom that I memorized.

Dear Helen

I had to go away. Here are some of the places that I hope we can go to someday.

Warm Regards
Isaac

I lined the monuments along the edge of my desk. I wasn't sure how to read them. The letter was curt—the gesture suspiciously grand. The farthest I had ever traveled was to St. Louis with my parents.

I rearranged the order of the monuments, moving the White House to the center and placing the Golden Gate Bridge right next to it, then trying other combinations: New York and San Francisco; D.C. and New York. I became so absorbed in my made-up geography that I didn't notice David watching me.

"What are you doing?" he asked me.

"Practicing," I said.

I handed him the letter that Isaac had sent, hoping he could help me interpret it.

"Is he serious?" he asked me.

"Look at the letter. It's typed. That has to mean something."

"Yes, that he didn't have a pen. That he has a fondness for typewriters. That his handwriting is terrible."

He pointed to the monuments on my desk.

"And he sent you those as well?"

I was almost too embarrassed to say yes. I waited for David to tell me that Isaac was delusional, but he fingered each of the monuments without lifting them.

"Who knows, Helen. Maybe your Dickens is on to something," he said.

He squeezed my shoulder before turning back to his office. As soon as he was gone, I picked up the phone and called Isaac. He picked up on the fourth ring. I felt my right eye quiver when he said, "Hello."

"Isaac."

"Helen."

"You're back."

"You received my package."

"I'm looking at it right now."

"Were you surprised?"

"I didn't know where you'd gone. You never told me you were leaving."

"I didn't know until the last minute. I will tell you about it."

"This evening?"

"Yes, this evening. If you are available."

"I'll be free after six," I said.

I had planned to visit Rose and a young single mother of two whose file I had just opened that afternoon, but at 3 p.m. I was still sitting at my desk. I had spent the hour after hanging up imagining what it would be like to be alone in a room with Isaac again—what his arm next to mine would feel like, what his voice would sound like—and then I started trying to picture us in New

York and in San Francisco and D.C. I'd lived in this country my entire life and had never come close to any of those places. All my trips were strictly middle-of-the-road.

I hadn't read Isaac's file since we met. There was hardly anything in it, to begin with: a single loose leaf of paper with his name and date of birth and a brief paragraph stating he was here as a foreign-exchange student. His was the only file like that in our office. Our other clients came with criminal records and hospital records, income-tax reports and psychological evaluations. In comparison, Isaac's single-page life story had seemed like a blessing when I first saw it.

I read his file two more times, and each time came up with a part of his past that appeared to be deliberately missing. There was no month or date of birth, only a year. His place of birth was listed only as Africa, with no country or city. The only solid fact was his name, Isaac Mabira, but even that was no longer substantial: any name could have filled that slot, and nothing would have changed.

I left my office a few hours earlier than I had planned and decided to take a drive through town—or, to be more precise, past all the places where Isaac and I had spent time together. I drove past the diner, and then the Goodwill store where we'd picked out his couch and kitchen table, the post office, the grocery store. That was the bulk of what we had; I had forgotten how poor we were as a couple. I tried my best to draw a solid image of Isaac, first alone, and then together with me, and when that wasn't enough, I drove to the university and parked near the library, where I hoped the memory of him on his first day in Laurel would remind me of who Isaac "really" was when I wasn't a part of the picture.

The campus had gone back to what it had been during my freshman year—a clean, calm, and ordered sanctuary of semi-

Gothic buildings and great towering trees that even when bare had given me a measure of solace. There were no protests on the lawns or banners draped from the windows, as there had been during the past two years. A few weeks just before I graduated, guardsmen and riot police had been stationed outside of all the main buildings; there were days when the entire campus had been closed off and traces of tear gas could be seen from blocks away. I had watched that on television, from the safety of my mother's living room, convinced that I was missing out on something important, but now I thought maybe I hadn't missed anything at all. The students that I could see from my car seemed content with what life had given them, and there was no trace of any of the anger that only a few years earlier had seemed so important. One war had ended; that was enough for now.

I watched five black students settle on the library steps in a semicircle, with the boys two steps above and the girls fanned out beneath them. Had Isaac been younger, I still couldn't have pictured him among that crowd. They were, for all their mystery to me, no different from the other students sprawled out on the steps, confident in their aimlessness, convinced that the future would provide. There was never the slightest trace of such cool confidence in Isaac. He told me once that he'd accepted the fact that there was no place in the world where he felt fully at ease. "When I lived with my parents, I used to take long walks by myself, even when I was very young and was forbidden from doing so. I couldn't help it. I was restless. I always felt out of place. I didn't know it was permanent, though. I thought eventually I would find a house or a street that seemed to have been made just for me. I think I have walked more miles than just about any man I know, and I have learned that if I were to walk every day for the rest of my life, I would never find such a place. That is nothing to be sad about. Many people have it worse. They dream of belonging to a place that will never have them. I made that mistake once."

I didn't feel sorry for him when he told me that, but, watching those students, I did think that, if it were possible to grant the small measure of entitlement that was theirs to others, then that would be worth fighting for. I didn't have the words to explain it at the time, but as soon as the thought crossed my mind, I knew it was wrong. There wasn't a protest in the world that could have done that for them. The right to claim their small share of this country had always been theirs; they knew that long before the rest of us. I wondered if the same would ever be true for someone like Isaac.

I decided to make a tour of the campus before returning to my car. I expected to feel a bit of nostalgia for my college days, but instead I had the feeling I was walking past the perfectly manicured lawns, with their wilting tulips, and the roughly carved stone buildings for only the second time in my life. The first had been with my head down, and although I had taken my time, over four years I never thought to look up and really notice what surrounded me. It wasn't nostalgia but regret that guided me through the campus that afternoon. All that time lost—not to have done more, but to have seen better.

I was thinking of the dozens of afternoons I had spent sitting on the lawn as a student when I noticed a man slowly walking down the steps of the science building. I could only see the back of his head, but that was enough to know that it was Isaac.

I followed him to the campus parking lot. He had a slow, dreamy walk. Classes across the university were ending, so it was easy to hide among the students, but even if the campus had been empty, Isaac would never have seen me. His gaze wasn't fixed so much as it was indifferent to anything that wasn't immediately in front of him. He walked to the rear of the lot to a dark-blue sedan parked in a numbered space. He took a set of keys out of his coat pocket, unlocked the door, and got behind the wheel. I didn't believe he would actually drive away. For months I had driven him around the city since he had no car and, according to him, had never learned to drive. "You Americans amaze me," he said. "Tell me the truth. Are you born with your cars?"

He turned on the ignition, adjusted the rear and side mirrors, and slowly reversed out of the space. I knew that I had been lied to, but I couldn't help smiling. Whatever he was playing at, it was a wonderful performance. I had to admit that.

ISAAC

I left the hospital on a Sunday, and Isaac was there waiting for me. He had thrown what few belongings I had into a pair of grain sacks and was standing in the parking lot with them, and that was how I knew I was also homeless. The other patients in the hospital were fed and had their wounds dressed and cleaned by their family. Mothers, wives, and children brought lunch, dinner, and extra gauze to change the bandages, while a few other men, who, like myself, had no one to tend to them, looked on in longing. I had learned from watching those patients that even if I did have a place to sleep it was hardly a home, and after Isaac's visit, I was confident that when I left I wouldn't have that. If Isaac knew I had been beaten, then everyone who lived in our corner of the city did as well, and there was no explanation in the world that could convince a group of people already in fear that a broken and beaten stranger like myself wouldn't bring more trouble into their lives. My landlord, Thomas, was a kind, generous man even with his bad habits and many flaws, and he had taken me in though no one knew me. Had he let me return, I knew it wouldn't have been for more than a few days.

As I walked toward Isaac, I felt nothing for the tiny room that had been lost. I moved slowly, one strained step at a time, and as

I did so I thought of my mother and father and all my younger siblings, who were growing into strangers. After countless nights of deliberately trying not to think of them, I now felt a distant and detached affection that I knew I could carry harmlessly. They were gone, and whether I would ever see them again no longer troubled me. My world was weightless, more so than I had ever thought it could be. I owned practically nothing and was obligated to no one; I felt more alive than I ever had before.

Isaac and I met on the edge of the parking lot. There were cripples and beggars, each limited to a few square feet of space they must have staked out long in advance, given how meager and yet precious that ground was; in the center were a handful of wasted old men who looked as if they had chosen that spot to die. In a few weeks there would be dozens more like them, except they wouldn't be old. They would be as young as Isaac and I were, and they'd be struggling to hold on to what little life they had left, but there would be no one to save them: the hospital by then would be full of men, women, and boys just as wounded and desperate not to die.

One of those crippled men reached Isaac the same time I did. He carried himself on a single wooden crutch, as weathered and thin as the deformed leg he dragged behind him. He spoke to Isaac in Kiswahili. Before he could extend his hand, Isaac pulled from his pocket a bundle of bills that looked as if they had been printed that day and handed him one from the middle. The man tried to prostrate himself before Isaac, but Isaac grabbed him by the elbow just as he was trying to bend his one good leg and in English said to him, "Please don't, Grandfather," with a tenderness rarely heard from men of any age. Before I left the hospital, one of the nuns had come to my bed to thank me for money that had been given in my name. "We don't ask our patients to pay for their care," she said, "since most are too poor to do so, but we're always grateful to those who can." She said she and the other nuns would pray for me, and as a sign of their gratitude she pressed into my palm a white plastic rosary. I hadn't known what to do with it, but I felt ashamed, and so I quickly put it in my pocket, where it would have remained for days, until the shame had passed and I could throw it away. Now I took it out and handed it to Isaac. He was far from being a saint, but there was more decency and kindness in him than I had assumed, traits that both of us were learning to suppress.

He held the rosary up with one finger.

"What am I supposed to do with this?"

"A nurse gave it to me to say thank you."

He folded the beads into his pocket. "I'm not the one they should thank," he said. He took a few steps back from me.

"You look good. I'm going to call you Ali from now on."

"I've been exercising."

"How do you feel?"

"Now that you're here, okay. I was afraid I was going to have to walk home alone."

"You're out of a home," he said.

"I can see. Did he say why? Does he know I haven't done anything?"

"I thought you knew by now that doesn't matter. The prisons are full of people who say the same thing: I'm innocent, I have done nothing, I was just on my way to work. It's stupid to talk like that. You know what your landlord told me when I came looking for you?"

"That I'm not much of a fighter."

"Everyone knew that already. He said that you're in trouble with the government. That you came here to cause trouble. When I went back and said you were in the hospital, I don't think he believed me. I went there to bring you some clothes, and he gave me these bags."

"Did you pack them?"

"He never gave me the chance. He wouldn't let me inside. He said he was sorry. He has enough problems and his family to think about."

"And what did you say?"

"I told him if he wanted to protect his family he should turn himself in to the police right now. 'Why should I go to prison?' he said. 'It's you who are causing all these problems.' "

"And?"

"Nothing. He was angry. He wanted to hit me. He was scared; he knew I was right. That was the best thing I could do for him. Maybe he'll be smart now and hide a little money where only his wife can find it. Or he'll see what's happening and he'll pack up his family in the middle of the night and return to his village."

Isaac picked up my bags and began walking toward the road.

"I have nowhere to go," I said.

I remember thinking I had expressed a rare honesty in that statement, but that was hardly the case. With Isaac near me, I may not have known where I was going, but there was always a destination waiting.

"Don't worry," he said. "I have everything taken care of."

I had never seen the capital from the inside of a car. Like most, I made my way by foot or, on occasion, an overcrowded bus that stretched the limits of how close you could stand to someone before feeling violated. The small blue-shelled, white-roofed taxis, even the most dilapidated ones, belonged only to the rich and to the white. The taxis stood in long lines outside of the capital's two largest hotels, day and night; for the drivers, all it took was a couple of good fares to make the hours of waiting worthwhile. If I did have the money for a ride, what driver, seeing me on the side of the road, would have believed I could afford it? I came from the wrong caste, and money alone couldn't buy my way out of it. Once we reached the road, Isaac raised his hand, and a taxi parked outside a café a block away came directly to us. I looked to Isaac for an explanation, but then I understood. I saw what the cabdriver saw—a young, confident man whose clothes and spotless shoes were the telltale signs of at least moderate wealth.

We drove for maybe two, three hundred feet, lurching and stopping the whole way. That was all it took—three blocks—before I knew I was finally seeing the city as I had always imagined it, both from afar and while living there. I had imagined crowds composed of men in suits and women in blue and purple dresses, and here they were, along with the traffic cop in white gloves I added from time to time. Of course, I had seen them all before—I had stood on at least two occasions at the very same intersection we were idling in—but until that moment I had never understood that I was living the fantasy I had built out of books and radio shows. I was too busy being a character to see that.

We often think of the dead as ghosts who have the power to hover indifferently above us. My dreams of life in the capital weren't so different; in those dreams I floated above life. Riding in that taxi was the same. I had the feeling I was gliding above the city, which was there for me to admire without my having to dirty my hands.

Isaac gave the driver instructions every few blocks. Our route was deliberately circular: we made unnecessary right and left turns when we could have just as easily gone straight. And just when the driver was growing angry, Isaac leaned across the front seat and threw two bills onto his lap. Soon we had come to another part of the city I had never been in before. The houses were new, each hidden behind a concrete wall that left only the roof and a few second-story windows visible. The bigger houses had their gates lined with barbed wire and shards of broken glass, and the last house on that narrow gravel road, where we finally stopped, had two men posted on the roof.

"Welcome home," Isaac said.

More money was exchanged. I didn't bother to see how much; it was more than what should have been paid, and I knew it didn't matter. By the time we opened the doors to the cab, the gates to the house had been dragged open, and from behind them an almost elderly gray-haired man in a dark-blue uniform emerged to take my bags. His face and bearing reminded me of my father, who had been a soldier in the emperor's army when the Italians attacked. His time in the military had lasted less than a year, and yet, like all the men who served with him, he was left with an unyielding devotion to the rigor of his military days.

That old man saluted Isaac before taking my bags, just as my father would have most likely done in his position. My father's attachment to those codes had always struck me as foolish and at times embarrassing, but at least he wasn't alone. There were other loyalists still out there.

Isaac nodded his head in return. We were nothing like them. They were a scarce and dying breed that, had I not been on crutches, I would have again gone running from.

For the next two nights, Isaac and I were the only ones who lived in that house. Guards came and went each evening without speaking to us. Every morning, a young girl with her hair wrapped in a white shawl brought food in a large pot and left it on a gas burner in the kitchen; we all ate from this pot, but who remained and who left, who cooked and watched over us, was never our concern.

In the morning, Isaac helped me from my room on the third floor, my arm draped over his shoulder as we wound our way down the uneven curved stairwell that was the most obvious proof of how quickly the house had been built. We had tea and coffee in the courtyard, next to a stone fountain that each afternoon attracted a steady flock of palm-sized golden birds who splashed and dipped their black beaks into the pool of water as long as no one was nearby. I waited for Isaac to explain to me what I was doing there and how he had become a part of that household himself, but it was clear by the time we had finished our first cup of coffee that he was in no rush to do so. He didn't want to talk about politics or the people he was involved with. He didn't want to talk about the money that had sustained him and had paid for my care and now my life, or what he had done to get it. He wanted to talk instead about all the places in the world that he hoped to see someday.

"I'd go to Egypt first," he said. "I want to see those pyramids. Even if they're not as great as people say, it was still Africans who made them. And then London, so I could see the queen. There are many things I'd like to ask her."

He talked about Rome and Paris and New York. He had dreams of Hollywood and movie stars.

"They could use someone like me there," he said. "I'm a great actor. I could be famous—I'm sure of it."

I had had similar delusions while bandaged in the hospital. I had thought of America and Europe, but in vague, monumental ways, of towering buildings and white marble memorials. I'd imagined finding a foreign wife here in Africa who would take pity on my broken body, a doctor with blond hair and blue eyes who fell in love with me, though we came from opposite corners of the world and I had nothing to offer besides my poverty. Rescue—that is the true heart behind romance and fairy tale; the spontaneous love that frees us from the tower, hospital bed, or broken world is always only the means to that end.

We knew there wasn't any chance of leaving that house, much less the capital and country, anytime soon. A large, empty house in which we were free to dream was as close as we were going to come to a different and possibly better life.

For those two days, Isaac and I lived in an increasingly magical world. We spent the bulk of our second day imagining ways we could improve the house. "A pool," Isaac said. "Right here where we're sitting. And more grass."

"The stairs," I said. "I'd tear them down and make them all the same height." Isaac wanted to paint the house red. I suggested that gray was more appropriate, and for the next half-hour, we argued about colors. By the time evening came, we were down to wishing for more comfortable beds to sleep on, food that contained more than chunks of fat with a hint of meat attached to the ends—a bit of lamb for Isaac; a piece of chicken, preferably grilled, for myself.

We took our dinner into the courtyard. Isaac made a show of carrying our dinner plates from the kitchen, with a rag draped over one arm, one plate resting on the other. This was as close as we had ever come to eating in a restaurant, and since the impression was good enough, it made for one less thing to long for.

We ate quickly, the same bland mix of rice and withered vegetables that we'd eaten every day. When we finished, Isaac went back for more, but by the time he returned to the kitchen it was too late: the guards had already eaten the rest of the food.

"One last wish," Isaac said. "It's a simple one. I think even you'll have to agree with me. I don't want to go to bed hungry ever again."

We raised our glasses of water and made a toast to that.

"To the end of hunger."

"To the end of hunger."

Before we went to bed, Isaac told me that tomorrow we had to be at our best: the men who owned the house were going to arrive in the morning.

HELEN

I knew Isaac would be home by the time I reached his apartment. I was already a half-hour later than he expected. I had taken my time walking back to my car, and before parking near his apartment, I circled his neighborhood, looking for the car he had driven off in. I sped down his block in case he saw me through the windows, but I took the other dozen blocks slowly. An older white woman, who must have been one of the last remaining in the neighborhood, was sitting on her porch; she stared at me as I inched past her house, but as soon as she saw my face clearly, I knew she wasn't worried: I was a young white woman in a used but respectable four-door sedan. I circled that block a second time, for no reason other than that I still hadn't found Isaac's car and was reluctant to give up my search until I did; the second time, we waved to each other as I passed.

I admit that, for the first hour, I loved playing detective. I now knew at least one of the reasons why David had followed me from the office. From the moment I saw Isaac get into his car, I had felt an irrepressible urge to smile, run, dance, jump, anything to put the extra energy I felt to use. He wasn't the only one with secrets anymore; I had my own as well. I was a spy; in the parking lot I had actually lurked in the shadows.

I made a partial list of all my doubts about Isaac. If I had tried to name them all, the harmless fantasy of mystery and intrigue would have broken, and only the fraud would have remained. I played it safe and went for the obvious deceptions. I thought of his abrupt disappearance, his mystery trip across America, his spotless apartment, his car, and the single-page file at the office that revealed practically nothing other than that he existed. Taken together it could mean only one thing—he was a spy, or perhaps working undercover, which meant that the real question wasn't who he was, but whom he was working for. Was he friend, or foe? I had a hard time deciding. There was something classically romantic about falling for the enemy—the risks were greater, and so were the odds against a happy ending. But I could see a possible happy ending if Isaac was on our side; I could be not only his lover but his confidante, and who could ask for a better cover than a woman like me? Adventure versus romance—not being alone won out every time.

I parked in front of Isaac's building rather than around the corner, as was my habit. His apartment was on the second floor; all the windows faced the street. I could see the lights in the bedroom, but before going inside, I wanted to see him once more from a safe distance. I turned on the radio. Bob Dylan was singing. I looked up and saw Isaac standing in the window. I turned off the engine and got out of the car. Before crossing the street, I looked up again and saw him staring directly at me. I expected him to smile or at least wave, but there wasn't a trace of joy on his face.

· · ·

I never made it up to his apartment. I stood on the curb trying to decide whether I should leave; before I could come to a decision, Isaac was in front of me.

"Now is not a good time," he began saying, but before he could finish he had taken hold of my arm and was leading me back to my car. He was calm, morose. When he took my arm I had the feeling that Isaac was trying to protect me, the same way my father often wrapped his arm around me while we were crossing the street if there was a car anywhere near us. The intention didn't matter, though; as soon as he grabbed my arm, we both felt the breach, and without thinking, my entire body recoiled.

Isaac tried to apologize: "I'm sorry if I surprised you," he said.

And I did as well: "You didn't surprise me. You just never know who's watching."

But it was a poor defense. No one was watching. Our fears and prejudices were ingrained deep enough that we didn't need an audience to enforce them. I had thought there could be nothing worse than our lunch at the diner, but I was wrong. What was worse was being alone in public and, for reasons you were reluctant to admit, feeling frightened because your lover held your arm.

I wonder whether, if before meeting Isaac I had tried to challenge the easy, small-time bigotry that was so common to our daily lives that I noticed it only in its extremes, I might have felt a little less shame that evening. It's possible that I might have been able to release some of it slowly over the years, like one of those pressure valves that let out enough steam on a constant basis to keep the pipes from bursting. It's also equally possible that such relief is impossible, that, regardless of what we do, we are tied to all the prejudices in our country and the crimes that come with them.

As Isaac turned away from me, I wished that there were some way I could vanish or simply slip out of my skin, keep my flesh but without the exterior that came with it. The shame was so complete that I didn't notice until Isaac had actually gone through the front door and I had heard it close that while he was outside with me the lights in his living room, specifically the lamp next to the dining-room table—the one I had brought from my own house after he told me that his living room was too dark to read in at night—had been turned on.

ISAAC

On the day the owners of the house arrived, the guards who had spent the past two days half asleep at their posts were up before dawn, raking the gravel in the courtyard. I watched the four of them from my bedroom window as they scraped the ground to reveal the fine red dust that lay beneath. They were meticulous to the point of obsession, running lines over the same few square meters of earth over and over until every bit of gravel was gone.

I watched them for at least half an hour, waiting for them to slacken their pace, to turn their rakes to the side and make meaningless observations that, bit by bit, would devour the time; but they remained committed to their task for as long as I watched them. At first I thought they did so because they were grateful finally to have something to do, but then I leaned my head out the window and saw Isaac standing against the sole tree in the courtyard, watching them, his legs crossed, a cigarette dangling from his lips. He was, without effort, the perfect vision of an overlord, a man who wielded his power casually, as if it had always been his right to do so.

I took my time getting dressed. My injuries had healed enough for me to take the stairs on my own, but I still missed having Isaac there to lean on. As soon as I stepped outside, I understood what all that tedious raking had been for. A wide, sweeping arc of nearly polished earth leading from the gate to the front door had been cleared to make a red carpet of dirt that looked like a half-drawn heart; this gave the house a dignity I would have thought impossible had I not seen it myself. I had to admire what Isaac had done. He yelled out to me from his tree, "Look at what we've done." The pride wasn't his alone—there was more than enough to go around. The guards stopped raking and looked at him with admiration and gratitude as well.

Isaac clapped his hands, and one of the guards brought a chair to the tree for me to sit on.

"We don't have much time," he said. "They'll be here in a few hours."

I had vague notions of who "they" were, and the images I did have were borrowed from the glimpses of powerful men I had experienced in my life. The men I pictured wore gold-rimmed sunglasses and had hefty stomachs they were proud of. They wore matching loose pants and button-down shirts, and the oldest or wealthiest of the group carried a walking stick topped by a shiny gold handle. I had seen those men on numerous occasions, stepping out of their cars in the capital. They may have been business-men, army men, or government ministers. Street spectators like myself never knew and were too afraid to ask. Their mystery was a part of their power, and even though I was in that house with Isaac, the same rules of hierarchy applied.

When the courtyard was finished, the guards began work on the rest of the grounds. They gathered the fallen leaves and emp-tied the dirty water from the fountain. The young girl with the white headscarf who brought us our meals appeared, with two other girls her age. When I saw those girls, who couldn't have been older than sixteen or seventeen, a harsh, sarcastic voice in my head said, "There is your Hope and Patience." They spent the morning and afternoon carting buckets of water from the kitchen in the back and later scrubbing the floors on their knees, while Isaac watched. I wanted to know what their names were but avoided getting too close to them; every time I caught a fleeting glimpse of either, I thought, Patience is on her knees, or Hope is out back looking for water.

Isaac asked only one thing of me: "You have to look your best today," he said. "Go to my room and change."

He pointed to the sling that I still wore on my right arm to keep my ribs from moving too much.

"Do you need that?" he asked me.

And suddenly I was also desperate to impress and to be rewarded.

"Are you joking?" I said. I slipped my arm out of the sling and did my best to raise it above my head. The pain was far greater than I had expected. "I never needed it."

He smiled. He gave my injured arm a gentle pat. He didn't say it, but I felt that I had made him proud.

By midafternoon, all the preparations that Isaac had been able to think of had been made. The house shone, and every half-hour or so the grounds were swept again so that they were as spotless as they had been that morning. There was nothing left to do but wait.

"They'll be here by three or four p.m. at the latest," Isaac said. In anticipation, Isaac had the guards and girls who had spent the morning cleaning and cooking line up in two perfect rows outside the front door. They held their place for at least an hour; at three, when no one had arrived, Isaac had them line up parallel to the house instead. He kept them there for a few minutes before deciding that it was all wrong.

"It's unacceptable," he said. "Look at them. They look like they just came off the streets."

He took the guards apart one at a time. He began with their shoes, spitting on each one.

"This isn't a slum," he said. He took the scarves off the girls' heads and gave them to the guards so they could polish their shoes with them. When they were done with their shoes, Isaac pointed to the dirt on their faces. He grabbed the youngest of the guards—a man who was still at least a decade older than him—by his ear. "You must be deaf," he said. "Look at your ear." Isaac took the same scarf the man had used to wash his shoes and stuffed it into his ear, and when that wasn't enough, he began to shine his forehead and cheeks with the scarf.

I watched Isaac's nervous, irrational rage unfold from the sidelines. I told myself that if he did the same to the girls I'd protest, but he exhausted whatever violence he had in him on those men, and I suspect that I knew he would do so all along, which was why I felt free to set those terms to begin with.

Fortunately, we had night on our side. As soon as the light began to dim, Isaac relaxed. He knew we wouldn't have to wait much longer; no one wanted to be on the road at night, not even the soldiers who patrolled the streets. If you were far from home at dusk, nothing in the world seemed crueler than a setting sun, especially if it was a stunning one, with thin vestiges of purple and red clouds streaked around it. Beauty at times like that was a reminder of nature's—or, for the faithful, God's—indifference. The greater the splendor, the more terrible the absence and terror that came with it. I remember the sun that evening as being more remarkable than most, but only because there were ten of us safely grouped together to admire it. We all felt touched by its grace, to different degrees and for different reasons.

No sooner had the sun vanished than the first traces of a heavy engine and tires crushing gravel could be heard. The guards responsible for opening the gate turned toward it, as if longing to perform the one task they were certain they knew how to accomplish. Isaac stared directly at each of the guards and, by doing so, kept them in place. At the last possible moment, Isaac clapped his hands and set them free. All four scrambled to lift the locks and pull open the gates. In their haste, they trampled the perfect driveway they had spent hours creating. Isaac wasn't troubled in the least bit, though. I saw him smile as they ruined what he had demanded they create.

"Look at them," he said. "They're like children." But there was no affection behind his words. Though he called them children, I was certain that what he really meant to say was that to him they were like dogs.

The gates opened and three black Mercedes slid into the court-yard. They looked beastly in the semi-darkness of early night, with their pale-yellow parking lights shining over us. I doubt I was the only one who felt an instinctive desire to run. They are only men, I said to myself, but there was no comfort in that. If there was anything to fear in this world, it was men who came in under the cover of night, who sat in expensive cars behind tinted windows, with the engines running and the lights on, while they measured their safety and our value to them.

At least a quarter-hour must have gone by before the first car turned off its engine and the second and third followed. None of us moved or spoke. By now it was dark outside. That's what they had been waiting for. When the car doors opened, all I could see from my place on the porch were the silver door handles and the outlines of the six men, who exited in pairs from the back of each sedan. Four were wearing dark suits and were as tall and almost as thin as I was. The two who had exited first, from the last car, were short and barrel-chested; their military decorations and caps stood out as clearly as the pistol each was holding at his side.

After all the anxiety and preparations, the men came and disappeared in a matter of minutes. They stood in the courtyard, talking among themselves, and then, without so much as a single glance at the guards, or the grounds, filed into the house. Only one stayed long enough to acknowledge that any of us were there, and even that interaction lasted a matter of seconds. That man was by far the youngest of the four men in suits. He paused at the entrance to shake Isaac's hand. I knew immediately I had seen his face before.

"You've done a fine job," he said, clasping both his hands around Isaac's. His voice was familiar; he had a real British accent. He avoided looking directly at me, but I remembered where I had last seen him. He had been sitting at the table across from Isaac and me at the Café Flamingo. He was the one who had ordered the beating to stop. When I walked past the café, alone or with Isaac, I looked to see if he was there. He never was, and so I never mentioned him to Isaac. I wasn't sure what I would have said had he been. That man there saved you from being beaten to death, or that man there watched for several minutes as those boys nearly beat you to death.

Isaac walked him to the door. One of the soldiers opened and closed it quickly, and then took his place in front, while the other hovered restlessly around the cars. Having decided the house was safe, they slid their guns into their holsters. They made a show of looking professional; they wanted it to be clear that they were officers, not hired guards at the end of their career.

I followed Isaac back to the tree, where we had left the chairs we'd spent most of the afternoon on. It was a warm, slightly humid night. Miles away, near the center of the city, we could see at least a half-dozen bright white lights that had been raised to trap the grasshoppers that had just begin to come out. It was hunting at its simplest: the grasshoppers swarmed around the lights and knocked themselves out by the dozens on the metal sheets that surrounded them. They were collected in barrels and then sold by the handful in little brown bags or plastic sacks, half dead or freshly roasted, a delicacy for even the poorest. It was said the president ate them by the dozens, roasted or boiled and then dipped in chocolate.

Isaac was staring at the lights as well. He had told me once how as a child he had tried to create his own little grasshopper farm to profit from, by taking all the candles from his grandparents' house and lighting them in the yard. "I caught three grasshoppers," he said, "and then I almost died of malaria after a hundred mosquito bites."

"We're missing out on all the fun," he said as he pointed toward the lights. He was sincere, and full of nostalgia. I was relieved to hear him talk like that.

"There's always tomorrow," I said.

"Second day is not as good," he said. "You want them on the first night, when they've just come out."

I let him dream about grasshoppers and the riches he might have made off of them. It was one of the rare times in my life when a part of me wasn't concerned with how many minutes or hours had passed since someone had last spoken. I knew the doors to the house weren't going to open anytime soon, but more than that, I knew that once they did it would be harder—not impossible, just harder—for both of us, Isaac especially, to drift into the past so easily. I let him have that for as long as I could. Eventually, though, I had to ask him: "What happens now?"

"We wait," he said. "They have things to discuss inside that don't concern us."

"That man," I said.

"Which one?"

"The one who thanked you."

"What about him?"

"I've seen him before. He was at the café that afternoon."

"His name is Joseph," Isaac said. "The Flamingo is his café."

"Did you know that when we went there?"

"Yes and no. I didn't know what he looked like or his name. I wouldn't have had that fight if I knew he was watching, but it worked out anyway. After you left, he came back. I was on a table in the kitchen. He brought a doctor to see me. He said he liked my courage. He asked what I was doing with myself. I told him I was a student at the university, but he knew I was lying."

"Why did he care?"

"He didn't. He just felt sorry for me. I kept going back there, though—whenever I wasn't on campus I was there. He gave me little jobs to do: I moved boxes around, I cleaned the floor in the kitchen. After a few weeks, he asked me what I thought about what was happening to the country. I knew who his father was: I saw him once before I came to the capital. Everyone in our village loved him. He was supposed to be the first governor of our district, but then, just before the elections, he disappeared. The president said that it was rebels, or maybe even the British who did it. The president put a cousin of his—a colonel—in his place. Joseph was still in London at the time. His father was smart—he kept him there while he was running. I don't think most people knew he had a son.

"I didn't tell him that I knew who his father was. I knew I could say anything I wanted to him, though, so I told him the truth. I told him that I thought it was worse now than it had been under the British. He liked that, but he told me I was wrong. 'It's better to be killed by your own devil than by someone else's,' he said. He gave me a list of names and asked me if I knew who any of those men were. I told him no. He asked me if I was lying. I said I was from a small village; I didn't know who anyone was. 'Even better, then,' he said. 'Remember to act as if you always believe that. Even when it's no longer true.' I started picking up and delivering messages for him. Only at night, or early in the morning. It was normally to one of those men inside the house, although this is the first time I've seen them. There was always a guard or a maid who met me at the door.

"I wanted to stay with him all the time, but he told me he needed me on the campus. 'The students have to know what's happening,' he said. 'They can't just read about it anymore.' "

"And that's how the protest began?"

"I'm surprised," Isaac said. "You haven't recognized any of the old guards."

"Why should I?"

"Two of them used to work on campus," he said. "They were the first ones to attack us that Friday. Since you were running, you wouldn't have had time to look at them."

"We were all running. I didn't know I wasn't supposed to."

"Don't take it that way," he said. "You had to run. I wanted to tell you what was happening, but I couldn't risk it. Joseph spent a lot of time and money finding two guards he could trust. The rest was easy. Once they felt they were being attacked, all the student groups joined in and made their own rally. I barely had anything to do with that. I just had to be there to watch. I was surprised when you showed up."

"I didn't know what was happening. I don't think I would have come if I did."

"I know. But you stayed. You were loyal. When I heard you were in the hospital, I thought it was the soldiers who did that. The ones outside the gates weren't going to do anything"—Isaac pointed to the uniformed man standing by the cars—"those were his men. But there were so many others on campus who weren't with us. I told Joseph you were beaten leaving the campus that night. That's why he let me bring you here, why he gave me money for the hospital. You can't tell him it was because you were walking down the street. It's dangerous for him now. The same for the other men as well."

"And what about you?"

"It's hard to say. I don't think so, but I can't be sure. You're lucky. Right now you have nothing to worry about. No one has any idea who you are."

HELEN

I drove my car around the block and parked on the opposite side of the street, half a block away from Isaac's building. I was prepared to wait there all night. If Isaac left, I would follow him and then surprise him—or surprise him and then follow him. I didn't know how it would work out. I didn't have a plan and didn't want one. If my mother could see me she would have said, "Helen, what are you doing? What's your plan?"

I believed that my not having a plan was what separated us. Her hair was long and dark brown, almost black. Mine never went past my shoulders; it was lighter, and in the summer almost blond. My mother had thick calves and narrow little feet. My legs were slender, and I hadn't been able to fit into my mother's shoes since I was a teenager. I went to college; she was pregnant and married two years out of high school. I sang all the time; the only music I ever heard from her was during the Christmas season, when she hummed the same two songs—"Silent Night" and "White Christmas." She had small hands, with long, delicate fingers that I imagined could easily break. My palms were large, and so were my fingers—man's hands, a boy in grade school had called them. The only book I ever saw her read was the Bible; she believed deeply in God. I never cared about him and went to church most Sundays because she wanted me to. She had a round, perfectly oval face that was pretty, not beautiful, when she was young. I had the same face she did when she was my age, but I promised myself that when I got older I wouldn't let it sag and fill with weight as hers had. She was a profound sleeper. I woke up several times each night. She cried easily. She hated to drive; she kept both hands on the steering wheel and even on empty country roads in the middle of the afternoon, stayed at least five miles below the speed limit. I could spend hours in my car. Her parents' named her Audrey, after her grandmother. My father named me Helen for reasons he said he couldn't remember. Those were all only superficial distinctions. She had always been a cautious woman; until now, the same had always been true of me.

Another set of lights came on in Isaac's apartment. He was walking back and forth across the living room, rubbing his hand over his head. He turned toward the picture window, but from my angle I couldn't see his face clearly.

I reminded myself that if I were my mother I would have left by now.

I rolled down my window. I wasn't positive, but it looked as if his mouth was moving. He might have been talking, laughing, or crying. Whatever he was doing, he wasn't alone.

I leaned the top of my head out of the car so I could see better. There was a shadow on the wall that wasn't Isaac's. It was much shorter, rounder, and when seen against the wall, had little or no hair.

I heard my mother's voice again. This time she was telling me to run, to close my eyes and drive away, but what good would that have done? Had I driven all the way to the coast, east or west, I would still have been sitting on that block, watching the shadows.

I took the key out of the ignition and threw it into the glove compartment. I thought of slashing the tires of my car, unplugging wires from the engine. I didn't trust myself not to run. After a while I closed my eyes. David was right—this wasn't the type of neighborhood to do that in. Every time I felt myself drifting off, I looked back up to Isaac's window. There were small surprises. It looked briefly as if the shadows in the living room weren't just talking but arguing, with arms raised and fingers pointed. Then, seconds later, everything seemed perfectly calm. For twenty minutes, Isaac sat on the couch and hardly moved while the other shadow sat opposite him. I realized I felt more comfortable when I thought they were fighting.

I never took my eyes off the window, but at some point I fell asleep. When I opened my eyes, there was no one sitting in the living room. I had just begun to worry that I had missed out on something vital when the man who looked liked the shadow on the wall left Isaac's building. I saw him for only a few seconds, while he was standing under the porch light, looking for his car. He was much older than I had expected, bald, but not as fat as I thought.

As soon as he got outside, he lit a cigarette and took his keys out of his pocket. He started walking toward me. I slipped to the bottom of my seat, but my window was open. I heard a car door near me open and close. I heard the engine and could see the headlights. He had been parked on the other side of the street, maybe two or three cars behind me. I could feel the car as it neared me, but just in case I'd missed him, the man rolled down his window and said, "Good night, Helen," as he passed.

ISAAC

Isaac and I were half asleep on the chairs by the time we were allowed back into the house. By then the girls and the house guards had gone off to the servants' quarters. The cicada lights had gone off, as had all the lights in the city. It was two weeks since the government had started cutting off the streetlights after midnight, but I had never noticed until then how complete the blackness was. Looking out at the capital from our secluded corner reminded me of a story my father had told me about a city that disappeared each night once the last inhabitant fell asleep. He was good at telling stories—not great, like my uncles and grandfathers, who reveled in the theatrics. Compared to them, a story was a solemn occasion delivered in a calm, measured voice that nonetheless left a lasting impression on anyone who was listening. He told me that story about the city that disappeared at night shortly after I developed a sudden, irrational fear of the dark. I must have been ten or eleven at the time, old enough to have known better than to be afraid of something so common and simple as the end of the day, and well past the age of bedtime stories, but for the first few nights of my terror, my father indulged me. He told me one night about the countries thousands of miles to the north of us where months went by without the sun setting—hoping I would find comfort in knowing that the world didn't end simply because the lights went out in our village.

According to my father, the city in the story was once a real place. "I'm not inventing this for you," he said. "Everything I tell you is true." I believed him in that semiconscious way that children have of dismissing reality in the hope of finding something better. "For hundreds of years," my father said, "that city existed as long as one person dreamed of it each night. In the beginning, everyone kept some part of the city alive in their dreams— people dreamed of their garden, the flowers they had planted that they hoped would bloom in the spring, or the onions that were still not ripe enough to eat. They dreamed of their neighbor's house, which in most cases they believed was nicer than their own, or the streets they walked to work on every day, or, if they didn't have a job, then of the café where they spent hours drinking tea. It didn't matter what they dreamed of as long as they kept one image alive just for themselves, and in many cases they would pass that image on to their children, who would inherit their house, or attend the same school, or work in the same office. After many years, though, people grew tired of having to dream the same image night after night. They complained. They bickered and fought among themselves about whether they shouldn't abandon the city altogether. They held meetings; each time, more people refused to carry the burden of keeping the city alive in their dreams. 'Let someone else dream of my street, my house, the park, the intersection where traffic is terrible because all the roads lead one way,' they said, and for a time, there were enough people willing to take on the extra responsibility. There was always someone who said, 'Okay, I will take that dream and make it my own.' There were heroic men and women who went to sleep each night when the sun set so they could have enough time to dream of entire neighborhoods, even those that they had rarely if ever set foot in, because no one else would do so. Eventually, though, even those men and women grew tired of having to carry all the extra parts of the city on their backs while their friends and neighbors walked around, carefree. They also wanted other dreams, and one by one they claimed their independence. They said, 'I am tired. Before I die, I want to see something new when I sleep.' Then the day came when no one wanted to dream of the city anymore. On that day, a young man whom few people knew and no one trusted went to all the radio stations and shouted from the center of the city that he alone would take on the burden of keeping their world alive each night. 'Don't worry,' he said. 'I'll dream of everything for you. I know every corner of this city by heart. Close your eyes at night and know that you are free.'"

From then on, everyone in the city believed they were free to dream about foreign lands, countries they had read about or that had never existed, the lovers they hadn't met yet, the better husbands or wives they wished they had, the bigger houses they wanted to live in someday. The people gave that young man their lives without knowing it. They had given him all the power he wanted, and even though they didn't know it, they had made him their king.

Weeks, months, and then years went by. People dreamed of living on the moon and the sun. They dreamed of castles built on clouds, of children who never cried, and while they dreamed each night, their king erased a part of the city. A park disappeared in the middle of the night. A hill that had the best view over the city vanished. Streets and then homes were erased before dawn. Soon the people who complained about the changes went missing. One morning, everyone woke to find all the radio stations and libraries gone. A secret meeting was held that afternoon, and it was agreed that the city should go back to the way it had been before. But by then no one could remember what the city had looked like—buildings had been moved, street names were changed, the man who ran the grocery store on the busy intersection had vanished. There was another problem as well. When asked to describe what the city looked like now, no one could say for certain if Avenue Marcel and Independence Boulevard still intersected, if the French café owned by a Mr. Scipion had closed or merely moved to a different corner. It was years since anyone had looked at the city closely—at first because they were free to forget it, and later because they were embarrassed and then too afraid to see what they had let it become.

Those who tried to dream of the city again could see only their house or their street as it looked years ago, but that wasn't dreaming, it was only remembering, and in a world where seeing was power, nostalgia meant nothing.

I thought of telling Isaac that story, but I didn't know how to explain it to him without sounding foolish. The president cut the lights at night, he might have said. So what? He did it because it made it harder to attack. And though that was the obvious reason, I would have wanted to argue that there was also something far worse happening. The city disappeared at night, and, yes, he wanted to protect his power, and what better way to do so than to make an entire population feel that just like that, with the flip of a switch, they and the world they knew, from the beds they slept on to the dirt roads in front of their houses, could vanish.

When the doors to the house opened, Joseph was standing on the other side, his tie undone, as if he had just finished a long night at a wedding, drinking and making speeches. He looked at once exhausted and relieved; whatever doubts I had about being welcome vanished as soon as I saw him again and he waved us in with a generous smile and dramatic sweep of the hand. Had I paid closer attention, I might have noticed that, as before, I hardly registered, and that all of his attention was devoted solely toward Isaac.

"You boys must be tired," he said. "I apologize for making you wait outside like that. I hope we didn't offend you. My colleagues are a bit nervous and aren't used to speaking in front of others."

He was the only man I had ever met who spoke like that. It wasn't the accent but the words themselves that were striking, at once formal and yet seemingly more gentle, as if he were trying not just to communicate but to elevate whomever he was speaking to onto the same privileged plane on which he existed.

"We didn't mind," Isaac said. "We would have been happy to stay outside longer."

It had been decided that Isaac and I would share my room on the top floor, and Joseph, the three other men, and the two soldiers with them would take over the rooms on the first and second floors.

"We are going to need all the space we have," Joseph said. "This is just the beginning."

As he talked, two of the house guards quietly entered, carrying a mattress that must have belonged to one of them. Joseph stopped them just as they were climbing the stairs. He had them turn the mattress over so he could see both sides, and then said something in Kiswahili that made both of them smile and Isaac turn away in embarrassment.

That was the second time Isaac and I shared a room—the first had been back in the slums, after Isaac was kicked out of his house. Neither of us had slept well that night, fearful about what would happen next. I felt a similar fear that second night, though it was hard to know what lay behind it. We were safe in that house, at least for the moment, but there was something else at risk. Isaac seemed to know that, too. He didn't say a word to me after we entered the room, just undressed in the dark and went straight to his mattress, which had been placed opposite mine, next to the door. It fell to him to say that everything would be okay, even if we were both certain that it wasn't. As tired as I was, I couldn't sleep while he was visibly disturbed. I turned my back to him so he couldn't see that, though I was lying perfectly motionless, I had both eyes wide open.

Either my performance was better than I thought or, after an hour of silently waiting, Isaac no longer cared. Sometime around 3 a.m., Isaac rose from his bed. I didn't turn around to see him, but I could hear him pull back the sheet and put his pants on. He opened the door just enough to slip out; not until I was certain that he was gone did I turn over.

Whatever I had been afraid of left with Isaac. With him gone, I was asleep in a few minutes. I suppose I knew that night where he had gone, and I suppose I also knew that he was trusting me not just to keep that knowledge to myself, but to ignore it altogether. There was no secret to guard, nothing to deny, because, according to the deal we had silently struck, nothing had happened.

When I woke the next morning, Isaac was back in his bed. His pants and shirt were strewn on the floor just as he had left them when he arrived. He was, to my surprise, deeply asleep. I had never felt protective of him before. I had seen him injured, beaten, and knocked unconscious, and all I had ever felt was pity or sadness and maybe a bit of envy for his reckless courage. He had never needed me to come to his defense, and to be honest, I wouldn't have known how to. Had I woken him up and told him that when it came to me he was safe, he had nothing to worry about, he would have kicked me out of that house, and we would never have spoken again. I wanted him to know that, though, and so I did the only thing I could think of: I picked his clothes up from the floor. I folded his pants and shirts, just as my mother had done for my father and for me—a seemingly insignificant gesture that was still one of the things I missed most about living so far away from home. It had something to do with knowing that even in your sleep you were watched over, and that each morning, no matter what mistakes you might have made, you had the right to begin again. I laid Isaac's clothes next to his bed, which was how my mother had always done it; before leaving, I swept my hands over his shirt and pants to shake off the dirt and smooth out the wrinkles as best I could.

HELEN

"Good night, Helen." It was a simple, seemingly harmless statement, and yet as soon as the car turned the corner I realized I had
been holding my breath since hearing my name. I didn't move
until I felt certain the car wasn't coming back, and then I pan-
icked. I looked for the keys in the ignition and slapped the steering wheel when I didn't find them. I searched my pockets and the
passenger seat before I remembered I had thrown them in the
glove compartment. I imagined Isaac and the bald man looking
down at me earlier and laughing. I told myself I was frightened,
but really the embarrassment was the hardest thing to bear.

I took my time putting the keys in the ignition. If Isaac was
watching me, I wanted him to see me calmly drive away, and so
I did my best to imitate a woman of composure. I fastened my
seat belt, I adjusted the mirrors, and I was about to turn the
key when the front door of Isaac's building opened. He came
out slowly, or at least he appeared to. I noticed he wasn't wearing a coat. He tucked his hands in his pockets, and his shoulders
hunched together. I remembered that this was his first glimpse of
winter, and that he had worried almost since the day he arrived
how he would handle the cold. He had asked me in September
if the weather would get much worse. "You have no idea," I had

told him, not knowing that for him there was nothing humorous about winter. The temperature had been dropping all evening; my fingers and toes felt almost numb, even though it was still above freezing. I wanted to tell Isaac that he should go back upstairs and get his coat.

He turned to where I was parked. I couldn't decide if I was relieved or disappointed that he knew immediately where to find me. I didn't hold on to the question for long. His standing under the light meant I could see him all too clearly. He made no attempt to hide his grief; I could feel it splayed across his face as surely as if he were lying next to me.

Isaac got into the car, and we drove away. How we came to that point without speaking doesn't matter, although David would later insist that it did.

"You had no idea what he was doing, who he was with, or where he had been," David said. "Please, tell me at least he apologized."

"He didn't say anything," I told him.

"That makes you either a saint or an idiot," he said.

I wasn't either. I simply saw a man in need, and knew I could do something to ease that.

We drove past Isaac's apartment, made a loop around the center of town, and within ten minutes were on the ramp leading to the highway. I didn't have a destination in mind. The farther we drove, the heavier Isaac's breathing became, and for a while, that was all I concentrated on. The rapid fall and rise of his breath would eventually have to break, and shortly after we got on the highway it did. First one short sob, followed by another, after which he finally gave in and cried openly. I drove faster. I knew as soon as he stopped crying he would be embarrassed, and I thought that if I drove fast enough we could pretend it had never happened, or was already such a trivial thing of the past, miles behind us, that it was no longer worth speaking about. I drove like that across two county lines; there were signs I had never seen before leading to Kansas, St. Louis, and Chicago. Had Isaac needed me to, I would have gone on longer, but the weight began to lift. His breathing returned to normal. He wiped his face clean with his forearms and placed one hand on my shoulder.

"Who was that man with you?" I asked him.

I drove for several miles waiting for an answer. When none came I tried again. "Can you tell me why he knows my name?"

"What did he say to you?"

" 'Good night, Helen.' "

Something nearing a smile crossed his face.

"I thought he was joking when he said he wanted to say hello to you. His name is Henry. He didn't mean to alarm you."

I had heard Henry's name mentioned in reference to Isaac before. He was the man behind Isaac's visa, who had brought him to David and our town.

"What did he want?" I asked him.

"I didn't know he was coming," Isaac said. "He was waiting for me when I came home. He drove three hours to tell me in person that a man I cared for deeply back home had died."

"Someone you were related to?"

"We were very close," he said. "He was like a brother and a father to me."

"I'm very sorry," I said. I was going to add, "If there's anything I can do . . . ," but despite Isaac's grief, his loss felt too remote to me to allow me to say more.

"It must be difficult being so far away," I added, but what I really wanted to say was that I was worried for him and for us. Nothing traveled better than death. Grief thrived in isolation, and I was afraid of being all that Isaac had.

"He did not have to die," he said.

"Maybe not," I offered, "but there's nothing you can do to change that now."

"You don't understand."

"Then tell me."

"He could have left. He could have been here."

I squeezed his hand. I looked at him tenderly. I didn't believe him; it was the standard refrain of mourning: He could have . . . She would have . . . If only . . .

"What was his name?"

Isaac turned his attention to the window. It was pitch-black outside, but even if it hadn't been, there was nothing to see other than flat, vacant farmland stripped clean at the start of winter.

I repeated the question: "I asked you what his name was."

Minutes passed. I counted to twenty and back. I began to imagine what I would do if he refused to acknowledge me: pull onto the shoulder and demand a response before driving any farther; scream; slam on the brakes.

"He loved nicknames," he said. "He had at least a dozen for me, but I only ever called him Isaac."

ISAAC

When I came downstairs in the morning, Joseph was standing near the front door, talking to the guards as they rearranged the furniture in the living room. I saw him when I was halfway down the steps and thought immediately of going back to my room to wait for Isaac to wake up, but I was afraid that if Joseph saw me retreat he would find it suspicious; if anything caused me concern, it was drawing attention to myself. I was a stranger in that house. Other than Isaac, no one would care if I disappeared. My life story since coming to the capital consisted of standing on the sidelines, and I could have continued to do so had I not seen Isaac leave our room in the middle of the night.

Joseph waved me over to him. He had traded in his suit for a pair of dark-khaki pants and a white shirt that had his initials, J.M., embroidered on the pocket. It was a small extravagance, nothing compared with the gold watches and necklaces that other wealthy men indulged in. He wasn't one of the true revolutionaries that Isaac and I had admired on campus, but he wasn't a privileged fraud, either. He was special. He belonged to a class entirely his own.

We shook hands while furniture was moved around us; he gripped my shoulder with what seemed to be genuine affection.

"Did you sleep well?" he asked me.

"Yes. I was exhausted. I was asleep minutes after I reached my bed."

He laughed. I couldn't decide if he did so because he knew I was lying.

"And Isaac? I haven't seen him this morning."

"He was sleeping when I left."

He pretended to be disappointed, shaking his head, but it was obvious he didn't mean it. He motioned with his hand for me to follow him outside. The morning was brilliant, cloudless, sun-drenched, and too bright for normal eyes. I had to keep my head bent toward the ground as Joseph spoke.

"I would like to speak honestly," he began, but even with one hand over my brow I could hardly bear to look up at him.

"Isaac wants to keep you near him, so he would never tell you this, but you can leave. You are under no obligation to remain here. If you leave, you should go somewhere very far from here. You should leave the country. Go back home to your family. I'm sure you know this already, but this city is a bad place for young men like you. If you remain here, with us, it will only get worse. I can have someone drive you to a town near the border; Isaac can accompany you the whole way, and then, who knows, after all this is over, perhaps you can return to join him."

He spoke with what seemed like genuine concern, and even remorse, as if it pained him to suggest I was better off leaving. For that reason alone, I didn't believe him. Such attention was more than I deserved, and I had come to believe that the only thing worse than being ignored was the suspicion that you were being watched closely.

"I would like to stay," I told him.

He said something to one of the guards moving the furniture. The guard bowed in response, and I wondered if Joseph had demanded that type of servility or if it was given to him freely.

He moved a few inches closer to me.

"Do you know why?" he asked me.

I pretended not to understand the question and just stared at my shoes, hoping he wouldn't ask it again. When he did, I asked him, "Do I know what?"

"Is it because of your friend or because you have nowhere else to go that you want to stay?"

He put a hand on my shoulder. I wanted to give a bold, definitive response—the type that came easily to Isaac—but none came to mind. A few seconds passed before Joseph leaned in and answered his question for me:

"It's both," he said, "and that's fine for now."

This wasn't a threat, or a warning, but a precursor to both. He squeezed my shoulder while describing how the house had been built.

"My grandfather used to own this land," he said. " 'Own' isn't the right word, since everything back then technically belonged to the British and could be taken away, but he had paid and signed for it when nothing was here. He thought that when independence came no one would want to live in the city anymore. He said the capital was built for the white people, and once they left, people would want to return to the land and live as their ancestors had. It was a silly and brilliant idea at the same time. When independence came, he was already dead, and there were more people in the capital than ever before. My father sold this land one plot at a time; it was suddenly fashionable for the rich to want to live away from the center of the city, and like that we became very rich. He built this house for his mistress to live in. She's an old woman now. She returned to her village to die there in peace, and now she is the only one who knows we are here. If the government knew this house belonged to my father, they would have taken it for themselves by now."

That was the longest conversation I would ever have with Joseph. He kept his hand on my shoulder the entire time, and after a while I found its gentle pressure reassuring, as if it were part of the force keeping us tied to the ground. By the time he finished talking, we were standing next to the tree in the center of the courtyard, looking back on the house, which meant much to him and nothing to me. I had no conviction I could point to, no house to look back on and say: That is why I am here; this is what I'm willing to fight for. If I understood the intent of Joseph's story correctly, I had only so much time to change that.

He shook my hand before leaving. "Make yourself at home," he said. "Stay as long as you like, but let's keep this conversation to ourselves."

He was gone before I could respond, but my answer was irrelevant to begin with. The ease with which he hardly bothered to distinguish fact from fiction told me that.

The preparations for Joseph's war began in earnest that afternoon. I knew from Isaac that something violent was being planned, but that on its own was hardly remarkable. Violent dreams and more plausible violent plans were burning all across the capital, and I assumed this was merely the version I had stumbled into.

Over the course of a few hours that morning, the scale of Joseph's maneuvers became evident. Pairs of men arrived in what felt like timed half-hour intervals. By the time Isaac came down and joined me in the courtyard, there were eight new bodies tucked away somewhere in that house, conferring in one of the rooms I implicitly understood were off limits. The presence of so many new faces was the kind of distraction Isaac and I needed. I had worried over how to approach him, and now here was something more extraordinary than his departure from our room in the middle of the night around which we could meet. Men in suits and men in fatigues. Men with pistols fastened at their belts. I should have been thinking of the fighting to come; instead, I was grateful for the distraction it offered.

"What do you think?" Isaac waved his arm across the courtyard and house as if it were a scenic view that he had made.

"Who are they?" I asked him.

He grinned and then threw his arm around me.

"They are the beginning," he said. "Very soon there will be many more."

The meeting that took place in the house that afternoon was the second-most-important conference in the capital's history since independence. I had missed the first, but dreaming of the writers who had once gathered at the university had brought me here to begin with. I came for the writers and stayed for the war. The difference wasn't as great as I would have thought.

Isaac did his best to narrate the movements for me.

That man is a colonel in the army.

He has a gold mine in the south.

That's the brother of someone in Parliament.

I've heard he is a general in Tanzania.

And so it went on, until the entire second floor of the house had been filled with serious men whose guards and valets stood quietly in the living room. When the last guest arrived, the front door was closed; the gate was sealed shut. If Isaac was disappointed at being left outside, he didn't show it.

"This feels very familiar," he said, "like we've done it before."

"I was thinking the same," I said. "Do you know what they're talking about this time?"

"I can guess," he said.

And so could I. In a certain context, it was entirely predictable.

"What do you think would happen if I went inside?" I asked him.

Isaac looked around at the various guards stationed around the doors. He pointed to a tall, skinny man whose face was largely hidden behind gold-rimmed sunglasses.

"He would tell that guy standing next to him to shoot you."

I looked closer at both men; it would have meant nothing for them to do that.

"And what if you tried?"

"Maybe they would let me in," he said. "And then, immediately afterward, someone else would shoot you."

"And what if I tried to leave?"

Isaac laughed.

"Then everyone here would take turns shooting you."

He thought about it a second longer.

"And if that wasn't enough, they would want to do the same to me next."

I didn't dare ask Isaac what guaranteed his safety. Without intending to, he had made it clear he could do little or nothing to protect mine, and so it was time I found a way to do so on my own.

·　　·　·　·

The conference on the second floor broke before lunch. The orderly procession entering the house turned into a struggle to leave it. Armed guards fought to get their charges through the gate; I assumed this meant that things had gone poorly for Joseph and his movement, but just as the first group was leaving, he appeared in the doorway, beaming, and suddenly there was a second rush back to the front door to shake his hand goodbye. I noticed deference similar to the bow the guard had given him that morning, but now it came from privileged and powerful men who nodded their heads discreetly, as if catching sight of stains on their shoes that had appeared that instant.

"That's it?" I asked Isaac. "It's over already."

"Joseph is very efficient," he said. "He lived in England."

Efficiency was only half the equation, however. There was a desperation not to be seen together outside for too long, even if it was in the courtyard of the house they had just met in. No one trusted even semi-private spaces; it was windowless rooms or nothing at all. I wondered somewhat romantically if that was how the writers who had met in the capital had felt—not wanted or hunted, but like outlaws.

Mere minutes after the last man left, three pickup trucks carrying loads draped under brownish-gray tarps pulled quickly into the courtyard. They had been waiting nearby for the congregation to vanish before entering. Isaac was right: England had made Joseph efficient. Isaac whispered into my ear, "Joseph wants you to see this."

I could feel Joseph watching us from the doorway; knowing he was watching me gave me something to do.

Two men left each truck and set about untying the tarps. I

had made no assumptions about what was underneath; I was so busy acting I didn't know how to feel about the crates of unripe bananas and yams that lay in the trucks.

"Food for an army?" I asked Isaac.

"Something like that," he said.

The men threw the boxes of food onto the ground; no one was troubled about the broken boxes or the damage done to the food. The piles of bananas and yams stood taller than me when, finally, the men reached the second load, buried beneath. They unloaded these crates carefully, one at a time, in teams of two, straight from the back of the trucks to the living room, where they were lined up in perfect rows. When there was only one box left, Joseph came out from the doorway and motioned with his hand for the lid to be opened. I couldn't see the contents from where we stood. I had to wait for Joseph to dig in and pull out a body-length strip of bullets. He held it up as if it were a prize catch plucked from the sea, but it didn't look like a fish, or even a snake gone limp. It looked like hundreds of metal casings clipped together. He held it up, I believe, specifically for me to see.

After the food was hoisted back into the truck beds, no one, not Isaac or Joseph or any of the guards, ever said that we were sitting on a large cache of weapons, enough to wipe out our neighborhood, a village, or to make at least a semi-valiant last stand if we were attacked. The closest we came to acknowledging the contents of those crates was later that evening, after the pickup trucks had left, blankets had been thrown over the crates, and the furniture moved back into place to hide it all. One of the guards carried in a crate of Kenyan beer. Joseph personally handed everyone a bottle.

"What should we toast to?" Isaac asked. I expected Joseph to say something like liberation, or freedom, or to our future victory, but he knew how trite and conventional that sounded. He raised his bottle and looked at everyone in the room. "We don't toast to anything," he said. "This isn't a celebration. We're trying to end the nightmare this nation has become." We drank our beer, one after another. When Joseph left the room, Isaac whispered to me, "Maybe instead of guns we should have gotten him an alarm clock." I raised my bottle to Isaac and said, "To never oversleeping." Our bottles clinked just as Joseph came back in. I was afraid he would be angry to see us toast, but he was a light drinker, and the three beers he had quickly downed had softened his mood. He came over and put his arms around both our shoulders and said, "Be careful—tomorrow is an important day. I can't have either of you lying in bed all day."

"Don't worry," I told him. "I'm going to be Isaac's alarm clock."

We had to avoid looking at each other to keep from laughing. Briefly, it felt like we were back at the university in the months before the protests, when our most pressing concern was how to keep our mock revolution going. Enough time hadn't passed for us to be nostalgic, but there it was. That period in our lives was officially over, and if there was anything I wanted to toast, it was that.

Joseph squeezed our shoulders affectionately. "I have to sit," he said. "My body has grown weary."

He took a seat on the couch and had one of the guards bring him another beer. I imagined him feeling nostalgic for his own college days in London, which would have explained why he spoke like that.

"That's how he talks when he's been drinking," Isaac said.

Before drinking again, Joseph crossed his legs and stretched his left arm over the cushions. He took a long look around the room—not at the people, but at the furniture and bare walls, the windows and door. He looked up at the ceiling and said in a voice just loud enough for Isaac and me to make out, "I hope I don't blow myself up sitting here."

HELEN

I took the first exit off the highway, onto a narrow two-lane road, then drove for another half-mile or so before pulling over. I had expected some sort of shock to seize me, and had left the highway in anticipation of that, but now that we were on an unlit country road, I realized it wasn't going to happen. There was no shock or surprise waiting: I had known all along that there was something fraudulent about the man sitting next to me; the only real surprise was how he came to tell me.

I left the engine on. I needed to feel like we were still moving.

"Do you want to tell me the rest?" I asked him.

He finally turned to me. It was almost pitch-black in the car, and the only thing I could see clearly was the outline of his nose and traces of his eyes.

"I can," he said.

"But you would rather not?"

"I'm not sure how to answer that."

I swung the car around and headed back to the highway, but I reached over and took his hand briefly in mine. He had lost enough for one night; I didn't want him to risk losing us as well, and there was no guarantee that he wouldn't if he told me more.

"Where are we going?" he asked me.

"Wherever you want," I said.

"Can we go somewhere and sleep? Without going back."

I chose the first motel we came across, two exits away, on the out-skirts of a town I had never heard of. I didn't have the slightest fear that anyone I knew would see me, but Isaac insisted on slid-ing to the bottom of his seat as I pulled into the parking lot.

"Even if they don't know you," he said, "they still might not like what they see."

I didn't say it, but he was right. He understood this about America more intimately than I did.

The motel was half a city block long and two stories high. When I remember it, I think of it as being forcibly conscripted from some generic B-movie about a couple on the run, a place where transients and criminals go to hide.

I asked for a room on the ground floor, on the far end of the motel if possible. There were only two other cars in the park-ing lot, so both my wishes were granted. Our room number was 102—the exact number of students in my high-school graduat-ing class. I took that as a good sign, and every time I returned to that motel, with Isaac, I always asked if room 102 was available. On almost every occasion, it was. The few times it wasn't, I made sure to avoid seeing who came and went, or what noises were being made on the other side of the blue door, so I could hold on to the fantasy that the room was exclusively ours.

· · ·

Isaac and I had the whole night ahead of us, and so, for once, we took our time. We kissed just on the other side of the door until our legs were tired, and then fell onto the bed; in another first, Isaac was the one to undress me. I had assumed that passion and speed were the same: the faster you flung and thrust, the more desire; maybe the difference between fucking and making love isn't just a question of the heart but of the hands as well. Lovers fumble all the time—especially in winter, through all the layers. It's a comedy of hands first, and then heads caught in sweaters and undershirts, and then shoes that stubbornly refuse to come off. If you can bear that with more than just an awkward grin, with a renewed desire, then a nearly vacant motel off the highway may feel like a sacred place at that moment, and for many years afterward.

We finished just as we had begun, unashamed and nearly laughing. We had left the lights on and could finally see each other with our eyes, not just our hands, and for what felt like hours all we did was stare at each other's bodies.

"What were you thinking about," Isaac asked me, "when you were sitting outside, watching my apartment? Did you think I had another woman? Another Helen who looked like you?"

I thought about what I could safely tell him. I looked him in the eyes; his grief was still with him. Unlike many men, Isaac was never a wall; he could only block so much. When he tried to hide his emotions, they leaked out on the sides. At his strongest, he was a cardboard box: it didn't take much to figure out what was inside. That made it so much easier to forgive and love him, and when the time came, that much harder to let go.

"What was I thinking about?" I said. "Many things, and all of them were about you."

·　·　·

What followed next was the start of a brief golden phase for Isaac and me, a winter and then a spring of long, almost nightly embraces, not cut short simply because it was after midnight. We called each other several times over the course of any given day, just to say what was obvious: that the night before had been marvelous, the days spent apart were too long, and there wasn't an hour that passed when we didn't think of each other. We spent the first weekend in December wrapped in blankets that we carried from the bed to the couch. Isaac said it reminded him of winters back home. "We love blankets in our family," he said. "I think that's one of the things I miss most. Seeing my mother or grandmother wrapped in a blanket anytime there was rain. They had blankets for winter and summer, and when I was little I'd try to hide under the blankets when they walked."

I stood naked on his bed while he showed me how to wrap a blanket over my shoulders and around my neck so my arms were still free to flap around. I raised my hands over my head and looked in the mirror.

"You think I can fly?" I asked him.

"Of course," he said.

I flapped my arms, then ran, jumped off the bed, and landed in his. I forced Isaac to turn around so I could see us together in the mirror.

"If you're a bird," I said, "then together we make a penguin."

When my mother asked where I was spending my nights, I did my best to tell her the truth. "I've met someone," I said.

I had come home early that morning and had hoped to leave before she woke up, but she knew my new routine and was waiting for me in the living room when I came downstairs with my coat already halfway on.

"Why didn't you tell me earlier?" she asked me. "Don't you think I worry about you?"

She was troubled, hurt. It wasn't a reproach, but I took it as one.

"You never asked," I said.

"How can I, if I never see you? Who is this person?"

I pretended to struggle with the sleeves of my coat. What could I tell her? I didn't know his real name, but I knew him to be a kind, decent man, none of which would matter if she knew where he was from. I wanted to spare us both the disappointment.

"I'm going to be late," I said.

Though she wasn't standing in my way, she stepped slightly to the side so I would know I was free to go. The last thing she said to me before I left was "This isn't like you, Helen."

"It's okay," I told her. "I know."

We barely spoke for the next few weeks, and when we did, it was never about where I went or whom I spent my time with. She missed me; she let me know that in her own quiet way. She left a new dress on my bed, a necklace of hers that I had loved as a child, all while I was away from home. When we saw each other in the mornings, she told me about the water stains on the bathroom ceiling, the lunch she had had last week, and I said nothing about Isaac.

If it had only been Isaac and me, I'd like to think we could have gone on like that until the day he was supposed to leave; and it's possible, if we had done so, that might have been enough so we could have tried to settle into a life together, maybe in one of those hippie enclaves in San Francisco, or in the chaos of a big city where no one's interest in us ran that deep. Isaac and I spent New Year's Eve drinking white wine in our motel room off the highway, and an entire Valentine Sunday in that room with a box of grocery-store heart-shaped chocolates and red and pink carnations. In April, it started raining hard a few days after Easter and didn't stop until almost two weeks later, by which point half a dozen towns along the river were covered in more than a foot of water. It was the type of natural disaster I would normally have wanted nothing to do with, given the scale and seemingly endless complications that came with it—from the vanished homes, to the devastated crops and factories forced to close—but when David asked if anyone wanted to go down and volunteer with another relief agency, I was the first to raise my hand. I thought I had lost the heart to take on that type of work, but I hadn't. I had simply let the muscles go slack. What I didn't know until then was that loving someone and feeling loved in return was the best exercise for the heart, the strength training needed to do more than simply make it through life. When I told Isaac I was going to work in the flooded towns that we had both seen on the news each night, he asked if the work wouldn't be too difficult. He imagined me carrying sandbags along a levee. "Of course it will be hard," I told him. I flexed both my arms. "Feel that," I said. He squeezed my biceps. "You're the strongest woman in the world," he said, which was exactly how I felt when I was with him.

I spent most of that April touring water-soaked homes, one house and family at a time. There was a stillness to the destruction that I carried home at the end of each day—a chair turned upside down floating in a kitchen, or a woman standing with her hands on her hips, knee-deep in water, staring at the ruined remains of what had been her children's bedroom. The rain and sandbagging had stopped days earlier, but the wreck remained, and it was in that wreckage that I found my place. Overnight, I became an agent of recovery. I waded in the mornings through drenched closets and chests of drawers, searching for important documents and mementos that could be salvaged, mainly for families who still didn't have the heart to do so on their own. In the afternoons and evenings, I pored through stacks of government and insurance forms. I itemized lives, made lists and charts of things lost, from cars, furniture, clothes, and homes to birth certificates, marriage licenses, deeds, wills, and mortgages. I loved what I did. I was hugged and cried on. I had the strength to endure others' misery, to bear some of it on my own so they wouldn't have to. Every time people told me, "I don't know what to do next," I held their hands and told them that was fine, they didn't have to, because I did. I made the drive back to Isaac's apartment three, sometimes four nights a week, on the days when I felt I needed him most. We took hour-long baths together.

"I'm starting to feel like a duck," I told him. "I'm soaking wet all day, and then I come here to sit in a bath."

When he opened the door in the evenings, the first thing I said to him was "Quack." Most evenings I was too tired to talk for long, so he read to me in bed until I fell asleep—never from the same book twice, since most books he finished in a single day. "How do you choose what you're going to read next?" I asked him.

"Simple," he said. "I walk down an aisle, close my eyes, and run my hand along the spines. Whatever book is there when I stop is what I read next."

I believed him at first, but then I saw the university course catalogue lying on the floor next to his bed. He had circled dozens of courses in different departments and was slowly making his way through the partial reading list that was listed next to each class. That was my Isaac at his best.

It was into that private world of ours that Henry stepped in. May was mercifully dry: eighteen straight days of brilliant sunshine, never too warm or humid. I went back to my office at the start of the month, when the bulldozers and construction crews arrived, convinced that, other than the five people who had drowned, nothing had been lost in all that water that could not be replaced. I had done a decent job until then of not counting the months that I had left with Isaac, but the change in season and weather and the return to office life had been so abrupt that all I could see was the end of summer. I skipped over June and July and went straight to the second week in August, when Isaac's visa was set to expire.

"We're running out of time," I told him.

"Let's try not to think about that," he said.

"And how do we do that? You're going to be gone soon, and I still don't know what I'm going to be left with." Which I suppose was my way of saying I was done with mystery; its charm had worn thin. What I wanted was a real person to hold on to and eventually miss.

He put his arm around me. "I'm not gone yet," he said, and with that I relented. A week later, Isaac called me at work to tell me he wanted us to have dinner with Henry, the only friend he had, other than me, in America. Of course, he was far more generous in describing him. His exact words were, "He's the closest thing I have to a past in this country."

Isaac claimed that he was the one who invited Henry to join us for dinner, but I'm certain that wasn't true. Henry was never Isaac's guest; if anything, Isaac was always his. The barrel-chested, balding, middle-aged man whose shadow I first saw from my car was the same person who had helped bring Isaac to America, the old friend of David's who had secured his visa and had him placed in our care. No, I don't believe Isaac invited Henry to dinner so he could meet me. He invited Henry to dinner because Henry wanted to know who the woman lurking outside of the apartment was.

Isaac played it well. For all the precautions we had set in place, from never leaving my car parked overnight in front of his apartment to having fixed times during the day when it was safe for him to call my office, I always wanted more from him. All he had ever told me about his family was that his father was ill, that it had been years since he had last seen them, and that he had five siblings that he knew of, though that didn't mean there weren't more by now. "We're good at having babies," he said. "Better than the Chinese. If we lose one, we have two more to make up for it. If we ever fought a big war, we'd double our population." He still wouldn't give the names of his family, and he had claimed he had no pictures to share. What he had instead was Henry.

"Are we supposed to be just friends?" I asked him. "I don't want to pretend in front of others."

"We don't have to hide," he said. "He knows about us already."

I'm sure I protested about the dinner initially, but not hard enough. I doubt I ever said no directly: I did sense the danger of letting someone like Henry into our life, but I was too curious, too desperate to know who Henry was and what he knew, to refuse the opportunity to meet him.

Isaac scheduled the dinner for six o'clock on a Friday. I arrived at five-thirty, and Henry was already there. My first impression when he opened the door was that he looked as if he had gotten fatter in the months since I had last seen him, but I knew I had no honest image of him. I wanted a brutish, crass man; what I got instead was a charmer—a man who took my jacket when I entered the apartment and hung it in the closet as if he were the host, which, for all intents and purposes, he was. We were in Isaac's apartment, but Henry brought everything to the dinner: the wineglasses on the table, the silver forks and knives, and the real cloth napkins that, in my mother's house, no occasion was special enough for. The chicken in the oven, he admitted, had been cooked by his wife that afternoon. "All I had to do," he said, "was throw it in the oven and keep it warm."

I came to dinner prepared to extract some vital kernel of fact about Isaac, but I was the one who spent the bulk of the dinner revealing myself. Henry asked me about my job, its joys and pit-falls. Those were his exact words. "Isaac tells me you're a social worker," he said. "I'm sure people ask you all the time to tell them about the joys and pitfalls that come with a job like that."

I was rarely asked to describe my job. David had told me never to tell any man I wanted to date what I did for a living. "Say you're a teacher, or a secretary. Men are afraid of women who seem better than them."

Henry had spoken with a wide-eyed earnest stare that gave the impression that whatever I had to say was of the utmost importance and the only way I could disappoint him was if I failed to say more. He was flattering me. I knew that, but after a while I didn't care.

"You really want to know?" I asked him.

"I do," he said. "Maybe in my own way I once tried to do the same."

"That's why you worked in Africa?"

"No. That's why I stayed long after I should have left."

We carried on like that for more than an hour, just the two of us, as if Isaac weren't even there. The more I talked, the more intently Henry listened, so that by the end I found myself seeking his approval. When I said, "What we need in our town is more people like Isaac," it was to Henry and not Isaac I was speaking.

Henry told me snippets about his career in Africa, enough to make me feel that he had also shared some part of himself. When I asked what it was like being a diplomat, he gave me one of those seemingly sincere, deep-hearted laughs that are supposed to imply humility.

" 'Diplomat' sounds much more exciting. To be honest, I was an old-fashioned government bureaucrat. I started off stamping visas in Tanzania. I hated it. Not the job, but the country. I used to say staying out of Africa was the smartest thing America ever did. I went there because I thought it would be the easiest way to get to Europe someday, but then independence came, and suddenly Africa seemed like the most interesting place to be. The French and British and Belgians were running out as fast as they could, and we became the biggest players in town. When I was moved to Kenya, I could pick up the phone and get the president on the line. I sat in hotels and gave lectures on democracy and our constitution. After a while, I didn't want to leave. When I'd come back to D.C., I'd tell my bosses that we could do more than just try to keep the Russians out. I thought we could get the whole continent on our side, if only we had the right leaders. That's when I was moved to London. When I asked my boss why, he told me I'd lost sight of our larger objective. No one in Kansas cares about what happens in Africa, he told me. I'd gotten carried away, which was a diplomatic way of saying I'd gone native.

"I met some of the most interesting people from the continent in London, though, including our mutual acquaintance Joseph. I suppose we should be thanking him for getting our friend Isaac here. He was the most remarkable person I met in London, and probably the only real friend I had.

"They wouldn't let coloreds into the club where all the diplomats drank, so we used to drink at the pub across the street. I had met his father in Kenya. He told me his son was studying in London, so I promised to buy him lunch if he looked me up. Of course he did. Africans always do. They love anyone who they think has power. I liked Joseph as soon as we met. On the outside, he was formal like an Englishman, but he disliked them as much as I did.

"We drank at that bar two, three times a week for almost two years. A bit more often after his father died. At least once a week,

Joseph would say, 'Henry, do you think if I were president they would let me into your club?' He didn't care about the club. It was the lies that it was built on that made him angry. 'They kill us and say it's adventure. If I raise my voice to a white man in London, someone will look at me as if I were an animal.'

"From time to time, at the end of the night he would cross the street and demand to be let into the club. I heard him say to the doorman, 'You should put bars on the windows. Everyone inside is a criminal.'

"I thought he would be president of his country someday. But Isaac can tell you better than I can how wrong I was."

Henry said more than he had expected. He began to grow cold, distant, as he retreated into other memories. I asked the only question I could think of:

"Did you like London?"

"No," he said. "I hated it. I was at a dinner one evening when someone asked me what I thought about taking back the colonies. I knew who he was—the minister of something or other—but I couldn't help myself. I said only little people on a little island would talk like that. He pretended to laugh. He said, 'Only an American would use the word "little" twice as an adjective in the same sentence.' I said, 'You're right. How about "Only tiny, ignorant people on a miserable little island would talk like that"?' I thought he was going to hit me. But you know what he said? 'This is the best dinner conversation I've ever had with an American.' We spent the rest of the night insulting each other. I was told the next day to stay clear of any official events. Six months later, I was reassigned to a consulate office in Canada. That's when I decided to quit."

When dinner was over and Isaac was in the kitchen, clearing the plates, Henry leaned over his side of the table and motioned for me to do the same. "Thank you for coming to dinner tonight," he said. "Isaac is lucky to have met you. I was worried about what would happen to him here. He's adjusted well. I think, wherever he goes next, he'll be fine."

"And where is he going?" I asked him.

He turned to see if Isaac was looking at us.

"I helped get him here," he said. "What he does next is up to him. After what he's gone through, I doubt he'll ever go back. I'm not even sure where 'back' would be for him. You probably know more than I do."

I tried to play along. I didn't know more, but I was afraid Henry would think less of me if I said that, so I smiled and leaned back in my chair as if I were trying to keep a secret close to my chest.

By the time Isaac returned to the table, I felt slightly light-headed. All the holes that I had allowed to exist between us were finally catching up with me. Isaac offered us coffee and dessert; I tapped the floor hard with both feet just to feel something solid beneath me, while Henry graciously declined both.

"I have a long drive back," he said. "I'm glad we had a chance to do this."

He came to where I was sitting and put his hands on my shoulders, as if he knew the last thing I wanted was to stand up.

"If you're ever in St. Louis, Helen, look me up." I promised I would. At the time, I thought I would do so first thing in the morning.

Isaac insisted on cleaning up. He said I looked tired and should go to bed, but I wanted to watch him when he thought I wasn't looking. I could read my mother's mood by the way she did the dishes. When she was sad, she spent minutes washing and drying each plate before setting it on the rack; that was how Isaac washed the plates that evening.

Later that night, in bed, my hands and then my entire body began to shake; Isaac wrapped his arm around me.

"What's wrong?" he asked me.

"I'm freezing," I said.

All evening the apartment had been uncomfortably warm, despite having the windows open in every room. As soon as I said I was freezing, I felt a genuine chill run through my spine, one strong enough to raise the hair on my arms. Isaac tried to comfort me, pressing in close to share his warmth, but the chill was still there. I closed my eyes and told myself to think of hot—not the feeling but the word, in big bold red letters as bright as a warning sign. Just like that, the goose bumps vanished, and I could feel again the humid, almost tropical air of the apartment. Isaac left the bedroom to get another blanket. When he came back, he asked me if there was anything else he could do.

"Yes," I told him. "Promise me you won't just disappear one day," and then, after I felt certain I knew what I really wanted to say, I added, "We've gone on like this long enough. You owe me more."

ISAAC

The next morning, there was an explosion near the center of the capital, followed, that afternoon and evening, by sporadic gunfire in four different neighborhoods. Those attacks had nothing to do with Joseph or his men. I knew because I watched the trail of smoke rising from the center of the capital with him and Isaac from a window on the third floor. Isaac asked Joseph if he knew who was responsible for the blasts and the shooting that followed. Joseph said he didn't know and didn't want to find out. "They have nothing to do with us," he said. "They are amateurs."

That evening, on the radio, we learned that the amateurs had punched a hole in the post office. They thought it was an important building because of the flag flying outside. Nothing was reported about the shootings.

"They died for nothing," Isaac said. Joseph disagreed.

"Everything is important," he said. "It makes the government look weak. It inspires others to follow."

Joseph wasn't looking in my direction when he said that, but I felt his words were aimed at me. Was I inspired? I didn't know yet, but I knew I wanted to be. I was the first one in bed that evening, and the first one awake the next morning. I could honestly claim ignorance of what might have happened during the hours in between.

Not knowing if Isaac had left the room in the middle of the night made the morning easier. Of the half-dozen books I had owned, Isaac had managed to rescue only one from my room. The loss was negligible. I knew the lost books almost by heart, and the same was true for the one with me. I took my copy of *Great Expectations* into the courtyard and sat near the tree. I didn't read the book so much as I recited it; I could have gone minutes without looking down at the page and not lost a word, just as I knew my father and uncles must have done with the stories they told me and their own children. The stories were lifeless until they made something out of them, and that was what I did that morning. London was now Kampala; Pip, a poor African orphan wandering the streets of the capital.

The silence that morning lasted until the sun was up and I could smell the onions the maid was cooking in the kitchen. I was just beginning to think of what moves I could make that day to convince Joseph I belonged here when I heard clapping and cheering suddenly erupt from the top floor of the house. The noise alarmed me, perhaps because it had been weeks since I'd heard anything like it, and I worried what it meant until Isaac's head burst through a window (the room we shared didn't look onto the courtyard).

"Come to the living room now," he said. "You have to listen to the radio."

We met at the bottom of the stairs. Isaac was wearing a dark-purple shirt I had never seen before. He placed the radio on the table in the living room and turned it up loud enough so that everyone in the house, from the maids in the kitchen to the guards at the gate and on the roof, could hear. The president's morning address was playing on a loop with nothing else allowed to interfere. His voice, as he spoke of the threats to the nation, the attacks on the state, and the emergency measures, from curfews to shoot-on-site orders, was certainly calm. I remember he said that we were all children of the revolution that had liberated Africa and that, as our president, he was determined that we remain free.

By the time Isaac brought the radio down, he had heard the speech several times. He had his favorite moments already: the sunset-to-sunrise curfew, the declaration of a state of emergency. After each one, he punched the table.

"The only real difference now," he said, "is that it is official. Now they do not have to pretend to have a reason to shoot you."

I didn't understand his enthusiasm, but I didn't fear it, either. I laughed when he did and smiled when I thought I should. I grew confident as I watched him. My feelings about what was happening didn't change; I had none that I was comfortable with, so as soon as possible I adopted Isaac's as my own.

"They are scared," I said.

I felt better saying that.

"More like terrified," Isaac responded.

"They're finished."

"It'll be over very soon now," he said.

After a brief silence, the president's address began again. I wanted to listen to it once more, to see if it was the exact same recording, or if perhaps there weren't multiple versions of the same words, inflected differently, the better to match the various moods of all those listening: a recording to instill fear, and one to bring comfort; one for the morning, and others for the afternoon and evening, with perhaps a softer, slower version that could be played throughout the night.

We listened to it a second time. Halfway through, I was convinced that Isaac and I had been wrong to speak so boldly about the government's demise—it was we who were finished. But then there was a slight pause in the speech that I hadn't heard the first two times—a second, or maybe only a fraction of a second, but long enough to create the image of a man sitting alone in a room rereading the same words out loud—and just like that, I returned to thinking it would be over soon. The government would fall, and we, or someone like us, would rise.

Joseph came downstairs just as it was ending. I was grateful to see him; I didn't want to listen any longer. Left on my own, I could find too many ways of reading what was happening. With Joseph present, there was only one.

He picked the radio up from the table and turned it off. It was the same shade of gray as the suit he was wearing. I wondered if that was a coincidence, or if Isaac had chosen Joseph's suit for him.

"This is an important day for us," Joseph said. "We have to act quickly now."

He held his hand out to me; I bowed my head before shaking it. I was part of the "we" now.

"How are you with maps?" he asked me.

Isaac put his arm over my shoulder. "He's a genius," he said. "He can do anything."

· · ·

Joseph had multiple offices throughout the house, and each one served a different purpose. He spoke to his guards in one room; he worked quietly alone in another. He left us for one on the ground floor, with instructions to wait in the living room or in the courtyard. We opted for the courtyard; we wanted to see who was going to come to the house that day. Isaac predicted more dignitaries—ministers, businessmen.

"He has many powerful friends who will support him now," he said.

We stood under our tree and waited for the procession to begin again; a half-hour later, we sat down. Noon came and went, and still not a single car had come to the house. The guards paced around the door and the roof; the maids hung sheets to dry behind the house. One and then two hours passed. It was too hot to sit outside, but Isaac insisted we stay where we were. "Something will happen," he said, and he was right. Minutes later, one of the guards who rarely left Joseph's side approached us. We both stood up as soon as we saw him. We couldn't see most of his face because of the large sunglasses he always wore, even inside the house, but I suspected that seeing us stand at attention, not out of respect but fear, pleased him.

He spoke to Isaac; when he finished, he handed him an envelope and made his way straight back to the house. I knew the envelope was for me by the way Isaac held it. He was hesitant to hand it over, but I wanted him to know that what happened to me next was no longer up to him to decide.

"It's fine," I told him.

He gave me the envelope.

"Joseph wants you to learn it," he said.

The "it" was an intricately hand-drawn map of a section of the capital I had never been in before. The dozens of narrow winding paths suggested a slum similar to the one Isaac and I had lived in, but several times larger.

"And then what?"

"I don't know," he said. "But you don't have long. It'll be dark in a few hours."

I was given a room on the second floor to study in. It was empty except for a thin, narrow mattress pressed underneath the window. I looked outside; there was an obstructed view onto the one road that led to the house. I knelt down on the mattress and, with my finger for a gun, pretended to take aim at the invaders coming for us.

It took what was left of the afternoon for me to memorize the map. There were thirty-four different paths, and a dozen smaller offshoots that abruptly ended. I memorized them by imagining myself walking along each one, and when I had walked them all once, I returned to them a second, and then a third time. But now I wasn't just walking the streets; I was living among them. I invented a second life for those roads. There was a street where my girlfriend lived, another that I walked down every Friday afternoon on my way home from work. I had family members—brothers, aunts, grandparents—that I visited regularly, scattered throughout the neighborhood. By the time Isaac came to tell me Joseph was waiting downstairs, I could close my eyes and see not only the map but the faces and the interiors of the lives and homes that I had made up.

Joseph's explanation of what he wanted me to do was kept to as few words as possible. I preferred it that way. He asked if I had memorized the map. I told him I knew it by heart. He took the map from me and said he hoped that was true. "You can't look lost," he said. "You have to look like you belong." I assured him that I wouldn't look lost, that I knew those streets as well as anyone who lived there. He told me he needed me to make a delivery. "We have things here in this house," he said, "that need to be moved." A car would be coming soon to bring me to the outskirts of the neighborhood. After that, I would have to go on foot, disguised as a fruit vendor. A wheelbarrow had been prepared. All I had to do was bring it to a particular house before sunset and the curfew went into effect. I would have to wait until the next morning to return.

When he finished, he asked if I was certain I wanted to do this. "It is your decision," he said.

I was confident I had nothing to lose. I was tired of being aimless.

"I'm positive," I told him.

The car arrived exactly when Joseph said it would: "It'll be here in ten minutes," he told me, and ten minutes later, a heavily dented and mud-stained white pickup truck was pulling into the courtyard. There wasn't much time left before sunset, and so we moved quickly. Joseph spoke to the driver; the wheelbarrow and its contents were loaded into the back, and I followed behind them. We were ready to leave after a few minutes, and would have done so had Isaac not insisted on coming along. He came to the truck bed, where I was sitting, and had begun to climb in when Joseph shouted at him to stop. Isaac stood on the bumper longer than I expected, and it's possible he might have even joined me had one of the guards not pulled him off. As soon as he was down, the car reversed quickly out the gates and onto the road, and the last image I had of Isaac was of him standing with his head bent in front of Joseph.

· · ·

The first five minutes were a difficult ride. I was almost thrown from the bed of the truck twice as we jostled our way along narrow back roads until we were far enough from the house to turn safely onto one of the main avenues. Traffic was light at that hour; as we picked up speed, I relaxed my grip on the rails and inhaled the warm air. We stopped at the traffic circle on Independence Boulevard just long enough for me to jump out and unload the wheelbarrow. There was less than a half-hour before the curfew went into effect, and the sidewalks and streets were crowded with people either rushing home or standing idle on the corners before being forced indoors. I slipped into that mass undetected. It was better than I expected. I knew exactly where I was, almost as if I were home.

I wound my wheelbarrow through the dirty, rutted narrow paths where my imaginary friends and cousins lived. The neighborhood was exactly how I had pictured it—all brown and gray, with every function of life, from the shit in the latrines to the sleep, sex, and fights of the bedroom, squeezed together. Loud voices and strong smells rose from every corner. When I came upon the house marked on the map—a single-story concrete home, identical to the ones next to it except for a faded Bob Marley poster in the window—I felt disappointed that I didn't have an excuse to keep walking longer.

As soon as I stopped in front of the house, the door opened. Several pairs of hands reached through and grabbed me by the neck and arms. I knew better than to shout, but I still tried to fight my way free. I swung my arms and legs; a powerful forearm wrapped itself around my neck and squeezed; another took hold of my legs and lifted me off the ground. I looked for the wheelbarrow, but it was already gone. That was how I knew I was in the right house.

I was carried into a room in the back. There were bunk beds lined against the wall, and a cot in the middle, but I was dropped on the floor. I was knocked unconscious. When I came to, I saw that I wasn't alone in the room. There were seven other boys in there, all of whom looked to be teenagers. Four were sitting on the bottom beds, while the other three sat in the corner and smoked. There was no window and only one dim light in the corner, so the room was rich with smoke thick enough almost to mask the other odors. One boy pointed to a cut above my brow, which had begun to bleed. He said something in a language I had never heard, and when I responded in English that I didn't understand, everyone laughed. I stood up. I turned to the door; poor homes rarely had locks, and my plan was to run as quickly as possible out into the street and find a place to hide. I never made it to the handle. All seven boys pulled at me, and when I was down, two stood in front of the door. They were as kind as they could be about it. They shook their heads and said no many times over, as if they were scolding a young child or a pet that didn't know its boundaries. I wasn't allowed to stand up again. I was given a bottom bunk in the corner. The walls were thin—on the other side, I could hear older voices shouting. I wanted to believe only the best outcomes were possible. I tried not to think of dying, but that, of course, was the easiest way of ensuring that it was all I could think about. There were occasional pauses in the shouting, signs that a conclusion was near. I closed my eyes and prayed that the door wouldn't open until dawn. When it did, ten minutes or maybe an hour later, my eyes were still closed, but I knew it was Isaac's voice telling me to stand. "We need to leave quickly," he said.

I followed the back of his head out of the house. I didn't look at the boys gathered around me or at any of the men in the other room. We slid quietly out the front door, and I heard a lock click behind us.

"Now it's your turn to get us out of here," he said. My map returned. I saw the exit I had charted earlier in my head and did my best to follow it, but nearly all the homes and stores had gone dark. Occasionally, a candle in a window gave off enough light so I could see the curve ahead, but by and large I was walking blindly. We were the only people on the road; the curfew had been in effect for hours. We turned left in what I hoped was the right direction. We made it a few hundred yards before we heard boots marching toward us, and then a familiar voice coming from a radio. We paused just long enough to hear the president's speech from that morning growing louder as it approached us.

Isaac took hold of my sleeve and pulled me toward a small blue house a few feet ahead of us that had its front door slightly ajar. He guided me inside and closed the door hard behind him. Sitting on the floor of the house a few feet from us were an elderly man and a young woman, huddled around a single bowl and a candle they had deliberately kept as far away from the center of the room as possible.

For all their obvious terror, neither said a word after we entered. They stared at me, at Isaac, and then at the floor rather than at each other, as if they had long since come to terms with the fact that on any given evening men could burst into their house and do something terrible to them. There's no honest measure for the toll that sort of knowledge takes, whether the scale is the breadth of a single room or an entire city.

Isaac did his best to comfort them. He crouched in front of the old man and, in the same tender voice I had heard him use with the beggar outside of the hospital, said, "Papa. Don't worry." He spoke to him for several more minutes in Kiswahili, the old man occasionally clicking his tongue in passive approval; eventually, Isaac stood up and told me, "We're going to stay here for the night."

"We can't leave before then?"

Isaac shook his head. He looked down at the young woman, who, I saw now, was practically just a child. She stood up slowly. It was only when she put one hand under her stomach that I realized she was pregnant.

"If we're all still here in the morning," Isaac said, "we will be lucky."

The girl disappeared into a room in the back. Isaac said congratulations to the old man, who for the first time smiled. He held out his right hand and for each finger uttered a few words before turning up and offering a prayer to his God.

"This is his fifth child," Isaac said. "Two are dead, and two he hasn't heard from in years. This one, he says, he hopes God will let him keep."

The man stood with what seemed to be his last remnant of strength. I had seen him poorly as well, thinking he was simply older when it turned out he was almost elderly. The years were evident in his feet—in the nearly nailless, bald toes and the shriveled skin that encased them. He made his way to the back room to join his child-wife. I had an image of the two of them lying together side by side on a mattress on the floor, an image that didn't inspire anger, as I would have thought, so much as pity for them, and, by extension, for us as well.

Isaac and I were standing in the middle of the room, which was bare except for a pair of wooden stools, a lone prayer mat in the corner, and a long hard wooden bench against the back wall, when we heard the first shot, followed by rounds of automatic fire. I was the only who looked around for a place to hide. Isaac didn't so much as twitch.

"Take a seat," he said. "We have a long night ahead of us."

HELEN

Isaac promised he would do his best to tell me what I wanted to know.

"I promise I won't leave abruptly," he said, but I never sincerely believed he would keep that promise, and so it meant little to hear him say it.

"I know that already," I lied, "but that's not what I want to hear."

He reached out to put his hand on my shoulder but I moved farther away before he could touch me. The last thing I wanted was to be comforted. I got out of the bed. I saw my clothes lying on the floor and tried to think of something he could say that would make me leave.

"Henry said I would know better than he did where you would go next, but that isn't true. I don't know any more than he does. What was the point of having this dinner?"

"I wanted you to meet. So did Henry."

"That's because he knows nothing about you. He doesn't even know where you're from. How is that possible?"

"He never wanted to know more."

"I don't believe you."

"When he met me at the airport, the first thing Henry asked me was 'Who are you?' He had a picture of my friend Isaac in his wallet—the same Isaac who died the night you came to my house. I told him the truth right then: The Isaac he was expecting was in a village in northern Uganda. He gave me his passport and visa so I could come here, because he never wanted to. I told him I became Isaac as soon as I stepped on the plane."

"And who were you before that?"

"That's what Henry didn't want to know. He said the less he knew about me the better, in case something happened."

"I'm not Henry."

"I know."

"Then why do you treat me like I am?"

He gathered the sheets around him. I wondered if I had actually hurt him, or if he was simply pretending to be wounded.

"I spent two days with Henry before I came here. We drove from the airport in Chicago to his house in St. Louis, where he said he would figure out what to do with me next. He had doubts about the story I had told him, and he said he would have me arrested and deported if he found out I was lying. I understood why he would say that. He had spent enough time in Africa to know there was no limit to what someone would do to leave. People risked their lives every day to get out. It was nothing to kill or steal from someone for the same reason.

"He made phone calls to find his friend Joseph. It was Joseph who had asked Henry to bring Isaac here. He thought if he could get him to America Isaac would be safe until the war was over. Early the first morning, someone from the British Embassy in Kampala called to say that Joseph was most likely dead, and that he and his army were rumored to be responsible for several massacres in the north of the country. I was sleeping on the couch when Henry received the call. He slammed the phone on the table. I thought he was pretending to be angry. He asked me what I knew about Joseph. I told him the truth. I said Joseph was dead.

"He sat down in a chair across from me. 'When will you people learn?' he said. 'Do you enjoy killing each other?'

"I admit I had had the same thought before. I saw many people killed, as if it were nothing. I thought at times that our lives were worthless, but, hearing Henry, I knew that we were both wrong. No one needs to learn how to kill, but it took the foreigners who came to Africa to show us that it meant nothing to do so. Henry's friend Joseph had many people killed before he died. I think now he had only done what the British had taught him.

"I said something similar to Henry: 'What do you think your friend Joseph learned to do in England, while he was with men like you?'

"He was surprised I had answered his question. I was afraid I had offended him, but then Henry smiled and said, 'You know what? You're probably right.'

"There was another phone call from the British Embassy, later that afternoon. The Isaac that Henry was looking for was a colonel or captain in the same army that Joseph had once led. They were hoping to surrender, but not to the government—they wanted to surrender to the British. Isaac was one of three who signed the letter asking for their help. That was all Henry would tell me.

"After he hung up the phone, we sat silent for a long time. I thought of my friend, who was alive but was unlikely to live much longer, while Henry debated what to do with me next.

"After almost an hour had passed, Henry said, 'I don't want to know anything else about you before you came here. As far as I'm concerned, you were born this morning, and your name is Isaac. That's the most I can do for you.'

"We began to like each other immediately after that. I was no longer a problem to be solved. He had no one to save or feel guilty toward, He asked me what I did in my spare time. I had never heard that expression. 'What do you do for fun?' he said.

"I told him I read Dickens. He loved that. He said he thought my accent sounded vaguely British. 'Dickens was the only good thing to have come out of England in a hundred years,' he said. Later that evening, he gave me advice about how to live in America. He told me not to stare at white people, to say 'sir' if I was stopped by the police, and to live as quietly as possible.

" 'This is a hard part of the country to have come to,' he said. 'You might wish you hadn't.'

" 'I will be fine,' I told him. 'I will live as if I am not really here.'

"When you and I became close, I still believed that was true. I thought the less I said the better."

"For you or for me?"

"For both of us."

"David said you must have done something terrible in your previous life to tell me so little about yourself. I never told him that I had doubts about your name. He would have begged me never to see you again if I had, which is probably why I never told him. I don't understand how you can live like this. My whole life is here, and if I left I'd probably always think of myself as Helen from Laurel."

"I understand. I had the same once, and I did my best to escape it. When I was born, I had thirteen names. Each name was from a different generation, beginning with my father and going back from him. I was the first one in our village to have thirteen names. Our family was considered blessed to have such a history. Everyone in our family had been born and died on that land. We fed it with our bodies longer than any other, and it was assumed I would do the same, and so would my children. I knew from a very young age, though, that I would never want that. I felt as if I had been born into a prison. We had one horse and a mule, which my father and I used to ride through the fields. It was beautiful land that had not changed in hundreds of years. We used oxen to plow it, and I knew if I stayed there my life would be no different from theirs. I begged my father to send me away to school, but he said my mother would never forgive him if he did, so I made my own plans to leave. I must have been thirteen or fourteen at the time. I never had many friends, and I had even fewer as I grew older. I was secretly preparing for my departure. I gave myself different names, which I copied into a notebook that I later burned. I practiced my English on the back of a mule and read what few books we had dozens, maybe hundreds of times.

"I stayed years longer than I had hoped to. There was a drought; we became even poorer. I began to believe the best part of my life had been spent dreaming. We heard rumors of soldiers revolting in the south of the country, but it meant nothing where we lived. Then men who weren't soldiers, who were the same age as me but had gone to university, began to visit our village. They held meetings that no one attended. Eventually, they came to our house and asked us if we thought it was fair that we should be so poor while the rulers of the country lived like kings in Addis Ababa. They promised us a socialist revolution, and asked me to come with them. The next day, my father said it was time for me to leave.

" 'I don't want you to stay here,' he said. 'If your brothers were older, I would send them with you.'

"He believed something terrible was going to happen to the country soon, and I suspect he is right. It hasn't happened yet, but I doubt it will be much longer now.

"When I left, he held me for a very long time. He used to call me Bird when I was a child. He said I lived high in the sky, far above everyone else.

" 'You'll come back,' he said.

" 'Of course,' I told him.

"I thought he was going to tell me to write. Instead, he kissed me four times, twice on each cheek.

" 'No, my little bird,' he said. 'I know you won't.'

"I went to Addis Ababa, and then took buses to Kenya and Uganda. I was no one when I arrived in Kampala; it was exactly what I wanted."

ISAAC

That was the first night of Joseph's war. The small arms hidden in the wheelbarrow ended up in the hands of the seven boys I had been confined with. Shortly after Isaac and I left the house, they began to kill the soldiers patrolling the neighborhood, one at a time. Those boys had the advantage at the beginning: It was their home. They knew where to hide and where to shoot from.

The soldiers fired back recklessly, blindly, in multiple directions at once. For every one that was hit, hundreds of shots were fired in return, not just down the streets but through windows, doors, and walls, regardless of who might be on the other side of them. Most of the dead died during that first hour, but Isaac and I weren't concerned with them. We listened to the fighting from a corner of the living room least likely to catch a stray bullet. Once there was a lull, we turned on each other.

I began with what I thought was the most pressing question: "How long were you at the house?"

"Twenty minutes," he said, "maybe less."

"And what would have happened if you hadn't come?"

"How can I know that?" he said. "I did come."

"Why?"

"Why did I come?"

"Yes."

"I was worried."

"Did Joseph tell you to?"

"He was concerned as well."

"That's not what I asked you."

"What do you want me to say? I'm here."

We ended on a loop. I had my doubts, every one of which Isaac could reject simply by pointing out that he was there, and I was alive, and both of us were in danger. He was carrying a gun of his own now—a black pistol with a snub nose, clipped to his belt. When we finished arguing, we had the fighting to return to. The silence had gone on too long; Isaac was growing restless.

"They can't all be dead already," he said.

A few seconds later, we heard a single shot. We were both relieved, although for different reasons. I thought I saw Isaac whisper, "Thank God," but it could have also been "My God," or "Oh God." Regardless, the heavy firing that followed was a good thing.

Isaac taught me how to read the fighting. The automatic weapons belonged to the government; the rifles were ours. "Our boys are more careful," he said. They were roaming the streets and roofs alone, or in pairs. They waited until they had an easy shot and then fired once, twice at most, before running off to another spot.

"Aren't they too young?" I asked him.

He laughed.

"They were in uniform until this morning," he said.

We knew when the first boy was killed because the soldiers started shouting. They cheered and fired into the air, and most likely again at the body. They did the same when the second died, a few minutes later, although this time a low, steady chant followed. The third wasn't killed until an hour later—a small miracle, given that soldiers from all across the capital had poured into the neighborhood and were occupying almost every corner. We saw the vague outlines of their forms running past the house. That was when Isaac took his pistol out and placed it on the floor next to him. The fighting needed to start again. As long as those four boys were hiding, everyone in the slum was vulnerable. We heard screams and shots from far away. These quickly became regular. Isaac whispered into my ear, "They're going door to door now."

I wanted to ask him if that was part of the plan, but I knew he would have said yes. The plan was to make war; anything that followed was part of it.

Had the remaining boys not found a house from which to stage a final attack, we would never have made it through the night. Doors were breaking all across the neighborhood, and it was only a matter of time before the soldiers made it to ours. The retreat, as it turned out, was deliberate: draw a large force into a narrow space, and then inflict as much damage as possible.

The boys from Joseph's army made their final stand within shouting distance of where we were hiding. They fired all at once, and continued to do so for as long as they could—dozens of shots in only a few seconds, and not a single one wasted. The barrage that followed must have leveled the house, and most likely the ones next to it. All the soldiers in the area converged on that spot and fired their weapons, if only to claim they had been a part of the battle. By the time they finished, there was enough light in the sky to make the road clearly visible.

"It's finished. We should leave now," Isaac said. I didn't agree or disagree. I was grateful to be alive; I was happy to follow orders.

We didn't see the old man or his wife before we left, although Isaac did leave a small offering of money for them on the floor. I expected the streets to be empty, but within minutes of leaving the house we came across groups of older women and packs of young boys, scouring the neighborhood for anything that had been abandoned or that could be honestly carried off, from shell casings to large pieces of broken glass. The first bullet-riddled body we saw was of a middle-aged man whose shoes had already been lifted from him. Other bodies were being carried off in wheelbarrows by sisters and wives so they could be put properly to rest.

We took the most obscure roads back to Joseph's house, steering wide of the city center and the hundreds of soldiers called up to protect it. We headed north for as long as we could before cutting west, straight through the old neighborhood where Isaac and I had once lived. Neither of us said anything to acknowledge this.

It was late in the afternoon by the time we finally neared Joseph's house.

"Eight hours," Isaac said. "You couldn't have found a shorter route."

"Not without another map," I told him.

We had nothing left. It hurt to speak—there was dust covering not only our bodies but our throats as well. Isaac pointed toward the house and tried to say something but decided it wasn't worth the extra effort to do so. Half a block before we reached the front gate, two armed men emerged from a car parked a few feet in front of us. They were Joseph's men, and Isaac raised his hand to wave to them. They stopped in front of their car and aimed their guns in our general direction as they yelled something; I couldn't understand the words, but it was clearly a warning not to come any closer. Isaac shouted back, and they shouted the same thing louder in return, this time making sure to refocus their aim squarely on our chests. Isaac held out his hand so I would know to stop walking. A volley of curses and threats that I was afraid was going to last until we were finally shot was lobbed back and forth between them. I begged Isaac to leave, but he refused to acknowledge me. He threw both his arms into the air to show he wasn't hiding anything; when that failed, he stripped off his shirt, and then his shoes and pants, until he had only his socks and underwear left. He was daring them to shoot him. And why shouldn't they? Many others had already died because of us that morning, and here we were, unscathed. How else to deal with that?

Joseph finally emerged, surrounded by a half-dozen armed men. I could barely see him through all the bodies and barrels. I expected him, after all we had gone through for him, to make a dramatic show of welcoming us back, especially Isaac. Instead, he stood outside the gate and motioned with his head for the guards to let us in.

As we passed the first two guards who had stopped us, Isaac spat at their feet and told them in English that they were lower than dogs. Once we walked through the gates, we saw there was practically nothing left of the house we had known. All the furniture was gone, except for a single couch in the living room; the spirit and mood of the house had been lifted as well. The courtyard was filled with men. There were dozens scattered under the tree, in the driveway, and around the open front door, most of them in uniforms with the Tanzanian flag on their shoulders.

"We've been invaded," Isaac said, "by our friends from Tanzania."

"They came last night?" I asked him.

But I knew the answer. Of course they did. Those seven boys were the distraction that got them here.

Joseph yelled out for Isaac from the living room. Once I heard his voice, I knew I was right to have been afraid of him. His guards still surrounded him, even as he lay semi-reclined on a couch in an otherwise empty room.

"I thought you two were dead," he said.

"No, not yet," Isaac said.

Joseph turned his attention to me.

"You are very lucky," he said. "You didn't have any problems?"

"None," I told him.

I felt almost equal to him as long as I knew we were both lying.

"We have to leave this evening," he said. He pointed to me. "That includes you as well."

I nodded my head, but only because I didn't know what else to do.

Joseph spent the rest of the afternoon sequestered in the living room; Isaac and I retreated to our familiar spot in the courtyard.

"Do you know where we're going?" I asked him.

"To his father's village," he said. "He wants to liberate that first and then work his way back to the capital. They're waiting for him already."

"There's too many of us."

Isaac shook his head. "Most of them are going to stay," he said. "They're not from here. They would look like a foreign army if they went into a village. Here in the capital, they can hide until we're ready to come back. When it's over, Joseph will give them more money and guns, and they'll go back into the bush."

"I could stay with them," I said.

Isaac laughed. "And what would you do?" he said. "There's already a cook."

He didn't say that to hurt me, or maybe he did. It was impossible to know for certain anymore.

We sat under our tree. Isaac leaned back and stretched out his legs. All he was missing was the uniform and sunglasses. After a few minutes of silence, I spoke.

"Joseph tells you everything."

He didn't respond.

"No one finds that odd."

He turned his back to me. He was offering me a chance to stop. I saw that and refused.

"You haven't known him that long. You've never been in any army. You're a poor kid from a little village. You have nothing he needs, and yet he treats you like—"

I wanted Isaac to see me. I wanted him to feel threatened and afraid as I had, and still did. Knowing where he went at night was my only weapon. Before I knew what I was going to say next, he broke my nose with his elbow. He spent several minutes after that drumming the right side of my face with his fist. I felt the pain; I didn't mind it, however. I didn't cry or ask him to stop. I could hear the men in the courtyard cheering him on, and I felt closer to them than I did to my own body. When Isaac stood up, he had his black snub-nosed pistol in his hand. He walked away without pointing it at me, but I knew he had thought of using it. Another man came over and kicked me playfully in the back and in the ribs. I didn't mind that, either. For once, I thought, someone was speaking to me honestly.

I tried to sit up but failed. My right arm collapsed under me. I looked up and saw Joseph's blurred form in the doorway, speaking calmly to Isaac. When they finished, Joseph made his way to me. It was hard for me to see if he had anything in his hands.

He squatted next to me so I could hear him.

"Isaac wants to know if you're okay."

"I'm fine," I told him.

"Good," he said. "Go clean yourself up. We're leaving in a few hours. What you do after that is up to you."

Joseph's last act of compassion toward me was to have one of his bodyguards bring me a wet towel to wash my face, and to have two others lay me down in a corner of the house, where I passed out, as much from the beating as from exhaustion, thirst, and hunger. I didn't fully come to until it was time for us to leave. I was helped into the back corner of a large open-air convoy truck. At least a dozen soldiers filed in after me; I had just enough room to curl into a ball. I drifted in and out of sleep until we were miles away from the capital, on the way to what would be Joseph's first liberated village.

HELEN

I came back to bed just as Isaac was telling me about the last time he saw his father. I wasn't sure if the distance between us hadn't grown larger the more he told me, and I hoped I could find the opposite was true if I lay next to him. When he told me how he'd felt once he arrived in Kampala, all I could think of was how small my life must have looked in comparison. My relationship with him was the greatest trip I had taken so far, and all it had required was that I spend my nights in another part of town, with a man whom no one would have approved of.

Just as I had wanted him to talk, I needed him to stop. I didn't know it earlier, but this was what had governed our silence—not that we couldn't understand each other but that we could lay ourselves bare and in the end each find a stranger sitting on the other side.

I asked him bluntly not to tell me more.

"I think you've told me all I can handle for one night," I said. "Maybe it's best if we go to sleep now."

"I'm sorry if I upset you," he said. "That was what I was afraid of."

"You haven't upset me. I just have a lot to think about."

We both slept poorly. It was hard to be in the same bed and feel incapable of reaching over, and so every time we drew close one of us pulled away, partly out of fear that the other would do so.

I woke up before sunrise. I picked up my clothes and dressed in the bathroom, and before leaving whispered in Isaac's ear that I had a lot of work to get to. Only when I was in my car did I remember it was Saturday; even though I had a key to the office, I knew I didn't want to be there alone. I drove to Bill's diner, which was the only place open so early on a weekend morning. From across the street, I sat and watched two older men who owned farms just outside of the town center. Many of the best memories I had of my father took place in there, which was the only reason why I returned so often. I knew it was unlikely that I would ever go back now, but this was marginally related to how they had treated Isaac. I would never return because I knew I would be remembered for having brought that man there with me. If Isaac stayed longer, or if we stopped being so private, I wondered what else would die because of him. There was only so much space in a town the size of Laurel; it wouldn't take long to ruin it.

Once the sun was fully up, I drove to David's house. I had been there many times before but never unannounced, even though he insisted that all of us in the office were welcome to drop by anytime, especially if we had something work-related that we needed to talk about. Other than myself, I doubted anyone in our town ever visited David.

He was on his porch, picking up that morning's paper, when I arrived. I took it as a sign that I had done the right thing, since the odds were that I would have lost the courage to ring his door-bell. He saw my car approaching; before I parked, he was using his newspaper to wave for me to come in.

"I won't ask what brought you here," he said. "You can tell me as little or as much as you want."

Everyone in the office had a similar line, which we used on new clients. It was David who had taught us its possible value. "It leaves the speakers in control of their story," he said, "and it shows them that our job is to listen, not to judge."

He led me into his kitchen; he poured us coffee.

"You look like you haven't slept," he said.

"I don't think I did. I woke up very early."

"Can I ask what happened?"

"Nothing happened. We had dinner. We talked."

"Let me rephrase that. If I asked you what happened, would you tell me?"

"I would."

"Denise asked me a few weeks ago why you spent so much time with one of your clients. She wouldn't say who, but of course I knew what she meant. We're not that different. She says 'that client.' I ask you, 'How's your friend Dickens?' You say 'we' as much as possible."

"You would rather we call him Isaac."

"No. I would rather we stopped pretending. I cringe every time I hear you say you're going to go visit a friend, or that you don't have any plans for the weekend."

"And what difference would it make if I said I was going to see Isaac?"

"I don't know. Maybe none. I heard you took him to lunch at Bill's. Denise and Sharon talked about it every minute you weren't in the office. I think the consensus was that your heart was in the right place; you just didn't understand what you were doing. That's the kindness you get when people have known you since you were born. I was very proud of you when I heard that story."

"And now?"

"And now I think of you sleeping in your car. I think you're fucked if you can't say more, even if it's only to me."

"You never gave me a straight answer about why you followed me when you thought I was going to see Isaac."

"I told you to use your imagination."

"I've asked you to do the same."

"What do you think would have happened if Denise knew you were having a relationship with Isaac?"

"I don't know."

"That's not true. Of course you do. Denise would whisper to Sharon, and Sharon would tell her husband and her sister. You would come to the office and find them whispering, and after a few days, you'd begin to think that it was about you. After a week, you would start to think that people all over town were looking at you strangely. You would notice them trying to look directly past you when you ran into them in the grocery store and on the street. When Christmas came, you would have only half as many cards in your mailbox, and at least once a year, junior-high boys would throw a half-dozen eggs at your window.

"If you think they wouldn't say anything, though, you're right. They wouldn't say a word. It would be rude and un-Christian to do so.

"I wanted to see you with Isaac for purely selfish reasons. Do you understand now?"

"I always did. I just wanted to hear you say it. I've wondered for the past year why you haven't left."

"I used to go to Mississippi in the summer with my father to visit his grandmother. They considered him a communist because he told them once not to use the word 'nigger' around his son. No one listened to him. My great-uncle took me to the black area of town the next day and said my father had some funny ideas in his head that he hoped to save me from.

"Most of the homes we drove past were nothing more than wooden shacks. I didn't know people were that poor in this country. 'Only niggers,' my great-uncle said, 'would live like that.'

"I asked my father why the black people didn't leave. He said maybe they didn't believe anything would change, or maybe they were waiting for the world to change around them and they wanted to be home when it did. It was the most eloquent thing he had ever said to me, and I knew he must have asked that same question himself and that was the best answer he could come up with. I would say both reasons are equally true.

"There's a spare bedroom upstairs. Why don't you get some sleep before you decide who to visit next?"

"And what if someone found out I had slept in the home of two different men in one day?"

"Will I see you at work on Monday?"

I didn't have a plan yet, but I felt certain that was unlikely.

"I don't know. But I hope not."

ISAAC

We drove west for several hours before cutting north onto a trail of dirt roads that wound their way through empty green hills and the nameless hamlets that sat at their feet. The sun had begun to set by then, and from the back of the truck I watched as the hills caught all the colors that came with that. It was a beautiful sight, even more so because I was the only one deliberately noticing it. I was in the war, but I no longer belonged to it. I stood and at times sat among a dozen other men who rarely looked at me, even as we were constantly thrown against one another with every rock and bump in the road. I took out the notebook Isaac had given me and tried to think of something to write, but then thought better of it when I saw I was being watched. I drew a crude picture of the hills instead, so I could remember them.

When our convoy stopped at the checkpoint leading into the village, the soldiers leapt out the back of the truck and took their positions around the sides. The ones in the truck in front of us did the same, leaving me alone to watch as the horizon turned a deep orange more striking than the purple and red shades that had preceded it. From that slightly elevated perch I could see the tips of all the thatch-roofed huts in the village—hundreds of them, lined up neatly on either side of the main road, and every one looked as if it were burning.

Joseph and those closest to him, including Isaac, were the last to leave their cars. They filed out of the two sedans, dressed in identical button-down olive-green uniforms. It was also an impressive sight, no less remarkable than the sunset ending right in front of us. The soldiers manning the checkpoint stepped forward and saluted Joseph. Another lifted the crude metal barrier blocking the road, and with that, the town had either been officially seized or liberated. It was an important moment for Joseph. He had made his move; his army was a real thing now. The same was true for Isaac. He had also become more. He had staked himself to Joseph, and now he stood a few feet behind him. Once everyone was out of the car, he whispered into Joseph's ear. I quietly applauded. I couldn't help it; I was proud of Isaac for having made something of himself.

Joseph led the parade through the center of town. The entire village stood along the sidelines, soldiers flanking the roadside in front of them. His power grew as he walked. It expanded outward to touch every ring surrounding him until it was returned in lesser form to the wildly cheering crowd of men and women singing and applauding his arrival. He walked slowly, turning his head from side to side so that everyone gathered along the road could claim to have seen him. At that pace, it took him nearly an hour to make his way to the town center. In the central square, a bronze fist rose from the ground; it had been erected on the first anniversary of the country's independence. There, in front of the fist, at the top of the four steps of the district headquarters, Joseph announced the start of the people's liberation.

· · ·

Joseph spent much of his speech listing the crimes and failed promises that had been committed since independence. There was vigorous cheering and constant applause, the lifeblood of a would-be demagogue. The most memorable parts of that speech came near the end, when he spoke of his father and the last time he saw him.

"He was a humble, simple man. He gave his life to defend and protect you," Joseph said, "and it is in his memory that I swear to do the same."

After he finished, the village's former leaders were brought handcuffed to the top of the steps, bruised but still able to walk on their own. Joseph pulled out a key and unlocked each of them himself.

"Our liberation begins with them," he said.

All those men were executed in their homes later that evening.

We took over the town's only hotel, a dilapidated two-story building with an open, terraced courtyard in the middle and a crudely made wooden sign in the front that read "Life Hotel" in faded, barely legible blue paint. Isaac slept on the top floor of the hotel with Joseph and his inner circle; I slept outside, on the ground, with the other soldiers. When Isaac came downstairs in the morning, he had a rifle slung over his shoulder.

Every evening for the next three days, a new garrison from a neighboring village arrived. They had either revolted, taking their senior officers captive, or simply switched sides: soldiers one day, rebels the next. Like Joseph and his colonels, all the troops that joined them had greater ties to the north. Isaac stood with Joseph and his colonels at the checkpoint to greet them. On the second day, Isaac led the parade to the town-hall steps; although he still left the speeches to Joseph, he was saluted and attended to with all the respect given to the senior officers in charge. I was free to spend my days wandering the village. I tried to make the most of my solitary strolls, imagining that what I noticed now I would write about later, in the shadows of the hotel courtyard, while the images were still vivid in my mind. I spoke to no one, but I watched how each day—and then, eventually, each hour— the villagers hid more of their belongings, anything the soldiers might consider to be valuable. On the first day, women slipped the silver bracelets off their wrists and necks if they saw any uniformed men ahead. Men stopped to tuck the bills in their pockets below their loose change. After three days of celebratory parades, the men who hadn't voluntarily joined Joseph's liberation army moved furtively through the streets, gathering their children around them. The only women I saw outside their homes were middle-aged or elderly. The soldiers had arrived with trucks full of weapons but nothing to eat, and after seventy-two hours they had devoured half of the town. On the third day, one man refused to hand over his last two chickens to a pair of soldiers who had arrived the night before. His chickens were slaughtered in front of him, and then his house was burned to the ground. I was in the hotel courtyard when Joseph heard the news. He ordered the two guilty boys brought to him; by the time they got there, each already had one arm broken. I doubt Joseph intended to punish them further—they were, like almost all the others, poor illiterate boys who by dint of a uniform and a week of training were called soldiers. Joseph was trying to decide their fate when Isaac shouted down from the balcony, "How can we be a people's army if the people are afraid of us?"

I looked up at him. I saw him briefly every day but so far had resisted getting too close. He slid past me a half-dozen times daily, and the only thing I had had time to notice was how rigid his posture and walk had become, how easily he seemed to slip into his new role.

Isaac came down to the courtyard, followed by the two young men who trailed him now everywhere he went.

"We have to set an example," he said, "or they will never trust us again. Which one of you set the fire?"

Those two poor boys looked only at each other. I thought neither of them was going to confess, and I prayed for their sake they wouldn't, but the taller and probably elder of the pair eventually stepped forward. Isaac pulled a pistol from his belt and shot the boy who had stepped forward once in the head, and then, a few seconds later, after he had time to look honestly at what he had done, the other. I knew then what all that violence had done to him. Life was trivial, and here he was trying to prove it.

He turned so I could see him holding the pistol near his face; it was the same one he had had when we were in the capital. At least twice he had weighed using it, once in the slum in case we were caught, and then at the house after he had beaten me. I felt grateful to him, while the right leg of the second boy he had shot twitched with the last spasm of life a few feet away from me.

Isaac ordered the bodies to be laid out on the main road—"so," he said, "the people know we are here to defend them."

I never imagined there was so much blood in the human head. I spent the rest of the afternoon watching it dry in the sun, reminding myself that I wasn't the one who had killed them.

That evening, Joseph held a party in the courtyard of the Life Hotel. He spent lavishly for the town in the hours before the party. He summoned everyone to the hotel who had given to the liberation and paid them in cash for what they had lost. He sat in the center of the hotel courtyard in what must have been the only plush chair in the village while a line of women and men stood waiting with their hands out. Once paid, everyone bowed. The man whose chickens had been killed and house burned was paid twice their value. By nightfall, half of the village was either in the courtyard or standing outside begging to be let in. Every half-hour, the crowd chanted, "Mabira, Mabira," just as they had when we first arrived. I expected to see Joseph playing to the crowd, but once the last person had been paid off, he spent the rest of the evening huddled in a corner with his bodyguards and colonels. It was only after they left the courtyard that Isaac came to talk to me. He had spent the past several hours standing near Joseph, drinking a clear bathroom-brewed liquor out of a glass jar. He was drunk, but not to the degree he wanted to be.

He squeezed my face with his free hand and examined my left and right eyes; both were still bruised but no longer swollen.

"You heal quickly," he said.

"I'm tougher than you think," I told him.

"That's probably true. I doubt I even hurt you."

"I hardly felt a thing," I said.

He had a pair of gold tassels hanging from his shoulders. I reached out to touch them.

"So you're a big man now."

"Yes. And so are half the men here. We were given promotions tonight. We've been saluting each other all evening. You want to be an officer?"

He pulled the pistol from his belt.

"You see that man over there with a mustache."

He pointed his gun in the direction of a heavyset military man with several rows of medals and buttons pinned to his chest.

"Shoot him," Isaac said, "and I'll make you a lieutenant."

As we stood there looking at him, four men led him away.

He was smiling and holding a beer in his hand when he stood up, but then he seemed to understand he wasn't coming back to join the party. I expected him to fight; he was clearly a powerful man, well built, with a large head buffered on both sides by bulldog-type jowls, but he had been in the military long enough to understand the futility and extra pain of doing so. He was led out of the hotel. That was just the beginning, however. Every ten minutes for the next hour, another man of rank was escorted out. After the sixth one, I asked Isaac if he could tell me what they had done.

He shrugged his shoulders. The alcohol had finally taken its toll.

"Then why take them?"

"They've been with the army too long. Certain people are convinced they can't be trusted."

After the seventh was taken away, he excused himself.

"I'm sorry. I have to go," he said.

He left the hotel with his two guards. He tried hard to walk straight but failed, which was fine—he didn't have far to go. Shortly after he left the courtyard, seven shots were fired. There was a brief silence across the hotel; it lasted for less than a minute after the last shot. Then the party really picked up. More beer and liquor were brought in. The soldiers drank and sang. Nine men had died; it finally felt like a real war had begun.

HELEN

I checked my watch when I reached Isaac's apartment; two hours had passed since I'd left. I didn't bother to knock or ring the doorbell. I let myself in. As soon as I entered, I noticed what a poor job he had done of cleaning the dining area the night before. My crumpled napkin, which had fallen onto my chair, was still there. There were bits of food on the edges of the table where Henry had sat, and a dark-orange spot on the white-tiled floor. I made a quick tour of the kitchen. The garbage can was nearly full with the scraps from last night's dinner, and inside the refrigerator, sitting alone on a plate in the center of the middle rack, was the rest of the chicken. One plate, two glasses, and a fork sat unwashed in the sink. I smiled; in my rush to leave that morning, I had missed them. It wasn't as large a mess as I had once hoped for, but it was close enough to count as proof of life—this time not just Isaac's, but ours together. I promised myself that before the end of the day I would call David and tell him I was wrong: "We're not fucked, at least not completely," I would say.

. . .

Isaac came out from the bedroom while I was making my study of the refrigerator. I heard his footsteps stop behind me, but chose to ignore him.

"You came back for the chicken," he said.

I laughed, but not too loudly. I straightened my face, closed the door, and pressed my back against it.

"It's Saturday," I said. I felt excited saying this. It was a beautiful morning, warm but not hot, the living room full of sunlight.

I had felt restless and scared since waking up, and now I had a vague idea of how to respond. "I think we should take a trip."

He folded his arms, leaned against the wall, crossed his legs, and even pursed his lips.

"I thought you had to work."

"I was wrong. I made a mistake."

I waited him for him to state what was obvious. I was lying. I had run out on him that morning in a way that had felt final to both of us, but he seemed willing to act as if none of that mattered anymore.

"Chicago. I've always wanted to go. It's the capital of the Midwest."

"I never got closer than the airport."

"Now is our chance," I said.

We disagreed on whether we should leave right away. As Isaac made his argument for later, I made a mental list of everything I wanted to do before leaving. When he finished, I said, "We can stop and rest along the way, but it's important we go now."

He didn't disagree. He asked: "Is that what you really want?"

"It is."

I told him to pack as much as he could, and not to leave behind anything that was important.

While he packed, I showered. When I finished, I saw his toothbrush on the sink and put it in my mouth. I yelled from the bathroom, "I'm using your toothbrush."

It felt more intimate than sex—a seemingly minor thing that any normal couple would have shared by now. But when I looked at myself in the mirror, I could see all the reasons why I had never done so staring back at me.

When I came back to the bedroom, Isaac had laid out on the bed the one suit he owned, the one he had been wearing at the airport. On the floor was the same suitcase he had been carrying. I was surprised at how little he still had, and then I understood that the suitcase had been empty when he arrived: all the clothes inside it now, he had bought with me. The only original item was the notebook that sat on top.

He was looking at the suit.

"Do you mind if I wear it? It was the last thing I bought in Nairobi. I don't want to fold it into such a small suitcase."

I wrapped my arms around him from behind and held my face against his back. I felt the urge to tell him I loved him; it wasn't the first time I'd had that thought, but it was the first time I was certain it was true. I pushed him onto the part of the bed that wasn't covered by his suit, and took off my towel as I undressed him.

He reached for a condom, but I pulled his arm back and placed it around me.

"Is this because of the toothbrush?"

"Yes."

He tried to pull me off him before he came, but I refused to let go. I looked ahead and had a sense of the doubt and anxiety that would follow, but when I looked beyond that for regret, I found none. I stayed on top of him for as long as possible. I saw him preparing to apologize.

"There is nothing to be sorry about," I told him.

I made eggs while Isaac showered and put his suit on. When I first met him I had wanted to laugh at the idea that someone would get so dressed up to come to this town, where most men wore suits only to church, and then just for weddings and funerals. I had missed how handsome he looked in gray, how a suit aged him just slightly beyond his twenty-odd years to a point better matched to the sometimes grave, formal aura that surrounded him.

"I thought you didn't touch eggs," he said.

"I learned while you were away."

I sat on the kitchen counter while he ate his breakfast at the table. I couldn't help thinking of the hundreds of times I had watched my mother sit next to my father as he did the same. His daily breakfast consisted of two eggs, fried or scrambled, with bacon and toast on the side. She nervously watched him eat from her side of the table, as if she knew that it was merely a matter of time before there would be a final breakfast; it would never be acknowledged as such, and so she rehearsed the end daily for years in order to soften the blow.

Here was another difference between us: I knew the end was near. I was making it, and trying to devour every moment left.

Before we left, I asked Isaac if he was certain he had packed everything he needed for a long trip. "Just in case I kidnap you and you never come back."

He held up his suitcase. "I've never had much to leave behind," he said.

· · ·

I didn't say where we were going next, and Isaac didn't ask. We skirted the center of town, drove past the new shopping malls to the eastern edge of Laurel, where my mother and I lived. I had never taken Isaac to that part of town, and I could tell from the way he stared out the window at the houses, which were larger than most homes in Laurel and were graced with wide, circular porches and acres of grass to look out upon, that this was new to him.

We pulled into the fourth house we passed.

"This is yours?" Isaac asked me.

I thought of it as my home, but never as mine. I don't think any of us who lived there had any strong feeling toward it. My parents were the second people to own it, and I never gave much thought to what I would I do when I inherited it.

"I live here," I said, "but it's my mother's house. My father didn't want anything to do with it after the divorce."

I asked him if he wanted to come in with me while I packed. He peered through the windshield as if trying to gauge the reception that would be waiting for him on the other side of the door. I knew better now than to guess what it would be.

"Is it okay if I just wait in the car?"

It was and it wasn't, but I said yes, because I owed him that.

The front door was already half open. I knew from experience that my mother would have parted the curtains in the living room or in her bedroom as soon as she heard a car pull into the driveway. Still, I was taken aback at seeing her standing on the other side of the door, in an ankle-length blue floral dress that she used to say made her look matronly, as if she were hiding children and possibly some pies underneath the hem. She didn't know what to do with her arms and hands. She unfolded and refolded them in the time it took me to enter and close the door.

"I heard your car from the kitchen," she said.

"I was going to call and tell you I was coming."

"This is still your home, Helen. Why would you ever do that?"

For all the love and affection that existed between us, we rarely hugged. Our gestures of affection had become increasingly girlish—we squeezed hands; occasionally, my mother held my forearm; I often caught her staring at me, waiting for me to notice she was watching me closely. I thought of that when I held my hand out to her. She took it, and I led her to the windows that looked out onto the driveway. The curtain was halfway parted.

"That's the man I've been seeing," I told her. "His name is Isaac."

She didn't look long; she had seen him as soon as we arrived and knew who he was to me.

"Does he always wear a suit?" she asked me.

"Only on special occasions."

She gasped. She held her hand to her mouth as if that could hide it. Only then did I understand how she had interpreted "special occasion." I began to laugh, harder than I should have.

"It's not what you think," I told her. "All we're doing is driving to Chicago." When that failed to calm her properly, I promised her that no other special occasion had been planned, or considered.

She moved away from the window. Her hands were confused again, twirling and tugging frantically.

"Is he coming in?"

"I asked him to, but he said he preferred to wait in the car."

Her instincts for proper behavior were off; she had no system of rules to apply. It was rude not to have him come in, but perhaps it was worse not to know how to respond if he did. I saw her worrying about where to sit and what to say, and how I would feel if she made no effort at all.

"Chicago," she said.

"It was my idea. I've never been."

"And do you have to go? I'm going to worry every minute about what may happen to you."

She was breathing deeply, with her right hand clenched tightly in front of her lips as if she was trying to work her way to anger in order not to cry.

I went to close the curtains, afraid of what Isaac would think if he saw us; but he was no longer in the car. I turned and caught sight of him just as his form was coming up the porch. My mother opened the door for him before I knew what to say.

"Welcome," she said. "My name is Audrey."

A portion of every minute of Isaac's life was spent acting, and so I shouldn't have been surprised that when a performance was needed he could easily fill whatever role was called for. Isaac entered as either the embodiment or a caricature of an English gentleman. He bent slightly forward when he introduced himself, and there was a hint of the accent I hadn't heard in months.

"My name is Isaac," he said. "It's a privilege to meet you."

I kept from laughing for my mother's sake and Isaac's. They were both performing; I couldn't have asked them to do more than that. Isaac complimented the house; "magnificent" was the word he chose. My mother downplayed the praise and then described the house as late Victorian, a phrase that I had never heard her use before, and which could only have been the result of having Isaac around. The house was as late Victorian as his accent. Only in the shortened history of the Midwest could these affectations thrive.

My mother suggested I take Isaac on a tour of the house while she prepared tea for us. I had lived in that house my entire life and never been asked to give a tour of it. It felt like going through a wedding album while the wedding was still going on: the past was all over the walls, in pictures and souvenirs, but because I was never far away, I rarely thought of them as markers of a time that had ended.

I led Isaac up the stairwell.

"I don't know why, but every house in Laurel has black-and-white photos by the stairs," I said.

At the very top were the only two pictures we had of my mother's parents, both of whom died shortly after I was born.

"We're the opposite of your family." I pointed to the pictures, which were shot from too great a distance. "We don't go back much further than this."

"Look at the size of this house," he said. "You're only just beginning."

Briefly, I saw the house through his eyes. It was built for a large family, for multiple generations to live together at the same time, and perhaps someday it would fulfill that design, but never with me.

I sent Isaac downstairs while I packed. I didn't linger over anything in my room, which had grown sparer and sparer over the years as I quietly unwound my attachments, carting boxes of clothes and photographs into the basement, where I knew they were safe, until all that was left was a bed, a bookcase, and a desk that looked out onto a large backyard overrun with weeds. I had never made any serious plans to leave Laurel, and yet long before Isaac, a part of me was gone.

It took me a few minutes to pack. When I returned to the living room, Isaac and my mother had already started their tea. They were hardly speaking; both were focused on getting their cups to their lips without spilling. The act had gone on long enough. I kissed my mother on the cheek and whispered that it was time for us to leave. She held on to my wrist and whispered back: "Helen, please be careful who sees you. If not for yourself, then for his sake."

ISAAC

When I woke the next morning, Isaac was standing over me, nudging me gently in the back with his foot. The courtyard was littered with still-drunk soldiers, many of whom had fallen asleep with empty bottles and their guns tucked in their arms. I had fallen asleep listening to a group of them debate whether they were revolutionaries or liberators. They seemed to split evenly down the middle until, finally, one pointed out that there was no rule saying they couldn't be both. "We are revolutionary liberators," he said, and to celebrate their new titles, they banged their bottles together, finished what was left in them, and then tossed them as far as they could over the hotel walls, to shatter on the road, where most children and many women walked barefoot.

I followed Isaac out of the courtyard. That we were leaving just before dawn, when there were still a few stars left on the northern edge of the sky, gave me hope that he had decided our life of war had gone on long enough. I had a general idea of where we were in the country, and I felt confident that if we had a car we could reach at least three different borders by midday, and that Joseph would be too concerned with his army's next advance to chase us. I had dreamed of big cities my entire life, but what I wanted for us was to find the smallest village possible—an idyllic, forgotten hamlet, like the ones we had passed in the foothills, but near a river or, better yet, within earshot of a waterfall. There was so much vast, empty space across the continent that I had no reason to believe it wasn't possible. We just had to find one of the dozens, or maybe even hundreds of hidden pockets where no one cared about borders.

I thought I had found a way to explain to Isaac why we had to leave. I was going to tell him that this wasn't the fight he expected, and that there were other things that could be done with our lives but to do them we had to get out while we could. I whispered his name as I walked up the main road.

"Isaac," I said, but, rather than turn around, he held up his hand and continued walking.

I was anxious but not scared. It was the best time to be alone in a village. There were a few signs of early-morning life in some of the houses farther up the road, and it was possible to believe at that hour that life here would go on as normal, that tea would be made and bread baked; men would go off to tend their fields while the women gathered water and dressed their children for school until the sun reached its peak and everyone retreated indoors to wait out the heat.

We continued up the main road in silence, listening to the last roosters left alive cackle at one another, until we reached the bronze fist where Joseph had delivered his speech a few days earlier. Once there, Isaac turned to me and said:

"Now we wait."

"For what?"

He motioned with his finger for me to stop talking.

· · ·

The sun was above the horizon when a man with a small boy and two donkeys trailing behind them emerged from the footpath that branched off the main road.

"This is where we say goodbye," Isaac told me. I looked at the man and child closely. They were clearly father and son, with the same wide, sloping forehead; on the child it seemed to take too much space, but it gave the man a gentle, almost feminine quality.

"Why now?" I asked him.

"We're leaving this evening," he said. "Joseph has other villages he wants to conquer."

"And where do I go?"

He pointed to the man, who appeared to be whispering something important to one of the donkeys.

"He has someplace safe to take you. Stay there. Rest. Get strong, and then go east. I've heard it's quiet there. Whatever you do, don't come back. Also, don't go south; I hear there are problems there."

"And north?"

"Not so good. There are more problems."

"And what will you do?"

He threw his arm around my shoulder. He pointed straight ahead and then slowly moved his finger from left to right, drawing an imaginary line across the horizon.

"There is nothing else out there for me except this?"

We had more we wanted to say—there were apologies that should have been made, forgiveness to have been granted—but the village was waking up, despite the late night. We could smell the charcoal burning in the gardens and hear people in the street. Joseph was certainly up by now.

"How long will you be gone?" I asked him.

"Joseph says it should be over in two days. He says there will be no resistance."

It was the wrong question to ask when saying goodbye. The talk of war turned him. He snapped back into form.

"Enough of this," he said.

He held out his hand. I shook it. He took a bundle of notes from his pocket and gave it to the man. They talked between themselves for a few seconds, and then Isaac gave him a pat on the back of his head. Before walking away, he said, "One donkey is yours if you want to keep it."

Isaac turned south, back to the hotel, while I headed west, along the same path the man and his boy had come from. One of the small wonders of village life was how quickly nature reclaimed its dominance, as if the life of a town was little more than a minor disturbance to an otherwise wild world. After a few minutes of walking, there was hardly any sound other than that of birds; by the time we had traveled a half-mile, the trees had all but swallowed the footpath we were on. We walked for more than an hour, until we reached a clearing where maybe a dozen thatch-roofed huts stood a few feet apart from one another, each surrounded by a wooden fence to pen in the chickens, and the children when the adults were away. It was the idyllic corner of the world I had been hoping to find, and though that vision was little more than the fantasy of someone desperate for refuge, I was determined to preserve it for as long as possible. I knew it wouldn't last; even if there wasn't a war on the horizon, if I stayed long enough I'd find all the petty complaints and frustrations of life here just as easily I had found them in the capital and in my own childhood home. But there wasn't much time anyway: Joseph's soldiers were going to take the next city that evening, which meant many of them would leave within the hour. If they won, they

would return within the next few days; if they were slaughtered, the army would finish the rest of them, holed up at the
hotel. In either case, it was only a matter of time before nothing
was safe.

During the three days I lived in that enclave, I learned there was
pleasure to be found in anonymity. Of the forty-five people that I
was certain lived there most of the year, all knew only one thing
about me—that I was hiding and had the money to pay not to
be found. I told the man who escorted me to the village my real
name, the one given to me at birth. Both he and his son laughed
when they tried to pronounce it, and each had his own variation. We had a few common words among us, which took all the
pressure off the silence and left me happily wordless. By the time
we arrived at the clearing, my name had been transformed into
Daniel—a Biblically familiar name among the devoutly Christian people who lived there. I enjoyed hearing the children say
it. It sounded like a song. They were the ones who spoke to me
most often. They watched me closely the first day I was there,
seemingly incapable of exhausting their interest in me and in the
pleasure they took in saying "Hello, Daniel," or "Okay, Daniel,"
every time I moved so much as an inch.

I stayed in a thatch-roofed hut next to where the man and
his son lived with a much older woman whom I took to be the
man's mother or grandmother. Unlike in most villages I knew,
women were scarce here, not men. Among the few there, most
were in the last half of their lives. There were dozens of children,
however, both girls and boys, so the loss of women was clearly
recent. It was easy enough to guess what might have happened,
but I refused to think too long on it. I wanted silence, and that
was what I had been given.

That first night alone, I had to contend with knowing Isaac was out there fighting. Initially, I found myself praying for his safe return, but I cut that thought short as well; his win could only be the product of someone else's loss, and the same held true the other way. Before sleeping, I settled on a simple enough prayer, made without fealty to any faith or cause: Have mercy on them all.

HELEN

My mother waved goodbye to us from the porch, with one hand on the screen door. She watched as Isaac and I got into the car, and was still standing outside as I steered us back onto the road. She waited until we were out of sight before letting go of the door. I knew that she would take either the wicker chair at the far end of the porch, or the rocking chair that sat in the middle. Whichever one she chose, she would remain there for hours. This was what she always did. We rarely had guests, and when they did come, she would walk them to their car and remain on the porch a while longer, as if she wasn't sure they were really gone, or was reluctant to go back into the house because they were. When I looked back and saw her still on the porch, I knew she would stay out there longer than normal, wondering if she had lost me, and if she had, how much longer she could bear living in such an empty house by herself.

I worried that I was being too quiet now that Isaac and I were alone again, but when I looked over he seemed equally removed, his gaze fixed on the soy fields outside his window. When we reached a red light, he asked if it was hard for my mother to live in such a big house. He didn't say she was alone, or lonely, but that was implied; he didn't say "big house," either. He referred to it as a house with so many rooms, as if it wasn't the scale that mattered but the way the space had been divided. I wasn't listening closely enough to understand the distinction at the time, but I knew he had chosen those words for a reason.

The simple answer to his question was yes, but I was unwilling to admit that. Her loneliness had multiple strains; as her daughter, I knew each and every one, and tended to them from a distance.

"Why would it be hard? She's very comfortable. She has everything she needs, and I still live there."

Comfort wasn't the point, though, and it was meaningless to claim to Isaac that I lived there.

"You are right. Forget what I said."

When we neared downtown, I told Isaac I wanted to make a brief detour to visit an old client. I had thought of Rose as soon as I had thought of Chicago, but never with the intention of visiting her. Like my mother, she lived alone, but she was much older and had far less space. At least a month had gone by since I had last spoken to her, more since I had gone to her house.

"You can wait in the car this time," I said. "It will only take a few minutes. She's an old woman. She's not comfortable with strangers."

I imagined finding Rose sitting on her couch, gracefully looking through old photos when I arrived. She would tell me that all was fine, her health and her home, and I would tell her that I was on my way now to Chicago with a man I loved, and that, in honor of her, we would stay at the Knickerbocker Hotel, perhaps in the same room that Al Capone had once lived in.

· · ·

David had warned me never to confuse my clients' lives with my own. "If your life is falling apart," he said, "don't think you can make it better by trying to save someone else's. And the same is true the other way. Be grateful when you're happy. Being miserable isn't required."

He had one expression taped to his door: "Why do [we] [they] think we can save them?"

And underneath that: *"Depending on your mood, circle one."*

My life wasn't falling apart, but I believed an important part of it was coming to an end, and I wanted Rose, with her photo albums and stories, to show me the brightest possible version of what that end might look like—not now, but twenty, thirty, fifty years in the future.

As soon as I turned onto her street, I knew I had made a mistake. The neighborhood, and in particular that block, had been emptying out rapidly in the past two years, as some of the older stores downtown began to close. The families who lived in this neighborhood worked in those shops, or in places that depended on their owners, and so they were the first to feel the loss. There had been at least three "For Sale" signs visibly displayed on front lawns the first time I visited Rose, and now here was a fourth, which I could tell even from the opposite end of the block had landed in front of Rose's house. I continued on anyway. There was a chance that Rose was there; in order to believe that, I avoided answering the obvious question: where would an eighty-something-year-old woman with no close family go after her house was sold?

· · ·

I parked across the street from her house, even though there were no cars in front of it. Rose's home could have fit comfortably on the first floor of my mother's. It was short and narrow, a sturdier, brightly painted version of a shotgun shack. The two windows on either side of the front door had been boarded over, as if the house had been blinded. It was hard to imagine someone had lived there recently, or would do so again anytime soon.

"Is this where you wanted to go?" Isaac asked.

I didn't want to answer him directly.

"This was where my client Rose lived."

I was afraid the state of the house said something about me as well.

"And where is she now?"

"She was very old," I said. "In her eighties. She was the one who told me to go to Chicago."

We remained parked across the street a while longer. My claims of caring, and not just for Rose, felt fraudulent. David knew when her file was closed, and had chosen not to tell me. It was part of the agreement we had struck almost a year ago. As long as I had Isaac, I had no funerals or hospital visits to attend to.

Isaac placed my hand on the gearshift. He thought I was mourning.

"I think this means that we should definitely go to Chicago," he said.

ISAAC

A slow, winding parade of tired and wounded refugees invaded the village on the fourth day. They emerged into the clearing shortly after dawn from a footpath on the eastern edge of the village. There must have been more than a hundred of them, but at least half were children, and as far as I could tell from behind the fence of my compound, many of the men and women were injured and could barely walk. Most of the village came out to witness their arrival, including the man and boy I was staying with. The man had an old rifle gripped to his chest, his son a pickax that he dragged behind him. When the boy saw me, he dropped his grip on the ax so he could wave to me with both hands as he said, "Okay, Daniel." His father turned to grab him by the collar, but by that point it was too late. A dozen other children standing in their own compounds had picked up the call and were waving with both hands, each shouting either "Okay, Daniel," or "Hello, Daniel." Their voices were a reminder of my place as a curious stranger—not totally welcome, but easily tolerated. It was a privileged perch. The previous evening, while trying to write for the fourth or fifth time the most general observations of what I had seen and done that day, I finally understood why my father had called me Bird: nothing made me happier than looking down, and in that village, that was all I had to do. I watched the old women pound maize in the morning while the children dug for ants and beetles and the men set off for work, either to their farms or back to town. When the children shouted hello to me that morning, I could hear the imaginary perch I lived on break.

The man who had brought me to the village turned his attention briefly toward me, as did the other men from inside their own compounds. Every one of them was armed—a few with guns, the rest with machetes, hoes, and axes—and I felt certain that when they looked at me each was thinking a variation of the same thought: Why have we let this man stay with us for so long?

I waved to the boy and his father. Neither acknowledged me, nor did anyone else in the village. Everyone was focused on the newest arrivals. They were a threat—both foreign and desperate and twice as dangerous as a result—but what to do with them remained, at least for those few minutes, uncertain.

The man who had brought me to the village stepped forward. As soon as he did so, a decision was reached. Every other man in the village came forward and joined him. They formed a parallel line of defense, twenty men strong, through which no one, regardless of how desperate, would be allowed.

The townspeople could have held their position until the crowd retreated back into the forest; they could have threatened the refugees by firing once in their general direction. But neither action would have solved the problem of what to do with that mass if they eventually returned, whether that evening or the next. Isaac was wrong: the problems were everywhere, and growing by the hour. New victims and killers were being bred far from the battlefields.

The men in the village knew what they were doing. They had

planned for this, or lived through it before. They spoke among themselves briefly, and then those with guns fired into the crowd without pausing to aim. The intent was to kill everyone, and so it made no difference who died first.

Among the refugees, those capable of running did so without looking back. I saw maybe a dozen women and children flee into the bush. Those who couldn't simply stood there, or sat, or draped themselves over the bodies of those who had just been shot, and waited to die. The few able-bodied men among the crowd attacked with knives. They were fired upon. None of them were hit, though two women behind them were. Had they stayed together, they might have stood a greater chance, but each man charged on his own, and each was quickly surrounded by three men from the village, and cut down slowly with machetes and hoes.

Every man in the village took part in killing those left huddled at the edge of the forest. They did so with hard blows straight to the head. I could tell by the way they slung their weapons that they were farmers. Once they had finished, the men lined up again and marched into the bush. They would kill the ones they found, and leave the rest to die on their own. I didn't stay long enough to hear them tell the story. The women and children began to drag the bodies into the forest. As they did so, I tried to write down what had happened. I thought of counting the dead, but I was too far away to do so. I tried next to describe one of the bodies, but all I could see was death—no eyes, no face, just a blank emptiness I didn't have the stomach to look at closely. When that failed, I tried to describe a woman dragging what looked to be an old man through the grass, but before I knew what to write, she was gone and then walking back, empty-handed. By the time I finally turned away from her, it was almost over. The bodies were hidden in the forest, which would swallow the remains before

anyone knew to look for them. I had no names, not even of the
village, which was too small to have existed on any map. And so
I did the only thing I could think of. I waited until no one was
watching me, and then left. As I walked back to Joseph's village,
I drew a map of the route. I recorded every bend in the road, and
the few forks that I came upon, along with sketches of a few long-
abandoned thatch-roofed homes barely visible from the path. It
was far from poetry, less than a journal, and worthless as history.

HELEN

One of the few games my father played with me when I was a child had us speeding through town as if we were outlaws. He would ask if I heard the sirens behind us, and as soon as I said yes, he would tell me to fasten my seat belt because we were going to drive so fast that no one would ever be able to catch us. As we pulled away from Rose's house, I was grateful to have found a fond memory of him to relive. I played that game silently, through two stop signs that I barely paused for and a yellow light I had no chance of making, until we reached the end of Laurel. I pulled over just on the other side of the sign that I had memorized when I was ten, and which had never changed since: "Laurel, Inc 1872. Pop: 15752."

I asked Isaac if he wanted to take one last look back.

"Turn around and enjoy the view," I said. "Who knows when you'll see it again?"

Recently harvested cornfields lay on both sides of the road, a silver grain silo a few hundred yards ahead. There were no cars in either direction. The emptiness was one of the things I loved most about the rural Midwest.

Isaac did what I asked him to do. He turned around and stared at the landscape, which was virtually the same as the one in front of him. As soon as he finished, I pulled away. He didn't know he was leaving, so I said his goodbyes for him. As I drove, I said good-bye to his apartment, to the books that he left behind, to the university library, to all the furniture we had bought together, to the apartment as a whole, and then to every place I could remember that we had gone to together, from the post office to the grocery store and Bill's diner, and then to David, whom he had never met, and his file, which he had never seen, and then to the rest of Laurel, the parts known and unknown to him.

I finished just as I reached the entrance to the highway. I was far from crying, but at some point several tears had crawled out from under my eyes. Isaac saw them running down my face. He smudged them against my cheek with his thumb.

"What's happening?"

I knew what I wanted to say: "I'm letting you go, slowly, in pieces, so it won't break me." I told him instead that I was thinking of Rose.

When we reached the highway, I asked Isaac to take out the atlas in the glove box and choose the route. He placed it on his lap and began to survey the country. He was delighted when he found a Cairo, an Athens, a Paris, and a Rome in America. He said we should continue going east, like all the signs suggested.

"This country," he said. "What don't you have?"

What we didn't have, for all that space, were many places where Isaac and I could publicly rest without fear of who was watching us. When we stopped for lunch at a restaurant off the highway, it was impossible not to notice the hostile glares of many of the men dining there alone. They were deaf and blind to the world until we entered; once they saw us, all they could do was glare over their coffee cups and from under the brims of their hats. No one said anything to us. Our waitress, who must have been near my mother's age, called us both "dear" and "honey" with the same general affection. Isaac and I were different with each other—not harsh or cold, as we had been during that terrible lunch at Bill's, just slightly separated by an invisible, but no less real barrier, a chest-high fence that we could still talk and see through rather than a wall that hid us completely from each other. We did our best not to be bothered. We didn't hold hands, we didn't touch, but we kept our eyes focused exclusively on each other as we ate our lunch and drank our coffee. At one point, when neither of us had spoken for several minutes, Isaac said, "On the count of three, laugh." At three, we began to giggle and then cackle, and then laugh with what felt like genuine delight. We left with the better part of us intact.

Before getting back on the highway, I studied the map; my plan had been to drive straight and then turn north, but I decided now we were better off leaving the southern part of the state as soon as possible. Without telling Isaac, I decided we would go north first, and then cut across.

"Chicago," I said. I thought of Isaac and me at the Knickerbocker Hotel with the ghost of Al Capone. We were the outlaws now.

We reached Chicago shortly before dusk. We drove along the lakeshore. I wanted to find the Knickerbocker Hotel but had no idea how to.

"It's not fair," Isaac said.

"What?"

He pointed out the window to the lake.

"You have oceans even in the middle of the country."

"It's not an ocean," I said.

"I know," he said. "Your lakes are my ocean. My forest is your jungle. America is a world, not a nation."

We slowed to a crawl just as Chicago came into view. I had never been in a city anywhere near that size; I had never seen so many cars. I grew anxious thinking about how many people there must have been inside them. I felt like we were driving into something alive, with white gleaming spires on top of its buildings for teeth.

Every time we came to a complete stop, I turned to Isaac. He was enthralled by the view, as I suspected he would be.

He pointed to the tallest building we could see through the windshield.

"That must be the Hancock Center."

He reached over and caressed my forearm. I took that as proof he had no idea what I was planning.

"This will be lovely," he said.

ISAAC

There was no one along the path back to Joseph's village. I expected that I would find traces of the war—more refugees, soldiers— but it was just as empty as it had been before. When I reached the band of houses that marked the town's northern border, I heard the lorry engines approaching. Assuming Isaac was still alive, he would be back by now. I didn't run, but I was desperate to see him again and walked as fast as I could while trying not to give the impression I was fleeing. When I reached the main road of the village, I saw that there were three lorries already parked, halfway in between the bronze fist and the Life Hotel. Dozens of soldiers were crowded into the beds of the first two. There was no crowd to greet them. The entire village had heard the engines and retreated indoors. The only truly communal knowledge was fear, and in this case everyone had the same response.

The soldiers descended from the back of the lorries; I was alone on the street watching them. The first to exit were clearly tired; they walked slowly and took time to regain their balance after landing, but they could do so on their own. That was true only for the first ones, however. Each group was more injured than the one that preceded it. There were the soldiers with minor wounds, cuts, and bruises across their chests and forearms, followed by those who had at least one limb badly injured—an arm in a sling, a thigh wrapped in bandages. Then, finally, came those who were almost dead, and those who might live but would suffer greatly for what little remained of their lives; all of these had to be carried out.

The third lorry was parked at the very edge of the road, under a large tree, just where the town began. There were no soldiers standing in the bed, but I could see through the slats part of a hand, a tuft of hair, boots, and patches of camouflage pants and shirts. A swarm of flies hovered over this truck, and I expected soon there would be vultures perched on the tree. I looked for Isaac among the living—the healthy and able-bodied, and then among the injured. I didn't see him anywhere; I decided that if he was among the heap of dead bodies in the back of the last lorry, I didn't want to know. I was prepared to accept his death, but not on those terms.

There is nothing left for me here, I told myself. I didn't know where I would go, only that I would never see the capital again. I decided to head south along the main road, in the hope that I would be able to pick up a ride to another village. I made it a few feet before two soldiers stopped me. One pointed to the lorry full of corpses. I pretended not to understand what he meant, and was trying to walk away when the other soldier took hold of my arm and pulled me back.

"Do you think you are special?" he asked me.

I shook my head no. I recognized him from the hotel. I was one of the soldiers who, under Isaac's orders, had taken the officer with the bulldog head away.

"Then why do you think you can leave? We go out there and fight for you, and now you want to leave." He smiled, as if the problem had nothing to do with the dead but was an issue of manners.

He turned to the soldiers behind him and pointed to the houses on the other side of the road. Each soldier entered one home and emerged shortly after with all the men or teenage boys inside it. Suddenly I was no longer alone; there must have been at least fifty of us now. The soldier holding my arm pointed to the last lorry.

"Go," he said. "And bury them."

"Is Isaac in there?" I asked him.

He squinted his eyes in either confusion or anger; either way, he had no idea who I was talking about. He had never heard of Isaac. He knew him by a different name, as did all the soldiers.

"The captain," I said.

He pushed me forward. I turned around to ask him another question, but he had already moved on; he had his hands around a young man's neck and was leading him on like a dog.

The youngest boys were sent to dig the grave while the rest of us formed a chain from the back of the lorry to the ground, where the bodies were stacked one on top of another. I was in the bed with the bodies—the second link in the chain, with a man much older than me whose thin arms were still defined by the muscles of his youth. Like all the other men, he performed his job in silence, without pity and with perhaps even a bit of gratitude that this was all that was being asked of him. He took the legs and I took the arms of each body passed to us, which meant that, whether I wanted to or not, I had to stare into every face to see if it was Isaac.

After the second body, I stopped paying attention to the features. I looked as long as it took to know whether it was Isaac, and if the body was clearly shorter, taller, or heavier than Isaac, I didn't look at all. I simply grabbed the stiff arms and passed them to the next pair of hands. After the fifteenth or twentieth, I decided to think of them as a single body named Adam. In my head I said, "You were a brave soldier, Adam. . . . Your mother and father will miss you. . . . You should have stayed in your village, Adam. . . . You had no reason to come here. . . . You could have gone to school and become a doctor, Adam." And when I ran out of alternate endings, I simply thought, "Adam, Adam," until we had carried the last body out of the lorry, and I could risk a small breath of relief: though there were more than a hundred Adams, there wasn't a single Isaac.

We pushed all of the bodies into the long shallow grave on the other side of the tree, facing away from the village. We took turns shoveling the earth back. When we were finished, the only priest in the village was brought from his house to say a prayer over the grave. He was a short, stout man dressed in black with a purple collar. He said his prayer without any devotion, as if he had either long ago lost his faith or didn't believe those men were entitled to share in it. Either way, when he was done, so were we. The soldiers who had been guarding us walked away as if they had finished watching a street performance that had only mildly held their interest to begin with. I thought I was done as well, and was going to continue walking south, as I had originally planned; but the second of the two soldiers, the one who had only pointed to the lorry without speaking, told me that the colonel was waiting for me in the hotel. I followed him into the courtyard, which was full of injured men lying on the ground, their open wounds festering in the sun. The soldier pointed up to the northwest corner of the balcony.

"Colonel," he said.

I was more relieved than surprised to find Isaac with his hands on the railing looking down at me. He was a colonel, a captain, or why not a general? Surviving was enough to have earned him that. We waved to each other—a simple thing that felt extraordinary, and I wished that we could have held that gesture for just a while longer, the way families and lovers did at bus stations and airports, whether someone was coming or going.

Isaac motioned with his hand for me to come up and join him. After a morning spent working on a mass grave, I felt I needed to stand on solid ground to make sure that I wasn't sinking, too. I showed him the bloodstained palms of my hands, and waved for him to come to me.

The only source of water in the hotel was a manual pump in the rear of the courtyard. Isaac met me there as I was filling a small bucket to wash myself with. He handed me a bar of soap, and the first thing he said to me was "Be careful with that. It might be the only one left in the hotel."

Before I dipped my hands into the water, Isaac told me to wait.

"Your hair is filthy," he said. "Lean forward."

I leaned my head next to the bucket, and Isaac poured water from a plastic pitcher over my head, then rubbed the soap deep into my scalp before rinsing it again.

"Now hold out your hands," he said. I stretched out my arms with my palms facing up. He laughed. "This isn't Europe," he said. "How much water do you think we have?"

He cupped my palms for me and slowly poured a handful of water into them so I could rinse off the blood before properly washing them. By the time I finished, there was a line of men waiting behind me. "Give me a few minutes," Isaac said.

I stepped to the side so the next man could take my place. Isaac washed his hands and hair as well. He did the same for a dozen men, until that last bar of soap was reduced to a nub no larger than the tip of a finger. He took what was left of the soap and rubbed it into his own hands until it had completely dissolved, and then rubbed his hands over his face. He washed himself with what little water was left in the bucket, and when he was finished, there were still streaks of soap along his right cheek.

"How do I look?" he asked me.

"Tired," I said. "And you missed a spot."

He rubbed the side of his face with his lapel, which was the one part of his uniform that didn't have an obvious coat of dirt on it.

"I was worried that you would come back here," he said.

"Where else was I going to go?"

"It didn't matter; any other place would have been better."

"I wasn't planning on staying long."

"Good. By tomorrow morning, there won't be much left."

Isaac took three fingers of my right hand in his. We walked out of the courtyard like that, and continued to hold hands until we reached the tree behind which the dead soldiers were buried.

"Why were they buried here?" I asked him.

He nodded to the hotel across the street. "The soldiers wanted it. They said their souls would never sleep after what they did if we buried them in the other village, and maybe they're right."

He saw me staring past him toward the grave, but he mistook my concern for pity.

"Don't feel bad for them," he said. "At least you helped bury them."

He walked to the other side of the tree and stood on top of the grave. I thought he was going to spit on it, but instead he dug the heel of his right boot into the mound of earth as deep as he could.

"What happened?" I asked him.

He pretended to ignore the question, focusing his efforts on pressing his foot deeper into the ground. After several minutes, he finally responded. "Why would you want to know more?"

I didn't have an answer, so I chose the one I thought he would want to hear. I pulled out the notebook he had given me. So far, I had filled six pages—four with a map, two more with half-finished sentences—but only I knew that.

"If you're going to write something, write something nice," he said. "Something that will make people happy. No one needs to read this."

He began to dig with his other foot. I let him do so for several minutes before interrupting to ask him the same question again: "What happened?" Or maybe the second time I said, "Tell me what happened." Either way, it wasn't the right question. The "what" was obvious. What I didn't know was what Isaac had done.

He kicked a mound of dirt into my hair without looking up at me. I took a few steps back, but that still didn't feel far enough, so I walked around his left side until I was standing several feet directly behind him. I tried again.

"Did you kill anyone?" I asked him.

I watched his right leg take a long swing back and then abruptly stop just before it hit the ground.

"That's a stupid question," he said. "If you want to know, you should ask how many."

"How many?"

"No. 'How many people did you kill?'"

"How many people did you kill?"

"I don't know," he said. "More than I can count. Too many."

I waited for him to turn around, but he didn't. He kept his gaze firmly fixed on the tree in front of him as he made a few more stabs into the ground.

"Ask me how we killed them," he said.

"How did you kill them?"

"We didn't shoot them."

"You cut them."

"Yes. We beat them. We burned them. We had no bullets left. Ask me if we buried them."

"Did you bury them?"

"No. We left them for the vultures and dogs. And then we ran back here so we wouldn't have to look at what we had done."

His right foot was buried past his ankle. I understood now why he was doing that.

"How deep is this hole?" he asked me.

"Not very deep," I said.

He pulled his foot out of the ground and shook the dirt from his shoes.

"Good," he said. "It's already more than they deserve."

HELEN

We set our sights on the Hancock Center and aimed straight for it. Isaac watched the city through my window, while I found it hard not to stare at the lake out of his. This was still the Midwest, but it didn't have the hard, firm earth that was supposed to come with it. The city ended abruptly, rather than trailing off into open fields like Laurel. This bothered me. I knew Isaac didn't see it that way, so I kept silent as we traced our way along the shoreline, past the center of the city, and around a tight bend. I followed the heaviest traffic onto Michigan Avenue, where we met the Hancock Center head-on. Isaac leaned against the dashboard to get a better look. It was all wonderful to him. He saw the great possibilities buildings like that promised, especially to men like him, who had no idea what it meant to scale them.

We parked three blocks away from the tower he admired so much. Once we were out of the car, I told him to lead the way.

"This is your parade," I said. He smiled. He had no idea what that meant. "It's my turn to follow you now," I explained.

Neither of us knew where we were. We had only the Hancock to orient us, and so of course Isaac retraced our route back to it. "I want to touch it," he said, as if this was a confession of a desire he was embarrassed about. I imagined a surface slick and oily against my hand, one that would linger for a long time.

"Then let's touch it," I said.

The distance on foot was greater than I thought. The blocks were long. The sidewalks were more like roads, wide and crowded; it felt dangerous to walk down them. While Isaac looked up, I watched the faces that passed us. We weren't holding hands, but we were standing close to each other. When Isaac caught something that fascinated him, he turned to me so I could share it with him. There were gargoyles, moldings, spires, and strange etchings on the sides of buildings, all of which could be seen if you walked with your head turned up. It wasn't just buildings, though. There was an antique red roadster parked across the street that he wanted me to see, and a fountain; every beggar we passed demanded his attention, but not his curiosity. I looked wherever he told me and just as quickly looked to see the reaction of whoever was near us. As far as I could tell, no one had noticed us. I thought this was what it felt like to be invisible, but when I subtracted Isaac I realized that, until he came along, this was how I had always felt. Not invisible, but a natural part of the background, entitled to all the privileges that came with ownership.

We stopped in front of the Hancock. Isaac wanted to see it from multiple angles, so we crossed the street, moved to various corners, and craned our necks to stare up the shiny black exterior.

"It is amazing," he said.

The awe was genuine. I wanted to know how he sustained it. We stood near the main entrance and rubbed our hands against the exterior. It was warm, polished; I wanted to say it was softer than I expected.

"Should we go inside?"

He shook his head.

"We can't appreciate it from in there," he said.

Isaac took my hand.

"Let's walk," he said.

We hesitated, looking at our hands, not each other, then gathered our strength and moved forward. We walked. It didn't feel like a victory over anything, but I was proud and, to an equal degree, scared. After walking one block like that, I was grateful for the feeling of his hand in mine, and even for the anxiety that came with it. After two more blocks, the gratitude had turned to sorrow that we hadn't had this sooner. All this time, I thought, we've been at best only half of what was possible.

I wished my mother could have seen us. I wished David were watching from around the corner.

"Are you okay?"

I wasn't crying, but the view ahead was blurred.

"I'm great. Wonderful," I said.

I squeezed his hand hard. He locked his fingers around mine. As long as we continued walking, I was certain that nothing could break us.

The light ahead turned red just as we reached the intersection. We slowed, and as soon as we came to a stop, a crowd formed around us. We were at the front of the pack, which was better than being in the middle, but still we were exposed. I noticed right away that the man next to Isaac and the woman standing closest to me were staring at us, and of course they weren't alone. I kept my head up without looking at anyone long enough to read their expressions. I knew what was there—anger, pity, contempt, maybe even envy—but I was convinced that there must have also been a touch of wonder, maybe even awe at the sight of us.

When the light turned green, Isaac held me back so we were the last to cross.

"Where should we go next?" he asked me.

It was obvious. He had his tower; I had my lake. I pointed straight ahead to it. The city masked its size with trees, and an expressway and more buildings, so that from where we stood the lake looked kiddie-sized in comparison with what we had seen in the car.

"I should tell you now, I don't know how to swim," he said.

"Don't worry," I told him, "part of my job is to save you from drowning."

We followed a party of young couples to the end of Michigan Avenue. They were carrying blankets and a picnic basket, and were dressed in sandals, shorts, and lightly patterned summer dresses.

"They're just like us," I said, "except we're better dressed."

I said it out loud, but I wasn't speaking to Isaac. I was testing out certain truths and seeing how they held up when they were no longer private.

We descended into the foot tunnel that led underneath Lakeshore Drive and onto the waterfront. There must have been at least three dozen of us in the tunnel—a two-way parade, with the overwhelming majority heading away from the lake. One of the pastel-clad men in front of us roared to hear his echo, and, for no reason other than that we could, we all began to join him, his friends first, until everyone in front of me and behind me, including Isaac, was roaring as we walked. We turned toward each other and roared. We looked up to the ceiling and roared at the cars passing over us. We roared at the people walking back to the city, and they roared back; then, as we neared the end of the tunnel, I roared at the distance opening up before me, at the trees, and then at the beach and lake. I could hear my voice—distinct and, according to Isaac, much more ferocious than all the rest.

"Another thing I love about you," he said once we were out, "your voice."

We walked down the tree-lined path that curved back toward the road before abruptly turning straight to the beach and lake. I had seen the beach from the car, but this was going to be the first time I actually stepped foot on one, and I wanted to make the most of the seconds leading up to it. When the view cleared and the sidewalk ended in a burst of sand, I realized I was wrong to have been so anxious in the car. There was nothing to be afraid of. The city simply paused at the water's edge. It ran alongside the lake for many more miles.

I tried to find a way to say that to Isaac, stopping him just before we reached the sand.

"It doesn't end as abruptly as I thought," I said.

I pointed north, to the buildings that continued along the shore. Isaac humored me. He took in the view and pretended that we were talking about architecture.

"Yes," he said. "The city is much larger than it appears."

He put his arm around me and tried to lead me onto the sand.

"I read somewhere it's bad luck to walk on a beach with your shoes on."

I made that up, but I had every right to: the common sayings and kitchen wisdom I had grown up with weren't enough. We sat down and pulled off our shoes and socks and buried our feet in the sand, which was harder and colder than I had expected.

"It's nothing like the Hancock," I said.

I pointed to the ground so he would know what I was talking about.

I wanted to say something about finding the opposite of what you expected.

"You mean the sand?"

"I thought it would be soft, and gold, maybe white. I thought you could sleep on it, but you can't. It's too hard. It's not the right color."

"Are you disappointed?"

"No. More like deceived."

It was a poor choice of words, given our history.

"I am sorry to hear you say that."

"Not all deceptions are bad," I added.

He gave a weak half-smile and turned his attention to the sand. He scooped up a handful and rolled it around on his palm.

"What was in your suitcase?" he asked me.

I remembered that he had carried it to the car and must have known as soon as he lifted it that it was almost empty. It was time now to explain why I wanted us to come here.

"You know why I wanted to come to Chicago with you?"

"I can guess."

"I thought I had a plan. I thought if I was the one who took you away from Laurel you would see there was no point in going back. You'd want to stay here, and I would help you do that."

"And then what?"

"And then I would promise to come back and visit, but eventually you wouldn't need me to. You'd make a life on your own here, which was what I was supposed to help you do in the first place."

"You did more than that."

"I don't know if that's true. There's only so much room in a town like ours. Helping you leave seemed better than watching us fall apart inside it."

"I would not let that happen."

"But maybe I would. Or maybe I'm afraid there is nothing we could do to stop it."

He placed his foot over mine and pressed them both into the sand.

"I am afraid for us all the time," he said. "I see the men at the other end of the beach and I worry that soon they will start to walk toward us. I worry—when you leave my house, when you come to it—that someone you know will see you. Until very recently, I worried about what you thought when you woke up. I worried about what I would think when you were asleep. I imagine things much worse than I would want to live with. That is why I packed everything, like you told me to."

"Because you wanted to leave."

"No. Not because I wanted to. When Henry taught me how to drive, he said it was so I could leave Laurel when I was ready to. On the day my visa expired, he said, I could drive myself to the airport, park the car, and disappear, or I could keep the car for as long as I needed, and leave when I was ready. 'I don't want you to feel trapped there,' he said. 'That might be just as bad as anything you've gone through.' That was when I told him I had met you. He was careful. All he said was to be honest with you, and to keep myself grounded, which I didn't understand. I thought he meant I should not leave the country with you, and so I promised him I would stay grounded. I thought, 'Why would we leave America when there is so much to see here?' which was when I decided to buy you those souvenirs. I showed them to Henry before I mailed them. He said, 'God bless you if you make it to one of those places.'

"I understood then what he meant by grounded. I sent the package anyway. I hoped to tell him someday he was wrong—that we had made it further than he expected—but it's okay if that never happens. We are here. We have gone far."

"That's what I tell my clients in counseling. I tell them, as long as they've done the best they can, they have nothing to apologize for. I say that when they feel guilty or they're grieving."

"You don't have to feel either."

"Right now I feel both."

Isaac stood. He took my hands and pulled me up.

"We haven't walked on the beach yet," he said. "We came this far. It would be a shame not to."

The view from the beach was a smaller deception. When I imagined my first walk on one, I pictured a sun setting in the water, but it was the opposite. The sun had already disappeared directly behind us, and we were left with its remains—purple clouds and streaks of orphaned light that did nothing for the water, which looked cold and gray, but made the sky a beautiful place to want to linger in.

We walked to the edge of the sand. There was a soft, shy quality in the way the water barely touched the shore before retreating.

"Is this a better view for you?"

"This is closer to home," I said. "I'm used to flat. I like to know what's in front of me."

Isaac laughed, a genuine, full-bodied one that had him throwing his head back.

"You speak in circles," he said. It was my turn now to be confused. I assumed that was part of the pleasure for him.

"It's a bad translation. It's what my father would say about someone who does not speak directly. They say the clouds are darker when they mean they are tired, or hungry, or lonely."

"And what do I mean?"

It was a simply question, with an obvious answer. Like most, I wanted to know what came next. Before I met Isaac, I more or less always did.

"It would be bad luck to tell you," he said.

"Are you making that up?"

"Yes."

I picked up his hand and began to swing it—gently at first, but then he joined in, and soon our arms were sailing over our heads. We were like birds, but instead of wings we had arms flapping. I knew what we needed to do, whether we stayed in the city or returned to Laurel. We had to invent new rules, phrases, and axioms to live by.

We swung our arms until our shoulders began to hurt. I don't know how much time went by. It was dark when Isaac asked me what we were doing.

I looked at my feet, and then his. I looked farther down the beach and saw the couples we had followed into the tunnel and, beyond them, the men that Isaac had been watching since we arrived.

"No one can touch us," I said.

Isaac squeezed my hand.

My plan was wrong. There was an alternate ending that I had been too afraid to consider.

"I won't leave you here alone," I said.

"What does that mean?"

"It means I won't be afraid as long as you are with me."

I saw myself driving back to Laurel, alone, in a couple of days, and returning to Chicago with suitcases and one or two of those boxes I had hidden away in the basement.

I started to swing our arms again, gently, and then with greater and greater force. I swung them high over our heads, as if we were declaring victory, which I know now we were. We had won and would fight to keep doing so.

As I held our arms in the air, Isaac asked me again: "What are we doing?"

I went back to swinging.

"Don't you see," I told him. "We're taking off. We're finally becoming ungrounded."

ISAAC

Isaac and I left the grave, and because I assumed we didn't have much time left, I took his hand as he stepped down and held on to it as we walked—a habit that had never formed between us in the capital, even though all the young men we had known did so with friends who meant much less to them. I let him lead us off the main road, onto one of the winding footpaths crowded with homes on both sides. At any moment I expected him to stop and abruptly say goodbye, just as he had before, except this time there wouldn't be a donkey to see me off, and I would go in any direction he wanted me to without arguing.

The paths were deserted. This part of the village was a smaller, more permanent version of the shantytown Isaac and I had met in—the same tight trails with rivulets of fetid water pooling out of them. I had learned my way through such neighborhoods by the voices and smells that came from certain corners. A latrine, a house crowded with children, one that smelled always of food were street signs. I had never been in such close quarters and had nothing to smell. I tried to say something about this to Isaac:

"Where did everyone go?" I said.

He looked around as if he were just now noticing there were no signs of life.

"I like it like this," he said. "It's very . . ." We walked for several moments before he found the word he was looking for. ". . . peaceful."

The path we were on gradually curved onto a wider red dirt road that ran along the back end of the town. It was the old market road—built with the village long before there were cars or colonists. I had been on that road twice since we arrived, once by accident, the second time by choice. On both occasions, I had spent the better part of the morning and all of the afternoon watching as the crowd peaked and ebbed according to the village's particular rhythm. There were thousands of markets like that one across Africa, which was what I wanted to be reminded of when I came the second time. Standing near a vegetable stall, I had written in the first blank page I opened to, "There are hundreds of places exactly like this." I knew I didn't really believe that, but I felt better having put those words down. Now that the tightly packed wooden stalls where slabs of meat had hung, and the rugs and mats from which the women sold their vegetables and spare goods were gone, I regretted those words.

I looked for traces of life accidentally left behind—a piece of fruit, a rotting stub of flesh—but everything had been stripped bare and then carefully picked over.

Isaac released my hand. He began to walk among the abandoned stalls, all of which were stained with blood at the base, knocking on every other one as if he suspected that someone was hiding inside.

"Joseph promised us a big feast when we came back. He said

we would conquer the town in hours and then return as heroes and eat until there was nothing left."

He knocked on two more doors.

"He was right about the nothing," he said.

"Where is he now?"

Isaac pointed to the last pair of stalls.

"Maybe he's hiding in one of them," he said.

I thought that was Isaac's way of saying Joseph was dead. I must have looked relieved at the thought, because just as quickly he added, "He's fine. He will be here soon."

It hurt him to say that. He didn't cringe, but a part of him recoiled. He picked up my hand and locked my three middle fingers in his.

"I want to show you something," he said.

We walked to the end of the market road; as it climbed, it curved slightly to the right, growing increasingly narrow, until, eventually, it connected back to the paved road that joined the bronze fist to the Life Hotel. We could hear the soldiers before we saw them. We stopped short of where the two roads merged. Isaac whispered into my ear, "Take a look around the corner." He waited in the shadow of one of the houses while I slipped my head around the bend. Gathered around the fist were all the soldiers I had seen getting off the lorry earlier that morning. They were sitting in a circle; the soldier who had told me to bury the bodies stood next to the fist, talking quietly but passionately, his right hand clenched as he spoke. I described the scene to Isaac, and then waited for an explanation.

"It's nothing," he said. "They are doing exactly what they said they would."

"This is what you wanted me to see."

He took my hand again.

"No. What I want to show you is much better."

We walked back toward the market. When we reached the last stalls, Isaac led us in between them onto a path that was barely visible and looked as if it led directly into the bush. Waist-high grass gave way to a dense pocket of trees. I expected Isaac to tell me that my only option was to take my chances in the wild, like the refugees I had seen that morning, but just as abruptly as the forest began, it ended. Before us was a wide, circular clearing, at least a hundred feet in diameter, in the center of which was a single-story house, made of concrete and wood and painted white on all four sides.

Isaac unlocked the front door, which was carved with signs and symbols that most likely were never intended to be put on a door; he used a lone key he had hidden in his shoe. He led me inside. All the windows were shuttered, but light flooded the main room through the skylights that lined the ceiling. There was no furniture. The floors were made of the same wood as the door and the beams on the roof; even with the dust, they shone.

"This is what you wanted to show me?"

"This is only part of it," he said.

He walked to the center of the main room, knelt down, and wiped a bit of dust with his finger.

"Joseph had floors like this in his home in Kampala," he said. "I wish you could have seen it. He had a woman who scrubbed it every day on her knees. He told me the wood came from a tree in Brazil. I asked him where Brazil was. I had heard of it, but I thought maybe it was in Africa. He showed me where it was on a map, and promised someday we would go there together.

"This is not the same wood," he said. "He used the trees outside. The floors in Kampala were made of mahogany."

Isaac led me on a tour of the other rooms, which branched off from the main room into two separate wings. Each room was virtually identical—wooden floors, white walls, windows that looked onto the back—but they had all been assigned different functions that distinguished them even when empty. Isaac named each one.

This was going to be the dining room.

This was for the servants.

This was the kitchen.

This was the library.

He did the same with the other wing of the house, except now he lingered a bit longer on each room we passed.

"These were the guest rooms," he said. "Joseph has little family left, but he has many friends all over the world. In Europe. Even in America."

The next room was Joseph's. We didn't enter: we stood in the doorway, as if afraid of disturbing someone sleeping inside.

"He wanted the smallest bedroom in the house. I asked him why build a house with so many rooms if you have such a small one for yourself. He said I shouldn't think of them just as rooms. Each one was a different part of his life. He had a room for work, for friends, for guests, and one to be alone in."

We continued to the last one, which was larger than Joseph's, and which was the brightest of all the rooms, with light coming in on three sides through the slats in the shutters. This time, Isaac entered. When he reached the center, he said, "And Joseph promised me this was going to be my room."

He took a few seconds to consider what he had said before turning to face me.

"You understand what I am telling you?"

I said yes without pausing to consider if it was true. Only later would I understand that Isaac wasn't confessing; he was telling me how much he was about to lose.

He began to make a slow tour of the room.

"Joseph wants me to go study in America. He's made all the arrangements. He says I could come back in a year and it will be safe—the fighting will be over. He knows he can't win, but he thinks the British will make it end, and they will make him vice-president or prime minister. He says this is the future of democracy in Africa. He thinks it will only be a matter of time until he becomes president, and then he can do whatever he wants. None of it is true, though. He will never be president. There will never be a house with enough rooms for us to live in.

"I asked him once, 'What kind of revolutionary has a woman scrub his floors?' He laughed at me. He said, 'That's why people become revolutionaries—so they can have someone else clean their floors.' What could I say to that? I was living in his house by then. For the first time in my life, every day when I woke up I had clean clothes, and something to eat two, three times a day, as much as I wanted. Once I had that, I realized my revolution was over."

Isaac opened the windows in what would have been his room. A banana tree right outside tempered the heat and allowed a slightly cool breeze to blow through. He leaned his body over the frame and stuck his head outside.

"He thinks I am already halfway to Kenya by now, but I wanted to see this house again. Neither of us will ever live here."

"We can leave now," I said.

"I promise, soon we will."

The sun covered the room in a yellow haze. Not since our first day at Joseph's house in the capital had I felt such peace. We knew to do our best not to disturb it. We took a place on the floor against the back wall and held that pose until dusk approached. The light shifted from yellow to a reddish pink, a sign that the air was full of sand and dust from a strong wind blowing in from somewhere.

Isaac stood up first.

"We should go now," he said. "Joseph will be at the hotel soon. I need to tell him we are leaving."

I didn't argue; I wanted him to have his goodbye if it meant he was free to leave. We took the shortest route back to the main road. When we arrived, we were exactly halfway between the bronze fist and the hotel. The dust had turned what would have been a common sunset into an occasion to color the sky a shade of red that was either glorious or frightening to witness. We stood at the intersection and looked up until we heard a large diesel engine and could see a lorry and a car trailing it, approaching us.

"Here they come," Isaac said.

"You don't want to leave now?" I asked him.

"There is one more thing I have to show you," he said.

We arrived at the hotel before the cars. Isaac said it was best if I waited for him in one of the other rooms while he spoke to Joseph.

"I will come find you when it is time to leave," he said.

The injured soldiers were still lying in the courtyard; three had passed away since morning, and their bodies were draped in light-blue sheets lifted from the beds. The soldier who had told me to bury the bodies was gone, as were many others, but there must have been at least two dozen able-bodied men remaining.

Isaac suggested I take a room on the second floor, where I would have more privacy. I climbed the stairs while he remained in the courtyard. He wanted me to stay in my room until he was finished, but I couldn't resist seeing Joseph again.

The lorry full of soldiers and the sedan trailing it stopped in front of the hotel. Isaac was standing in the middle of the courtyard with his arms folded, as if he were the owner waiting for his guests to arrive. When soldiers entered with their guns drawn and pointed squarely at him, he seemed more amused than bothered. They formed a semicircle around the courtyard, while a second wave of men entered, with Joseph securely hidden in the middle. They were the same guards who had been with him at the house in the capital—tall, powerful men whose loyalty had been bought. Once inside the courtyard, they opened up just enough for me to see Joseph. He was no longer dressed as a soldier. He had traded in his fatigues for a dark three-piece suit, a return to his original role as a politician rather than a soldier.

He walked directly to Isaac, who wasn't supposed to be there. From the smile on his face, he seemed grateful to find that Isaac had stayed. Joseph placed his hand on Isaac's shoulder, and with that the two of them, along with Joseph's bodyguards, walked off to an empty room on the ground floor.

I waited in the doorway for them to come back; after an hour had passed, I went to the bed and lay down; without intending to, I fell asleep. On a mattress propped up by a stack of wooden boxes, I dreamed of being in a large house that stood near the center of a city; I was late to meet someone but couldn't find my way out. I wandered through hundreds of identical rooms, or rooms that seemed identical, because I kept thinking, I've been here before, there has to be another way out. The dream was a nightmare in that it seemed I might never escape from it, and yet I wasn't afraid: as desperate as I might have been to leave, another part of me thought that all would be fine in the end, that whoever was waiting to meet me would wait for as long as was needed. I was still in the throes of that dream when Isaac entered. Half awake, I thought I was right not to have been worried. Isaac had waited for me after all. I didn't realize I was still in my dream until I heard Isaac's voice tell me calmly not to get up. I opened my eyes, and when I did, I saw him standing over me, but since there was no light in the room and it was night outside, I could see only his form. I stood up, though he had told me not to. For the first time he called me by the name my father had given me when I was born. "D——, don't get up. Stay where you are. It will soon be over."

I could hear soldiers shouting in English and Kiswahili. I understood the threats and curses in both languages.

"Don't worry about it," Isaac said. "It is finished now."

He hadn't closed the door fully behind him, and despite what he had said, he made no effort to stop me from going out. When I reached the balcony, I saw Joseph standing alone with what was left of his army surrounding him. I looked for his guards and saw them on the opposite side of the courtyard, talking among themselves; none of them were looking down. I turned around to look for Isaac, but he was in the room and wasn't going to come out.

Joseph was still dressed in his elegant suit; he hadn't been harmed in the least; only his tie was slightly askew. I looked at the soldiers surrounding him and realized there were many more now than there had been when we returned to the hotel, and that among them was the soldier who had spoken with his fist clenched. He was now in charge. This was one thing Isaac had wanted me to see.

That soldier took three steps toward Joseph, and as he did so, the rest of the men stopped shouting. He spoke while standing at attention. Though I couldn't hear, I knew he was uttering a list of crimes against Joseph.

I never thought about closing my eyes. I didn't blink as that man raised his arm and shot Joseph in the head, nor did I turn away as he stood over Joseph's body and fired twice more into his chest, because Joseph deserved at least that much, and because that was what Isaac had taught me to do.

I didn't weep for Joseph, but I mourned him nonetheless. I gripped the rails on the balcony until my palms almost bled. When I went back into the room, I found Isaac on the bed, staring at me calmly. There was enough light with the door open to see he had been crying.

"It had to be done. There was no other way," he said. And because I knew he loved Joseph, I believed him.

He made room on the bed for me. He handed me what I thought was his wallet. I held it close to my face and saw that it was a Kenyan passport.

"There's no picture in it," he said. "You will have to do that on your own after you cross the border. But it belongs to you now."

On the first page was Isaac's name attached to Joseph's: Isaac Mabira.

"This is what I wanted to show you," he said. "Joseph gave me that just before we left the capital. He bought a plane ticket and found a way to get me a visa, but I told him I would never leave. He thought I would when the time came, but this is my country. I don't know who I am if I leave it."

We didn't fight long. The argument wasn't heated. We never raised our voices. I begged Isaac not to do this. I promised to go to America if he left for Kenya with me, but no man of worth gives up his faith that easily, and in the sickest corner of my heart I was prepared to give up anyone in order to leave.

He gave me a satchel that I had noticed was lying on the floor. Inside was a notebook exactly like the one he had given me when I was in the hospital.

"Take the bag with you," he said. "There is money inside. I've written everything you need to know. All you have to do now is go, and tell me that we'll see each other again."

He stood and walked out onto the terrace.

"I'm not going to go any farther than this," he said. "So say it."

"I promise we'll see each other again soon," I said.

He put his hands on my shoulders. We kissed on both cheeks, and when that wasn't enough, embraced each other until our arms hurt.

He wasn't on the balcony when I looked up from the court-yard. The door to the room was closed, so he never heard the engine of Joseph's car as it pulled away. He had so much more than my leaving to mourn that I would like to think I slipped away as quietly as possible.

It took me two weeks to reach the Kenyan border. The car dropped me off hundreds of miles away, and from there I walked and rode in the back of several different trucks, all of which were crowded with others fleeing. Joseph's army was one of many fighting to liberate the country. Together, they left a trail of deserted villages, some of which were still smoldering when we passed, that lasted the entire journey. When I reached Nairobi, I opened the notebook Isaac had given me. It was just as he had promised: there was a list of everything I needed to know about going to America, from the visa at the embassy to the airline and how to find Henry when I arrived. Its middle pages were filled with notes he had written for me. On one page he rewrote his list of Crimes Against the Country, with an addition at the end: "It is a Crime Against the Country to forget this happened." On another, a list of names he had given me: Professor, Langston, Ali, ending with the one on the passport, Isaac Mabira, which is our name now. He had made a better record of our lives than I had ever done. He knew why he was writing. It was always for me. The last thing he wrote, dated the same day I left that village, which I read over and over as I made my way to Kenya and then again when I was on the plane to America, which I tore out and placed in the middle of the passport that he had given me, and which I read again after saying goodbye to Helen on a street in Chicago, and which was what I said to her before she left with a promise to return:

No one will have ever loved each other more than we did.

ACKNOWLEDGMENTS

I am indebted to my parents, Hirut and Tesfaye Mengestu; my sister, Bezawit; and my family in Ethiopia, America, and France. To my dear friends, colleagues, and editors: Mark Binelli, Jonathan Ringen, Jonathan Hickman, Steve Toltz, Julien Chatelin, Pierre Scipion, Manuel Gonzales, Stanislas Wang-Ghen, John Freeman, Ellah Affrey, Francis Geffard, Pervaiz Shallwani, Aamer Madhani, Julia Holmes (conqueror of the Erie Canal), Jessica Lamb-Shapiro, Marcela Valdes, Shawn McGibboney, Nam Le, Christian Lorentzen, Megan Lynch, Mih-ho Cha, Michael Bronner, Bhakti Shringapure and Brian Plazas. Thank you for your years of support. I am indebted to Andrew Rice's wonderful book, *The Teeth May Smile but the Heart Does Not Forget,* and to Mark Gevisser, for his brilliant essay "Edenvale," and to my colleagues at Georgetown University, especially Carolyn Forche, David Gewanter, Henry Schwarz, Norma Tilden, Mark McMorris, Penn Szittya, and Jessica Williams. I am also deeply indebted to Patrick Lannan, Jo Chapman, and the entire Lannan Foundation; as well as to Jan Vilcek, Marica Vilcek, and the Vilcek Foundation; the Baton Rouge Area Foundation; and the MacArthur Foundation, whose support was vital in the final stages. To the staff at Knopf, especially Caroline Bleeke and Gabrielle Brooks,

ACKNOWLEDGMENTS

thank you for all you have done to bring this book to life. And to my agent, P. J. Mark, and my editor, Jordan Pavlin, I can't thank you enough for your patience, wisdom, and support. And, of course, and above all, to Gabriel, Louis-Selassie, and Anne-Emmanuelle.